HYPER CARNIVORE

HYPER CARNIVORE

LAURENCE HAYE

AMOS
ARTHUR

First published 2020

This revised edition published 2022

 A catalogue record for this book is available from the National Library of Australia

ISBN 978 0 6488560 5 4 (eBook)

ISBN 978 0 6488560 4 7 (Hardback)

ISBN 978 0 6488560 6 1 (Trade paperback)

Cover Design: Amos Arthur/Cover Photo: Adobe Stock/Author Photo: B.C.P.

AMOS ARTHUR

ABN: 66009904213

AmosArthur@outlook.com

Pour
D.L.C.

Ma petite lionne...

THE SEARCH

THE SEARCH

Chapter 1

DENE SELKIRK GRIMACED AND sucked in air. Dark hair dangled over his forehead. Sweat stung his eyes. His arms burned and a web of fine blue veins wrapped his shoulders.

"That's it – keep going."

The woman's voice spurred him on. Bands of muscle pulsed beneath gleaming olive skin. His hips tilted in time as his spine rose, reared, uncurled and then fell forward again. His buttocks tensed and relaxed, driving the steady tempo.

"Nearly there. Don't you stop. *Don't you stop.*"

He arched his back, eyes clenched shut, straining to finish. He gasped and let out a shuddering sigh. He hung his head, catching rapid breaths that whistled through his lips. An orb of perspiration clung to the tip of his nose. A crimson flush bloomed across his cheeks.

"Jesus, Dene. Is that the best you can do?"

He glared at the woman, then swayed back and pulled one last, defiant hang-clean. He let the barbell crash to the floor and bent, hands on knees, chest heaving.

He glanced up. "I don't see you throwing any iron around."

Zanelle Argus leaned on a long, mirrored wall. Ankles crossed, hand on a hip. All sass and attitude. No-nonsense cute.

"I've paid my dues, pretty boy. Now I get to give the benefit of my experience to desperates like you."

Dene guessed what was coming. She tossed a water bottle, harder than necessary. He snatched at it and dropped it.

She said, "And if you'd done that set properly you wouldn't be able to lift your arms."

He squinted sideways. Sometimes she just needed a laugh. He picked up the bottle and lifted his arms over his head, yawning and flexing his biceps in the classic bodybuilder's pose.

"But I *am* very strong."

"C'mon Dene. You asked for my help and you've fought me all the way."

He dropped his hands. "Zannie, I've done everything you wanted and I haven't seen any results."

She shoved off the mirror. "Are you serious?" She scooped a clipboard from the floor and waved it. "Your reps are up, your strength is up, your bar velocity is up."

"But I need to see results on the stopwatch."

"Well, if you didn't cheat on your workouts, maybe you would."

Dene smeared perspiration across his face. "There's no such thing as cheating. There's working out, and there's sitting on your arse watching Oprah."

He used the English version of 'backside' but Zanelle's smirk was long gone.

She slapped the clipboard to his chest. "You are a waste of my time. I need to get to the station."

Zanelle headed for the exit. She strutted past a row of exercise bikes that took up one wall. Halfway down, she pretended to flick hair from her eyes and stole a glimpse in the mirror.

Dene grinned. Sleek black workout tights stretched over her thighs and hips. A red maple leaf on a white T-shirt faded to pink where it spread against her heavy breasts. Blonde, pixie-cut mop. Clear blue eyes. Flawless skin and full lips.

There wasn't much to fault.

She stepped over a pair of manila battle ropes and grabbed her gym bag from a desk beside the door. She hoisted it onto her shoulder and said, "Can you lock up when you leave?"

He answered with a surly look and a long guzzle from the water bottle. Riding his luck.

Zanelle stopped at the top of the checker plate steps that led down to the parking lot.

Sometimes he rode too hard.

She prowled back. Over the ropes, past the mirror, along the row of bikes. She took a fistful of tousled hair and pulled his head down. She kissed him hard. Then again, more softly.

"And it's Zan-*elle*...."

She turned and leered back over her shoulder. Dene tapped the clipboard against his knee. He pursed his lips and nodded.

Chapter 2

THE VANCOUVER WOLVES' HEAD coach watched the feed from a camera drone on his tablet. The images blanched in the early June sunlight but Roger Bartoli wasn't sure how to adjust the screen. He knew that said a bit about him, but didn't care. Overstuffed and frayed at the edges, he was near the end of his tether.

And the Canadian Football League's sixty-third season hadn't even started.

"No, no, no! Pete, look at this will ya?"

Pete Hoffman combed thinning sandy hair across his freckled scalp with twig-like fingers. He took two sideways steps and leaned over the coach's shoulder.

"Jimmy and Max are too far apart," said Bartoli, "and Clay's feet are all wrong. See what you can do."

Hoffman had twenty-five years in the program and split the quarterback and offensive team coaching role with Bartoli.

Once a red-hot running back, by six years out of college he'd been a reserve for every team in the NFC North. Back then they couldn't fix knees the way they can now.

"I'll take care of it," he said.

Bartoli marched off, rolls of fat jostling for room in his clammy Wolves polo.

"The Lions go up to Kamloops for *their* training camps. Us? We stay in beautiful, downtown Abbotsford."

Hoffman called after him. "Don't forget we've got a roster cut-down later."

"No time like the present," said the coach.

Bartoli stumped toward his defensive co-ordinator. Charlie Tait wasn't fat. He was a walking pie-stand. Which is to say, not a lot different to his days as a bone-crunching defensive end in the East Division. He met Bartoli half way. They looked like two pumpkins.

"Switzer's heart-rate is up again," said Tait. "Not sure if he's just tired, or still on the juice."

Bartoli grunted. "Doesn't matter – he's cut."

Unlike computer technology, Bartoli knew about drugs in sport. He'd watched a score of players spiral into obscurity after testing positive to one or more of almost two hundred substances on WADA's Prohibited List. He knew the strain on players to perform. And on coaches. He'd seen a few of those sacked amid drug abuse scandals, too.

He said, "Set up a triangle drill for me."

Tait ran his eyes over the players milling on the field. The session was winding down. "Conlan, Max. Over here. And you, Clay." The guys straggling for the showers picked up pace. "You too, Switzer."

Billy Switzer sulked like no strapping Aryan halfback should. Bartoli looked away. He'd been soft on Billy, but couldn't afford to be any longer. The kid was another disposable piece of merchandise on the football roundabout, but at least he knew it. He'd hung on as long as he could. Now his time was up.

The problem with guys who turned to drugs was that they always took someone down with them. They became pariahs in an industry that demanded rigorous moral standards. The CFL machine ran on network dollars, and Bartoli knew the rules. A squeaky-clean image was crucial, but ratings reigned over all.

The coach did a chubby pirouette, searching for a face. He found his target chatting with a pair of Hawaiian line-backers.

"Selkirk! Front and centre."

Chapter 3

DENE HEARD BARTOLI CALL his name.

"Shit."

The two Hawaiians almost hid the coach from view. Token and Totem Kainoa were twins. They sported different hairstyles, but otherwise they were identical slabs of hardwood bolted to six-foot three-inch frames. Dene dubbed them 'Kenny' and 'Tim' and the names had stuck.

He leaned sideways to see around their shoulder pads. "I wasn't looking forward to this."

"Don't worry, man," said Tim. "Just go for it."

"Think positive," said Kenny.

Dene set off toward Bartoli.

"Lid, brah," called Tim.

Dene remembered his helmet. Good start. He ducked back and picked it up, then trotted to the growing huddle.

"Coach?"

"We're gonna run one more drill."

"Sure."

"I want you to feint wide, then cut inside the blocker."

Dene nodded. Nothing he couldn't handle. He pulled his helmet on and joined the scrimmage. He settled behind the quarterback.

Not far enough to let the defence move up. Not so close that he wouldn't have momentum when he took the ball.

"Rogalski!" called the coach.

"Shit," said Dene.

A giant defensive tackle moped toward the coaching group. Eddie Rogalski was still more muscle than flab, but only just. A twenty-year stalwart of the league, he had a bad back and a bad temper.

And now it looked like he'd have a cold shower.

The players gathered to watch. Dene didn't blame them. It was fun to see someone else get smashed for a change. A rookie wide receiver darted about, letting everyone know he was on the roster. Kyle Ovens had mercurial speed and talent to burn, but he undid his good work with a smart mouth and dumb decisions. A high draft pick with a low IQ.

"*Sell-cock*, you in trouble here," said Ovens.

Dene thought the rookie might be right. His arrival had forced Dene to the bottom of the wide receiver depth chart. Now Bartoli was pushing him into the slot back role. The position required versatility, and he was floundering.

He glanced at Rogalski and checked his chin strap. He unhooked it and hitched it up again. Bartoli gripped the tackle's chunky arm and manoeuvred him away from the bunch. Dene wondered what the message was.

Bartoli said, "Eddie, it's gonna be another tough season. Lot more games than last year, anyway."

For a very few people, the *coronavirus* brought benefits. The terminated 2020 season had been a blessing for the league's veterans. Many of them spent their final years hopped up on painkillers, hoping for a last hurrah or one more pay cheque. An extended break gave the old stagers a chance to mend and freshen up.

Old stagers like Eddie.

"So?" he said.

"Well, the coaches are wondering if it's time to pack it in. They think maybe you're not up to it anymore."

Rogalski fixed his eyes on Hoffman and Tait. "Who thinks I'm not up to it?"

"Now, I don't agree with them Eddie, but if this guy gets past you...." Bartoli shrugged.

Rogalski turned and sneered at Dene. "This weed? No chance."

"That's what I like to hear," said the coach. The tackle swung away. Bartoli grabbed his arm again. "He'll feint wide and cut back inside."

Rogalski nodded.

Kenny and Tim mingled with the onlookers at the sideline. Kyle Ovens flitted through the group.

"Hey, *Sell-cock* – been nice knowin' ya."

The twins moseyed forward and crowded against Ovens. Even without the 'smack talk' he wasn't their favourite recruit. They shouted into the rookie's ear.

"C'mon Dene!"

"Turn him inside out, brah!"

Ovens shrank back. "Jesus, I'm on Easter Island."

Charlie Tait yelled instructions and waved his arms, and the formation set. Bartoli called the play.

Dene launched and took the ball. He jinked inside but Rogalski was ready. He seemed wider than Dene remembered. A lot wider.

The giant loomed up and slammed him to the turf with a brutal shoulder charge. Dene bounced and rolled into a heap.

It sounded like someone had slugged a mattress with a baseball bat. It felt worse.

The spectators heckled and jeered. Rogalski snorted.

"Run another one," said Bartoli.

Dene hauled himself up and wobbled to the coach. "What now?"

"Same again."

Hoffman and Tait studied their feet. Dene frowned.

Bartoli said, "He won't expect it twice."

The scrimmage faced off. Bartoli nodded at Rogalski and called the play.

Dene took the ball. He feinted, then switched back. Eddie suddenly seemed a lot quicker, too. He wrapped Dene up, ball and all, lifted him off his feet and crash-tackled him to the ground. The concussion shocked the air from his lungs and tiny gold stars danced before his eyes.

Rogalski shoved his helmet into the turf, then leaned on the grille and pushed himself up. "Pommie fag."

Dene lay on his back, legs bent. He dug his fingers under his ribs to massage the diaphragm.

"That's enough," said Bartoli. "Let's call it a day."

The coaches turned to their tablets and dissected data from the session. Downbeat figures filed toward the locker room in twos and threes.

England's finest looked up at the twins. He raised his arms and they lifted him to his feet.

"That didn't go so good," said Kenny.

"Coulda fooled me," said Dene.

The trio traipsed off the field.

"They gonna cut us all," said Tim.

Chapter 4

THE WOLF TROD A narrow path, brittle with pinegrass and fresh snow. She weaved through stands of mountain hemlock, then skip-hopped down a jagged fall of shale scree. She hunted long-familiar trails but didn't know she was a hunter. Didn't know she was a carnivore. She didn't know she was a predator at the top of her food chain.

Didn't know she was a killer.

Sleet-laden cloud hovered low between the peaks, veiling deep ravines and granite outcrops. The wolf eased along a slick, wet scarp, gliding through the snow mist. Rime stippled her mane and shimmered over a pelt the colour of steel dust. A canopy of crystal on a languid, lupine gait. A ghost on a ghost.

———◇———

THE CASCADE MOUNTAINS SCAR the American continent's northwest seaboard like a rocky welt. Ridges of proud flesh where tectonic plates grind their broken teeth. Their upper reaches spear into the heart of western Canada, icy spires erupting from the earth like upturned talons.

Or the jaws of a waiting bear trap.

Everything changed after the trappers came. When the fur traders forged inland from the Atlantic coast in the early eighteen-hundreds, they came for beaver, but discovered a living bounty.

The Cascades harboured elk and moose and deer; foxes and wolves; bears, lynx, muskrat and more. Fortunes changed hands as hides by the shipload were surrendered to the whims of Old-World fashion.

And the forests became a charnel house.

Then came the miners. They swarmed to strike after strike in the last half of the century, the hills yielding silver and copper and gold.

Forts and trading posts sprang up. The mining companies pushed farther into the mountains, building camps and access roads. Logging operations spread farther upstream. In 1885, the railroad came through, joining coast to coast.

Over time, the trappers and miners and loggers nudged the environment off kilter. The intruders feasted on venison, and trophy heads lined the walls of cedar plank cabins.

An already hostile world became even more perilous for the animals. Those that kept their skins were robbed of shelter. Then they ran out of food. When their habitats declined too far, they had few options. They could move on, deeper into the wilderness, seeking new territory, or they could stay and take their chances.

Or they could push back.

Chapter 5

ROYAL CANADIAN MOUNTED POLICE Constable Argus manned a communication console behind a pebbled-glass partition that divided the Chilliwack station's foyer from its operational function areas. She sorted duty rosters and filed incident reports.

Not her first choice of assignments.

She adjusted the buttons where her crisp, grey uniform gaped and thought about Dene. A popular pastime.

She loved his British accent, with its dash of the upper class – which he denied and tried to suppress. She adored his long, dark lashes. The straight but slightly flattened nose. His too-perfect teeth, replacements for loose or cracked incisors. His split and sutured eyebrows, another legacy of 'the game they played in Heaven'.

She liked that he wasn't hard work, even when sparks flew. He let her get away with a lot. Perhaps too much. She wondered if that was the attraction.

The phone rang. She snatched it up before it could ring twice.

"RCMP Support. This is Officer Argus."

She rocked in her chair.

"When was the last time you saw him, Mr Ellis?"

She pulled a report pad from the desk drawer and reached for a coffee cup full of pens.

"Have you checked the rescue shelters? Okay. What's your address there?"

She jotted on the pad.

"And what type of dog is he? Okay...Robbie? Robber. Got it."

She drew zig-zags beneath a couple of words and wiggled the pen between her fingers.

"Yes, I'll make a report and we'll keep a lookout for him. Try not to worry, Mr Ellis. He'll turn up."

Zanelle dropped the phone onto its cradle. She noted the time, signed the page and ripped it from the pad, then stepped around the partition.

A rangy Salish teenager wiped the reception counter with a damp cloth.

"Tom, did you take a call about a missing dog yesterday?"

An Auxiliary Constable had to volunteer a hundred and sixty hours a year to maintain their status with the Mounted Police. At his present rate, Tom Calder would knock that off in three months.

He pondered. "Um, day before I think."

Calder's crewcut head looked small atop a Modigliani neck, but Zanelle knew he was sharp. He embraced his First Nation heritage and studied BC's ecosystems by correspondence in his spare time.

She slid the report across the laminate. "We had a couple of calls last week, too. I wonder what's going on."

The young man peeled up the paper. He wiped over the counter-top again, his arm swinging in an easy arc.

"It'll be wolves," he said. "They come to town looking for food around whelping time."

Motivated by hunger, an average sized wolf pack would challenge mountain lions and bears, even wolverines. If desperate enough, a pack could bring down a grown moose. Domestic dogs were easy prey.

Zanelle lifted her chin and scratched her throat. "Hmm, okay."

"It's true," said Calder. "We'll see more once winter sets in."

He held out the report. Zanelle took the page and wandered back behind the partition.

"Poor Mr Ellis," she said.

Chapter 6

VANCOUVER'S LATEST SPORTS FRANCHISE was slapped together to maximise revenue from a newly brokered television deal with Mexico. The TV rights gave a lucrative boost to the Canadian game, but with only nine teams in the CFL it meant someone had a bye. After they added the Wolves, the league could offer an extra match each round.

More matches, more advertising.

More advertising, more money.

It didn't surprise Bartoli that the newest team in the league was also the least successful. Despite a glitzy launch, the Wolves remained a poor relation to the BC Lions. How could they not? The roster comprised rejects and second-grade personnel. The broadcast dollars hadn't yet filtered through, and for the small consortium of owners a minor investment was the prudent route. Easier to write off – if it didn't work out.

Bartoli won the coaching job because he came cheap, and it showed. They'd gone 0-18 their first year, and the less said about 2020, the better.

Bottom of the West Division. Bottom of the League.

Bottom of the barrel.

The coach's office contained a desk and three odd chairs. A cork board displayed newspaper clippings and photos of players reclining on a sponsor's product. Synthetic carpet. Most thought it a good match. Sticky tape held a league fixture to the desk, the home games circled in red ink.

A pile of Vancouver sweatshirts rested on a chair. Stacks of cardboard boxes filled with last year's merchandise leaned against the wall in a corner.

Thanks to the pandemic, the 2020 season was a fiasco. Lost gate revenue and concession money crippled half the teams in the comp. The league kept the Wolves franchise afloat with a bailout package, but everyone prayed things would turn around in 2021.

Bartoli and Hoffman stood in front of a whiteboard. Bartoli flicked the cap off a red marker and ran a line through a name.

Hoffman cross-checked the names on a tablet. "Yep, he's gone."

"Too right he's gone. Built like Tarzan, play like Jane."

Bartoli scribbled across another name. Billy Switzer.

"Yep."

The marker swiped through two more names. Token and Totem Kainoa.

"Yeah," said Hoffman, "Charlie's already spoken to them. They've been disappointing."

"They can't take a dump without holding hands. Too much trouble." Bartoli ran a finger down the board. He scrubbed another name.

Hoffman said, "You sure?"

"You saw what Eddie just did to him. And don't tell me Eddie's not past it."

"Kid's got some ticker."

The coach looked sideways at his assistant. "I'd prefer it if he had some talent."

"He's never played the game before and he comes halfway round the world to make it in the big time. That takes major *cojones*."

"But that's the point. He hasn't made it. The Niners let him go. The Hawks didn't even try him."

"We're not exactly the Hawks."

Bartoli's eyes flashed for an instant, but he let it slide. "He's determined, I'll give him that. But it's not enough, even in this league. And what is he? Twenty-nine?"

"He wouldn't be the first late starter to have a break-out year at thirty."

The coach snorted. "Look, I've asked him to come in. Don't worry, I won't burn any bridges."

Hoffman was fifty pounds lighter than his boss and a decade wiser. He leaned against the board and gave it another try.

"He's got pedigree."

"Yeah, his dad could play a bit. So?"

"A bit? The guy was a legend."

"Which makes it even harder for the kid. How often does a son-of-a-gun live up to his father's name? I'll tell you – never."

Hoffman looked at the list in silence.

Bartoli said, "Rugby's not the same game, Pete, you know that. Lotta guys have switched and hardly any make it. Look at the Australians. Good for punting and that's about all."

"It's not the same game *now*, Bart, but it's still the *origin* of our game. Doesn't that count for something?"

"Oh, give me a break. Since when did you get all sentimental?"

Hoffman rocked on his heels.

Bartoli held up a hand and tapped the marker to his fingers. "Pete, I've got Americans, I've got Englishmen, I've got Islanders. This is a Canadian league. I need to cut someone."

Hoffman raised his hands in surrender. "Okay, I'm not arguing anymore."

Bartoli's red marker circled above another name when Dene knocked on the open door.

"You wanted to see me, coach?"

Chapter 7

DENE HAD HEARD ALL the stories.

Some clubs cut players with an e-mail. Some put an envelope in their locker. One club left a player's gear in a heap outside the building. It hadn't happened to him, but that didn't make him feel any better. He'd been here before.

Bartoli lifted a porky thigh onto the edge of his desk. "Come in, young Selkirk. Take a seat."

Dene sat beside the pile of sweatshirts and hunched forward, elbows on the arms of the chair, hands folded together. He worked the body language, aiming for relaxed. Confident. Eager.

All the things he didn't feel.

He said, "Eddie caught me by surprise today."

"Don't worry," said Hoffman, "he's done that a few times over the years."

Bartoli laced his fingers in front of his gut. "Son, I wanna be up-front here. You haven't come on like we hoped."

Dene rubbed moist palms against his knees. He straightened in the chair. Whatever his faults, he could still look a man in the eye.

Think positive.

"But I run a lot better when I get into the clear."

"It's not that you can't run. It's that you're too easy to stop. You've struggled to get separation under good press coverage."

Hoffman leaned on the door. "Your yards after first contact are way down. A receiver might swing it, but not a running back."

"You need to be heavier," said Bartoli. "Stronger."

"I'm stronger than last year."

"But you ain't a whole lot heavier. It's not only you, son. Hell, three-quarters of the guys that try out never make it. They're a stone too light or a yard too slow. Or both. This league doesn't suit everyone."

Canadian football differed from its big brother down south. Pete Hoffman was right; the game *had* derived from Rugby Union, and it kept the larger dimensions of the rugby playing field. The extra space produced a faster, higher scoring match. Pure speed was a legitimate currency, but things weren't cut and dried. Unlike the NFL, there were only three downs, with teams of twelve, not eleven.

Dene knew it would be tough, but he thought he'd make it. Rugby teams used fifteen players. Thirty men running around instead of twenty-four. Logic told him it had to be easier, but he'd learned the hard way. Sometimes it got crowded out there.

Bartoli squirmed off the desk and stuffed his hands in his pockets. "I'm sorry, youngster. There's a lotta guys in the same boat. Not everyone can be Jerry Rice." He saw Dene's blank look. "Or Calvin Johnson." Nothing. "Derrick Henry? Anyway, bulk up a bit and you're welcome to have another go next year."

Dene dropped his head. He was sick of try-out camps, but at least they hadn't cut him off completely. He stood and looked at the assistant coach.

Hoffman held the door. "Patience and persistence, son. You'll get there."

Dene paused. He nodded at Bartoli, then shuffled out.

He lugged his bag across the parking lot. The twins propped themselves against his old Ford pickup.

"Well," he said, "that's that for another year."

"Coach has got it in for you," said Kenny.

"You think? At least I can come and watch you guys get your brains knocked in."

Dene chucked his kit into the rear of the truck. It tumbled over a pair of grungy duffels. He turned to the twins. "You too?"

"We were always borderline," said Kenny.

"But we thought you'd make it this time," said Tim.

Dene slumped against the Ford and gazed at the vacant stands around the empty gridiron. His dad would have a field day with this.

He said, "Let's get the heck outta here."

He slid behind the wheel. The twins crammed into the cab beside him. Nobody spoke. The starter-motor rasped and the pickup chugged toward the exit.

Chapter 8

THE WOLF PUSHED BACK.

She was a survivor. At five years of age she'd already delivered two litters and carried another, but she hadn't eaten for days. She trekked westward from the Skagit Range toward the Fraser Valley and its river flats. The lowlands teemed with men, but men had goats and sheep and dairy cows.

Men had food.

Her mate followed, never far away. Stoic and loyal. Just a year older than his partner, but more worn down. Half a ragged ear hung useless by his head, and his kinked tail flopped like a broken limb. When there's not enough to go around, you fight, or starve.

Two bony young males flanked the adult pair, and a couple of scrawny sisters from the last litter tagged along behind. As a group, a small pack needs less to eat; as individuals, they'll go hungry as soon as the rest.

The wolf led her clan through the forest deadfall to the edge of an open alpine plateau. She paused. In summertime, lupins, columbine and tiger lilies would blanket the meadow with scarlets and mauves and flashes of gold.

Now it was a waveless pond of white.

A dozen wary eyes combed the nearby woodland. Swathes of lodgepole pine nestled in the valleys and ranks of Douglas fir paraded up the slopes, marking time at the tree line. A stinging wind swept down from the peaks through rock-strewn gorges. It looped around clustered trees and drifted in elusive whorls, trailing wisps of a tell-tale scent.

The wolf lifted her head. Her nostrils quivered. She skirted the clearing through a scattering of red cedars. The dim shapes of her mate and their offspring hung back amid the darkened trees, their eyes a string of amber coals in the gloom. She crept onward, locked on the trace.

Compelled by an elemental urge.

Science had labelled this urge the 'prey drive', but the wolf didn't know that either. She simply obeyed. It was a biological circuit stamped on the DNA of all predators.

Instinct in its purest form.

Chapter 9

BENEATH THE OFFICE OF Prime Minister, the UK government comprises twenty-five ministerial offices and another twenty non-ministerial departments, beneath which are four hundred other agencies and public bodies.

The British Consulate-General in Vancouver operates under the auspices of the Foreign and Commonwealth Office, and is the government's representative in British Columbia, Yukon, and Northwest Territories.

David Selkirk was content to be a minor cog in the apparatus. He loped down a corridor on the eighth floor of the Consulate building on Melville Street. Thinning silver hair drooped over his ears, and the skin across his cheeks was the colour of old porcelain. A pale grey suit hung on his lean body, a faded flag in a feeble breeze.

He turned into a small alcove and stopped at his secretary's desk.

"Morning, Val."

Valerie Bedford shook glossy black curls from her handsome face and looked up. She smiled, but pulled her cardigan across a sheer silk blouse. She laid a wad of letters in her current master's hand.

"Hello, Mr Selkirk. Just these today. And upstairs is waiting for you to sign off on the latest security protocols."

In the existing climate, prudence dictated that public access to the Consulate should be by appointment only and, as Director of Security, Selkirk had wide-ranging powers. He could not, however, persuade Val Bedford to use his first name.

"Thanks, Val. I'll get onto it."

Selkirk shouldered through his office door. Government-issue furniture filled the room. A plain desk with an all-in-one computer. An ergonomic chair. Matching bookcases on either side.

Several volumes on official procedure reclined on the shelves and a couple of personal objects decorated the spaces in between. Framed photos took up prominent vantage points, lending splashes of colour.

Selkirk meeting the Queen.

Selkirk with Mandela.

Selkirk on the set of *The Krays*.

He tossed the mail onto his desk and dropped into the chair. He leaned forward and straightened a desk-top plaque that bore the gilt Crown and Brunswick Star of Great Britain's Metropolitan Police Service.

Young Davey Selkirk spent a decade on rugby duty for England, so his passage through probationary constable training took longer than the usual two years. The Metropolitan police didn't mind. As the golden boy of British sport, he was a walking billboard for the force.

Because of his size and athleticism, the Service assigned Selkirk to the Territorial Support Group, a replacement for the earlier Special Patrol Group. The remit of the TSG was 'public order containment'. It was a glorified riot squat.

First week on the job he volunteered to become an AFO – Authorised Firearms Officer. If the crazies came at him with razors and fire-bombs, he wanted protection. The two-week training course in the Glock-17 and the Heckler & Koch MP5 sounded a lot better than the eighteen weeks required to become a higher-graded Specialist Firearms Officer.

His cell phone burred. He rolled sideways, dug it out of his pocket and checked the number. He tapped the screen and put the phone to his ear. "What's going on?"

He rubbed his eyes with the heel of his hand, then fanned the mail on his desk.

"So, he missed out again. What about next year?"

He picked up a brass letter opener in the shape of a cavalry sabre.

"Okay, thanks. Any other news?"

He separated an envelope from the pile.

"Really? New sponsors already?"

He stabbed the envelope with the sword and slid it toward him.

"More money than sense. I wonder what they know that everyone else doesn't."

He sat back and grazed the blade across his cheek.

"Alright, I'll have a look. Thanks again. Keep in touch."

Selkirk ended the call. He picked up the envelope and slit the flap, then unfolded the page within and read its single paragraph. He shifted in his chair, leaned on the armrest and gazed out the window toward Coal Harbour.

After seven years, the TSG granted Selkirk a transfer to Protection Command because he was the only member of his unit not cited for excessive violence.

When he retired from the British Lions as a Hall of Fame inductee, many felt a knighthood was assured. Others were less certain. Whispers spread that he had 'flexible standards', though people doubted the allegations would to stick to a former captain of England.

When Selkirk finished playing club rugby he became a close protection officer for various diplomatic personnel. He joined the Parliamentary Security Detail, but there his rise stopped.

Then, in gratitude for two decades of discretion beyond the call of duty, someone pulled strings. They offered a role at the Consulate in Vancouver, and he accepted.

The posting could use more sun, but five years on, the job still fitted him well enough. For now.

He read the letter again, then slipped it back into the envelope. He reached across his desk and pressed a button on the intercom.

"Val, would you make an appointment with Dr Swift for me, please?"

Chapter 10

DENE ROLLED A ROCK from a heap of basalt until it balanced on the edge of the pile. He carried the rock through puddles of slurry and wrestled it into place on the top course of a low stone wall.

The wall extended across a sloping, semi-rural block north of Abbotsford. It turned in at either side of an asphalt driveway and followed it up to a large split-level home. Dene and the twins still had a solid week's work ahead of them.

Tim doled splashes of water into a rattling cement mixer.

He said, "Would you play for the Bears?"

Dene put a forefinger to his chin and feigned deep thought. The British Columbia Bears played in Canada's strongest domestic rugby union league, but it was still an amateur competition. As a top-flight winger in England's Premiership rugby comp, he was more than handy in Canada.

And definitely worth paying.

"Not sure I love getting beaten up enough to do it for free." He wasn't joking, but there was a greater truth he couldn't escape. "And I realised something else a while ago, too."

The twins flashed toothy smiles.

"This'll be good," said Kenny.

Dene aimed a finger. "If you two ever tell anyone this, I'll deny it – and you'll never work for me again."

"C'mon," said Tim, "spit it out."

Dene knew they wouldn't let him live this down. He grinned and looked to the sky. "I don't think that much of rugby anymore."

Kenny and Tim slapped their knees and hooted like schoolkids.

"No, really," said Dene. "Gridiron's a better game. And it's sure more fun to play."

"Ha! Woken up to yourself at last," said Tim.

"If you're gonna play it," said Kenny, "the first thing you need to learn is that it's not called gridiron."

"Okay, *football*."

"So, why don't you come to Honolulu and play?" said Tim. "I'll show you what sunshine looks like."

Dene's grin faded. He slid a bag of cement out of the pickup and dumped it beside the mixer. "Unfinished business."

"So, you *are* gonna try out for the Wolves again," said Kenny.

"Yep. But first I'm having a month off. Then I'm gonna step it up a notch."

"Tim?" said Kenny.

Tim shut down the mixer and leaned on the dented bowl. "Why go home when I can freeze my balls off here?"

Dene scuffed grit off his hands and settled on the tailgate of the Ford. He said to Kenny, "How about you?"

"Someone's gotta hold your hands."

"So, what's the plan?" said Tim.

"I've got less than a year to make it. Ten months, max. I'll work harder. Go all out for one more season. Sprints. Extra weight sessions. The lot."

Kenny scraped mud off his boots with a trowel. "I need a break from that place."

"They don't wanna see us again anyway," said Tim.

"Not the Wolves' gym," said Dene. "Somewhere else."

"Zanelle?" said Kenny.

Dene shrugged. It hadn't worked out with Zanelle. Not according to the Wolves at least. He remembered the line about doing the same thing over and over, and expecting a different result. He might not be too bright, but he didn't think he was insane.

He wanted to give himself every chance – and it was his last chance – so he needed to try something else.

"Dunno," he said. "Would Tallie take me on?"

"Too busy at the university," said Kenny.

Tim split the cement bag with a shovel. "Tallie won't even train us. Says we're like a pair o' girls."

"Fair call."

"Ha ha, *haole*."

Kenny pushed off the rock pile. He leaned into the back of the pickup and groped around inside his bag. "Switzer told me about a gym in town. Androgen something."

"Andropha," said Dene. "Mainly bodybuilders I think."

Kenny found a dusty business card. "That's it. Andropha Gymnasium. Mattson Lampard."

Tim said, "The power-lifter?"

Dene reached for the card. He flipped the creased paper and scrutinised the logo. "So that's Lampard's place." An idea suddenly called from the far, dark corners of his mind.

"Sounds like the go," said Tim. "How about it, Dene?"

Dene tried to ignore the voice in his head. He stood and spun the card onto the tailgate. "I don't think so."

"Some of the guys swear by him," said Kenny.

"Yeah, I've heard about him, too. From my father. His exact words were, 'steer clear'."

"Since when do you listen to your old man?"

"I know he's a pain in the neck, but at least he's on the right side of the law."

The air froze. Kenny and Tim stopped dead. Dene closed his eyes and bowed his head. He raised his hands, palm out, fingers up, and held them toward the twins.

"Token. Totem. I'm so, so sorry. I didn't mean that the way it sounded."

Tim started the mixer. "It's okay, man."

Kenny tapped his middle finger on the little cardboard square. He looked at Tim. "I'm gonna check this place out. Wanna come?"

"Sure thing."

The brothers turned to Dene. The idea sneaked from the shadows again. He said, "Maybe another time."

"C'mon, dude," said Tim. "Why not give it a go?"

He shook his head. "Because the guys that swear by Lampard are on steroids or peptides or some other shit." He dragged another rock from the pile. "And in case you hadn't noticed, they've all been cut."

Chapter 11

THE PREY DRIVE HAS five stages:

The Search...

The wolf lingered at the shadowed edge of the clearing. A crooked line of indentations pocked the snow. She followed the footprints into the barren glade. Cautious. Alert.

The Eye Stalk...

She halted, seeking an invisible prey. She inched forward on spatulate paws as broad as a big man's hand, but her weight sank through the crust of snow. A sound. A warning.

The Chase...

A snowshoe hare skittered over the hoary field. The wolf breached like a marlin, springing through plumes of frosted sea-spray. She bounded after her quarry, jagging right and left across the open space.

The Grab Bite...

She leapt on the hare in a gust of white, and seized its head in her jaws.

And the Kill Bite...

She crunched the hare's skull and cracked its neck with a savage wrench.

The wolf tore at the carcass. Her mate snatched his share. The pack converged, but held back. This was the alpha pair's meal. A morsel each and a mouthful of bloody snow for the rest. But enough to carry them to the next kill.

A sudden, anguished howl grappled with the wind. Not animal, not human. It echoed off the crags and swooped through the trees.

The wolf snapped her head up. Frozen needles bristled down her spine. Her muzzle pleated, filtering the scents on the frigid air. She scanned the summit, hard eyes full of menace. This sound was different, alien. But the message was the same.

A new rival.

A new threat.

The wolf and her pack trooped on. Constant. Resolute. Relentless. In some creatures, the prey drive must be encouraged, or even taught. In some – like the wolf – all five stages are perfectly formed at birth.

Survival of the fittest.

For centuries, novelists pitted man against nature, contriving victory over daunting foes. Rogue lions, crazed elephants, vengeful whales; in popular fiction, all have fallen to the hand of man. Some writers even declared man to be the supreme predator, but they were wrong.

He's not even close.

Not yet.

Chapter 12

THE BATTERED FORD DIDN'T look out of place wedged against one side of Dene's poky garage. Once holly green, the duco had wilted to wattle grey, and rust bloomed over scraped wheel arches. Stencilled lettering on the doors spelled *Selkirk Stonemasonry* in chipped white paint.

His unit shared a small block on the Vancouver side of Abbotsford. Old and shabby clapboard. Dry patches of lawn amid trampled dirt. The lock-up garage was a bonus; he didn't need to unload his tools every day to prevent them from being stolen. Hell, it meant the pickup wouldn't be stolen.

Or was less likely to be.

He wiped grime from his arms with a tattered sweatshirt and tossed it onto an old armchair crowded into a corner. He glanced at a speedball, then at a row of cast-iron dumbbells on the floor. The dumbbells made a set of eight, from forty pounds to seventy. The speedball hung from a frame screwed to the exposed studs and noggins of the wall.

When he worked the ball, the whole garage juddered and dust floated from the rafters.

Stuff it. He'd had enough dust for one day.

He squatted and gripped a pair of fifty-pounders, then stood and started an easy running motion. The dumbbells swung waist high. After a dozen swings he unlocked his elbows and hefted the weights to shoulder height. He rocked from side-to-side on bent knees, core braced tight against the momentum.

He reached a count of twenty. By thirty he was struggling. At forty his forearms began to cramp. Fifty was a good set. He'd go to fifty.

His cell phone rang.

He dropped the dumbbells onto the armchair, reached into the pickup, took his phone from the seat and checked the caller ID.

"Hello, Dad."

"I hear things didn't go too well at camp."

"That's what you want to talk about?"

Silence. Hesitation.

"Well, I just thought you'd want to discuss it. Your new goals."

Time to make a stand.

"My goals haven't changed. I'm doing what *I* want to do, not what *you* want me to do."

"For Christ's sake, you've been here three years. It was supposed to be one."

Dene looked down and stamped dry mud from his boots. "I don't want people saying I didn't have a go."

More silence.

"Why not play with the Bears then?"

Just what he wanted to hear.

"Oh, fuck the fuckin' Bears!"

"But you'd walk into their squad."

"I've told you a hundred times. Rugby was your game. It isn't mine, not anymore. I won't compromise."

"You've already compromised – you're with the Wolves. Go any further north and you'll be playing in the fucking Eskimo leagues. You tried, you failed. Why not give it up?"

Dene sagged against the pickup. "Inuit."

"What?"

"It's Inuit, not Eskimo. You don't need to insult everyone else as well as me."

"You don't understand, do you – I was a bloody champion. You'll never be as good as I was. You don't have the mongrel for a start."

"So I should stop trying, is that it?"

"Why not come back home? To London. We could start a security business and you could have a decent job."

"I already have a decent job. And there's Zanelle."

He heard his father inhale.

"Oh, tell me you're not getting married. Oh, *Lord* – please tell me she's not pregnant!"

Now Dene hesitated. He realised he hadn't thought that far ahead. He bounced his boot against a tyre. "How did you know about training camp?"

"I care what happens to you, you know."

"Are you spying on me? You do so much spying in your job that you think it's normal to spy on me too?"

"Of course not, Dene. It's nothing like –"

"When I think of the years I spent trying to earn your respect. I don't know why I bothered. Thanks for the pep-talk."

He jabbed at his phone and tossed it back onto the seat, then smashed his fist into the speed-ball. A cloud of dust wafted down. He snatched up the dumbbells and started swinging.

"And fuck you, too."

Chapter 13

ABBOTSFORD'S UNIVERSITY FORMED A network with twenty-five other public institutions across the Province. These organisations provided tertiary education to ten percent of British Columbia's population.

But Dene Selkirk wasn't one of them.

When his knuckles were raw and his fingers cracked and split from cement burns, or he hobbled around with frostbitten toes, he knew he should have taken a different path. He should have pursued a degree – perhaps something in medicine – but he'd cut off his nose to spite his face. Too bad the concept of 'give and take' was so foreign to his father. With Davey Selkirk, it was his way or nothing. Always had been.

Dene knew it was his fault as much as his dad's, but he still preferred to be led rather than pushed. Asked rather than told. Above all, he would have liked some encouragement, but now it was too late.

Now he was doing it his way.

He sent Tallie a text. Nothing came back, but how hard could it be to find someone on a school campus? He shaded his eyes and read the brushed aluminium signs outside the university's admin block. No joy. There had to be another means. He scanned the procession of students dawdling across green, sunlit lawns. Some chatted. Most peered at their cells.

Two girls drifted by. Nope. A single went past. Absolutely not. The intent of a grown man approaching college girls could be misconstrued.

For many of their generation the #MeToo movement was a flag-waving cause. Modern women made old-time feminists seem unambitious. Dene could hear his father now: *'Bless the empowered little darlings.'*

Everyone on the Wolves' roster received counselling about sexual harassment, but as a demographic harassed more than most, the footballers had little sympathy. They toed the company line, but didn't hide their opinions. It was victim mentality, sanctioned and weaponised.

He bailed up a full-bearded teenager in stovepipe moleskins. "Hey there. Can you tell me where the science labs are?"

"Biology or chemistry?"

"Ah...Talisman Kainoa."

"It's lunchtime. You want the gym."

"Do I?"

"Tallie's always at the gym."

The kid pointed behind Dene. "Third building that way."

Too easy.

"Thanks a lot."

"You're welcome."

Dene pulled on a heavy fire-door and strolled into the gymnasium. Shouts and laughter echoed from the high ceiling, and bright lights gleamed on a polished maple wood floor. Handfuls of students

lolled about at chromed exercise stations, joking through half-hearted workouts.

He spotted Talisman straight away. The big Hawaiian pressed up
and down in a steel dip frame with a sixty-pound plate suspended
from a chain on a wide leather belt. Full, explosive extension. Deep,
controlled dip. Perfect technique.

Dene stopped behind the action.

"Keep going, Tallie – one more."

Talisman Kainoa pumped out five more reps, then dropped to
the floor and turned. A mane of sable hair framed an impassive
face. Smooth, honey-bright skin glowed through glittering beads of
perspiration.

Athletic. Powerful. Imposing.

And arrestingly beautiful.

"Easy for you to say," she said. "What's happening, Dene?"

He looked her over. She had two inches on him. And carried
forty pounds more muscle. He'd played a lot of football; he was
accustomed to big bodies. But none of those was the next thing to a
Polynesian goddess.

"Not much," he said. "You heard about the training camp?"

Tallie unbuckled her belt and the plate clanged to the floor. She
unclipped the chain, picked up the plate and slid it onto a rack with
one hand.

She nodded. "Mmm."

"So. Wanna make some pocket-money?"

She peeled off her gloves and tossed them into a gym bag. "You're
gonna ask if I'll help you make the Wolves' roster."

"Well, I was hoping."

"Now, how can I work with you if I won't work with those brothers of mine?"

She slung the bag across her shoulder and made for the showers. Dene skipped a couple of steps to catch up.

"I thought it was worth a try. Kenny and Tim might like some help too, you know."

"Those boys need to be taught a lesson. Haven't seen their father in over two years. They gonna be stubborn, I can be stubborn."

"It can't be easy for them. I mean –"

Tallie corralled him against a rock-climbing wall with one enormous arm. She jabbed a thumb at the sweat-soaked tee clinging to her torso. Blood-red letters spelled out her favourite saying.

Life is Primal, Death is Final.

She said, "Sooner or later, we all gotta learn that it is what it is. Now, tell me straight. Are they really going to Lampard's gym? After everything that's happened?"

"I don't think they realise it's him. I tried to drop a hint, but...."

"Dene, I like you, but if he hurts those boys, you will surely answer to me."

He took in the blood-gorged arms, the bulging shoulders. A foot-hold on the wall behind him chiselled into his back.

"I don't want that either," he said.

Tallie straightened to her full height. "What you *don't* want is for their father to find out, or you are history. Family friend or not." She turned and batted the shower room door aside.

Dene breathed slowly in. And slowly out.

Feminists, shmeminists.

Chapter 14

DENE COULD HAVE MADE the drive from Abbotsford to Chilliwack in thirty minutes on the Trans-Canada. Instead, he took it easy on the Parallel Road and racked up forty-five.

Chilliwack's RCMP Community Office leased a municipal complex in a light industrial area on Airport Road, south of the city centre. Automatic sliding doors opened onto a concrete forecourt that expanded into a concourse with neat lawns at each end. Sturdy black bollards ringed the entrance.

He parked the Ford and sat in the cab. The more he thought about it, the more he liked the idea of Lampard's gym. Murky history aside, the man had a reputation for turning athletes around. The testimonials ranged from glowing to hero worship. So what if some fell by the wayside? Dene had no intention of joining them. Forewarned is forearmed, and if he wanted a career, he needed everything in his favour.

Everything.

He checked his hair in the mirror. He flicked his collar up, then turned it down again. Checked for messages on his cell. Nothing. He couldn't put it off any longer. If Tallie wouldn't train him, he needed to find someone else. Telling Zanelle would be the hard part.

He bumped the door open and swung his feet onto the asphalt. He stood and stretched, then dodged around the bollards, scuffed his boots on a doormat, and edged into the foyer.

He looked around. Public service posters covered the walls, and sporting trophies gleamed in a wooden cabinet. He approached a reception counter with a pale blue laminate top.

Tom Calder sprouted from beneath the counter and dropped a stack of ledgers onto the laminate. "How can we help today?"

"Hi. Is Zanelle Argus busy?"

The young constable called over his shoulder. "Zanelle? Someone to see you."

Dene walked a small circle. Zanelle appeared from behind the partition and met him in the middle of the foyer, concern in her eyes.

"You didn't call," she said. "I guess it's not good news."

"They still don't think I'm up to it."

She brushed her fingertips down his arm. "What are you going to do?"

"There's not enough work to get us through winter, so I don't know if I can extend my visa."

"What about your dad? Can he help?"

You've already compromised.

Dene glanced around. Calder ducked back under the counter.

"He's the last person I want to talk to right now."

Zanelle took his hand and squeezed his fingers. "You think, maybe it's time to let it go then?"

"But I know I can do better. Even you said I don't put in enough."

"I didn't mean that. You've been great with me."

The hard part.

"Yeah, well, I was thinking I might try another gym."

Zanelle's eyes widened. She dropped his hand, stepped back and folded her arms. "You said you wanted more speed."

"Well, now the coach thinks I need to be stronger."

"Okay. What if we make some adjustments to your program?"

"I'm just not sure. I mean, I want to try some heavy-duty stuff. I don't think you have the equipment I need."

Calder gathered up the ledgers and vanished into the squad room. Zanelle watched him leave.

"So, where will you go?" she said.

"There's a place called Andropha Gymnasium."

"You sure about that?"

"Apparently they get results. Footballers, bodybuilders, wrestlers. Lotta guys go there."

She pouted at the floor. "Okay. If you think it'll help."

"Zannie – Zanelle, it's nothing against you."

She planted her hands on her hips and nodded half a dozen times, like an angry bobblehead. "No, you're right. I've taken you as far as I can."

"It's just that I want to try a different direction, that's all."

"Then maybe you should try another direction in your personal life as well."

She spun and marched across the foyer. The linoleum squeaked beneath her toe as she swivelled around the end of the counter.

Dene took a step. "Listen, I need to get back to work, so I'll call you, let you know what's happening."

She said, "Don't bother," and disappeared behind the partition.

Dene watched her grey shape roil like a thundercloud in the foggy glass. He did a slow about-face, then slipped out between the sliding doors.

"Thought as much," he said.

Chapter 15

ZEAL & VIGOR HEALTH Club was the place to be seen when sweating it out in downtown Vancouver. A high-end gymnasium with celebrity cachet.

The evening cardio classes glowed with white smiles and orange tans. Slick and shiny executives battled slick and shiny machines on the exercise floor. Recreational triathletes admired each other's Vaporflys while cloned news presenters clustered together and laughed too much. Cashed-up joggers plugged away on treadmills that overlooked the city through a sparkling-clean glass wall.

Dr Paul Swift toddled on the treadmill farthest from the entrance, a black T-shirt with the gold Z&V logo bunched up around his waist. His rosy cheeks bobbed like apples as he gnawed on a muesli bar and gazed at a television screen.

Two out of five gym members are driven by vanity or the dread of dying young. For the rest, it's a dating game. A bricks-and-mortar storefront where you can market yourself, or get a better feel for the merchandise than you can when shopping on-line.

Swift fell into the 'dread of dying' group, though at forty-five he wasn't young, and he sure wasn't driven.

"How's it going, Paul?"

David Selkirk hauled his lanky frame onto the machine beside the doctor.

"Hey, Dave. Welcome to my home-away-from-home."

Selkirk tapped on his treadmill's touchscreen and began a lazy stroll. "Slow and steady. You'll get there."

"I've been going slow and steady for eight years. Ain't there yet."

"Could be your diet. Those things taste any good?"

"Like a vegetarian's turd – I don't recommend them." He poked the last of the snack into his mouth and munched like a beaver. "Did you get my letter?"

"Made an appointment as soon as I read it."

"Good. We'll reassess and schedule some follow-up treatment."

"Business must be going well – I couldn't get in for a month."

"Well, I only work three days a week. Don't worry, you won't keel over before then."

"Handy to know. I thought you might have those blood results."

"I do, but we needn't discuss that here."

"Okay," said Selkirk. "Have been thinking it might be urgent, that's all."

Swift blinked at the taller man. He shut down his treadmill and said, "Come with me."

Selkirk prodded the touchscreen. He stepped off his machine and followed Swift to the corner beneath the television.

A digital scale sat on the floor. Swift lifted himself onto the platform. Bright green numbers flickered. He gestured at the result and then stepped off.

"Now you," he said.

Selkirk stood on the scale. The men stared down.

"What does that tell you?" said Swift.

"That I'm lighter than you."

"And you're damn near a foot taller." Swift glanced around. "Dave, I don't want to alarm you, but we must face facts. You're very sick. But you haven't told me all I need to know."

"About?"

"About when you were playing football."

Selkirk had wondered how long he could avoid the subject. He stared over the doctor's head, massaging his cheeks with the thumb and fingers of one hand.

He said, "What does that have to do with blood cancer?"

Swift lowered his voice. "Blood cancer is an umbrella term for a number of conditions. The biggest problem is that half the time – literally fifty percent of the time – we don't know what causes it. What we *do* know is that exposure to drugs can be a trigger."

Selkirk scanned the room. Two lissom girls stood nearby, their heads together over a glowing phone screen. An effete man wrestled with an overloaded Pec Deck. A couple of spin cycles whirred in the background.

"You're right," he said. "Best not talk about it here."

Chapter 16

ANDROPHA GYMNASIUM OCCUPIED A cinderblock warehouse three blocks from where Highway One passed through the southern side of Abbotsford. It shared a parking lot with a take-away chilli joint and a store that sold motorcycle gear.

Dene swung his pickup onto the concrete pad and stopped a few spaces past the gym entrance. He stepped out of the truck and looked around. A couple of dozen vehicles ranged across the carpark in random bunches, noonday sun flaring off their windshields.

He spotted the twins' white Corolla in the row behind him. The Wolves players ribbed Kenny about his 'nun's car', but Dene knew it hadn't missed a beat. Not that the Wolves could say much right now. After three games of the regular season their for-and-against column stood at 19-72.

He turned and gave the warehouse a once over. Frosted panes of wired glass ran along the wall like portholes in a ship. A slender radio mast soared above the roof. An orange Chevy Tahoe backed against a roller door at the rear of the building, and a black Jeep Renegade sat beside an aluminium-framed door near the front.

A crude rendition of Myron's *Discobolus* loomed over the doorway. A sign showing business hours clung to dollops of Blu Tack inside the glass. Dene kicked his steel-caps against the step, dislodging flakes of dry slurry, and pushed the door open.

The reception area had faux wood panelling around the walls, and a remnant of coffee-coloured carpet lay askew on the floor. A couple of dusty, plastic pot plants fronted a timber counter. A first-aid kit hung on the wall. The sign next to it read: AUTOMATED EXTERNAL DEFIBRILLATOR.

Bass-heavy music throbbed from an adjoining studio. A blonde in red lycra leggings pranced down a ramp from the studio, ample breasts bouncing. Her eyes flicked over Dene and she smiled on autocue.

"Hi there," she said. "I'm Erin. Welcome to Andropha Gymnasium. How can we help you achieve your goals today?"

"Hi. Um...I'm interested in joining up. What do I need to do?"

Erin flounced behind the counter. "So, first you fill in some forms. Then we'll do an assessment and get you started on a program."

Dene glanced over his shoulder. He saw bodies hopping and jumping in an aerobic dance class, most of them out of sync.

"I might be in the wrong place. I wanted to build up a bit. For football."

"Oh, you'll want our Cast Iron membership then. But you have to apply. Why don't I get our manager to show you around?"

"Okay, fine."

Erin pressed a button behind the counter, then grabbed some photocopied sheets and marked crosses where she needed a signature. A door beside the first-aid kit opened and a six-foot walnut appeared.

"This is Marcus," said Erin. "Marc, could you take this gentleman and show him the weight room?"

"Happy to," said the walnut. He offered a craggy mitt, fingers splayed, palm down, asserting dominance.

Tosser.

"Marcus Quillan. Nice to meet you."

Quillan had thick lips and waxed eyebrows beneath a cap of dark, gelled hair. He wore a white singlet a size too small. Dense slabs of muscle writhed beneath his skin and full sleeve tattoos covered his arms. The guy would be right at home in the Wolves' locker room.

Dene extended his hand. "Dene Selkirk. Same here."

Quillan crushed the knuckles. Dene expected it, but it was still annoying. Someone with something to prove. It came with the ink, but the tatts were all for show as well. They were mock Yakuza, not authentic *Irezumi*.

"Come this way," he said. "I'll show you how a real gym works."

The manager rocked down a short corridor and into a cavernous space. Dene thought it was an aircraft hangar until he realised the mirrors on the far wall made it seem twice the size. An aggressive soundtrack thumped through the room. Battered frames and heavy-duty workstations. Racks of dumbbells. Mounds of chain. Tons of plates.

Wall-to-wall metal.

Twenty heavily muscled men, in pairs or groups of three, sweated and grunted while spotters barked encouragement. Their skin gleamed beneath a grid of bright lamps hanging from the rafters.

Iron, rust, testosterone, and attitude.

Dene had prepared himself to play it cool but couldn't pull it off. Heavily muscled? They were beasts. This was hard-core heartland.

"Impressive."

"No pussies here," said Quillan.

Dene grinned and tilted his head. "Thought I saw a few out the front."

Quillan opened his mouth in a soundless laugh.

"Motivation," he said. "You know how it is. Get the girls and the boys follow." He pointed at a door in the wall to the right. "Showers and lockers that way. You'll get a membership card and a key when you sign up."

A tall man in a black sweatsuit crossed the floor and disappeared through a doorway to the left of the weight room. The gym's logo covered the back of his track top, circled above and below by the words *Andropha* and *Gymnasium*, like the rockers of a full-patch biker.

Quillan anticipated the question. "Office area. Invitation only, I'm afraid."

Dene nodded and skimmed the room. He saw Kenny and Tim at a bench press station against the far wall. He waved and Tim saluted back.

"New guys," said Quillan. "Know 'em?"

"Yeah, I play football with them."

"Like I said – no pussies here. They'll hang in, or they won't." Quillan cuffed a rack of steel plates. "This place is full-on old school. We pump iron, and lots of it. It's the only way."

Dene nodded. When he mentioned football, most people asked if he was with the Lions or the Wolves. Quillan hadn't, so either he already knew or didn't care. If he knew, it would be from the twins. If he didn't care it was refreshing, though some people only faked disinterest. Quillan avoided the subject, so maybe that was his game. Of course, Dene still hadn't started in a single official match in the CFL, so....

Who's the tosser now?

The sight of a hulking figure pulling deadlifts in a corner distracted Dene from his self-reproach.

The man worked out alone. Wide shoulders, thick midriff, broad back and hips. From behind he could have been a wool bale. Not cut and muscular like the others in the room, but every inch as big.

Blotches of dampness spread over his baggy shorts and faded blue singlet. Legs like bowed fence posts disappeared into flat-soled wrestling boots. The spotlights shone against his pale skin and the hairless dome of his skull.

"Who's that?" said Dene.

"Serious lifter back in the day."

"Looks like it."

"That's the owner. That's Mattson Lampard."

Dene felt his stomach harden to cold porcelain.

Lampard hoisted a mammoth weight from the mat. The bar bent in his hands under the load. He lifted his chin and straightened to lockout, shoulders back, scapulae almost touching. He lowered the barbell past his knees, then heaved it up again.

The manager waited a moment before going for the close.

"So. Think you can hack it?"

"Yeah, sure."

"Okay then. Let's get you signed up."

Quillan turned back to the corridor. Dene lingered. He watched Lampard slide two more plates onto the bar.

"No problem."

Chapter 17

FEW PEOPLE WAKE UP knowing they'll die that day.

Barry Epstein wasn't one of them, or he wouldn't have pushed his old Hyundai through the darkness so fast. In Epstein's defence, he was under pressure. Tomorrow was the first of July. The fiscal year was already three months old, and it hadn't been a promising start.

The harried sales rep had called at every motel, bar, and restaurant from Agassiz to Hope, taking orders for some wine glasses and a box of drinking straws. The hospitality business wasn't booming.

Highway Seven mirrors the Trans-Canada's route from Hope, all the way to Vancouver. It tracks the northern edge of the Fraser River while Highway One follows the southern bank. Epstein worked the north side of the river going up, and planned to work the south side on the way home.

He ate a meal at his last stop, a roadside diner. He could have stayed the night in Hope but decided to make a run for Chilliwack. It wasn't much, but it was better than Hope. Besides, there'd be no traffic on a Wednesday night, and it would save him half an hour in the morning.

Ribbons of moonshine draped the clouds drifting over the valley. The highway meandered through the hills, damp surface gleaming with a soft pewter glow from the back-lit sky.

Epstein bumped the Hyundai's cruise control up past sixty. He searched the radio for some easy listening, then tugged at the wheel to correct when he veered across the yellow centre lines. He gave up on the radio and raked through the glove compartment for a compact disc.

The tired rep glanced up and steered his car around a gentle bend. He sensed a vague shadow extending across the road ahead.

A shadow with legs.

A full-grown moose ambled onto the bitumen, then halted, straddling the shoulder. Epstein wrenched the car into the middle of the road and swerved around the startled animal. He swung back into his lane, scanning the rear-view mirror.

"Holy moly! That was close."

The salesman laughed. Damn moose weren't harmless, but it didn't help if you drove into one. He peered through the windshield and checked that the headlamps were on high-beam, then gave the cruise control another tap. He delved back into the glove compartment and found his favourite album. He fumbled it open with one hand and popped the silver disc out with his fingertips. He lined it up with the CD player and saw the mechanism suck *Bookends* into its thin black mouth.

What he didn't see was the second shadow on Highway One.

The Hyundai slammed into a six-foot high, fourteen-hundred-pound bull moose at close to seventy miles per hour. The hapless creature's disembowelled guts exploded as it ripped the little sedan's top clean off. A rooster tail of blood and glass spewed into the air behind the car.

And Barry Epstein's head went with it.

The driverless vehicle skated across the road, through a gap between concrete barriers, and jounced up a steep embankment. It ploughed to a stop against a lofty white spruce, buried in a bier of drooping branches.

Pine needles fell soft as drizzle from the tree's shaking limbs, and a chorus of wolves howled in the distance.

————◆————

SEVENTY MILES WEST OF the highway carnage, David Selkirk sat in the gloom of his small apartment on Cordova Street. Single bedroom, single bathroom. It was all a single man needed.

A laptop screen powdered the living area with light. Selkirk stroked the trackpad, checking his stock portfolio. It didn't take long. He knew all the reasons he should diversify but he couldn't afford to. Paul Swift's message was getting through. He was in trouble. And cure or no cure, it was going to cost him money.

Money. It was all anyone wanted, but it could get you into strife. And then you needed more to bail yourself out again. His first marriage at twenty-two showed that. His second marriage only confirmed it. Weddings could be expensive in more ways than one. He'd left his first wife. His second had left him. Mistakes all round.

But he was the only one paying.

He did some calculations and scrawled notes in an old dictation pad pilfered from Val Bedford's desk. He'd put everything he could spare into a single blue-chip company, but the stock market had tanked big time and still hadn't come all the way back. Damn the bloody *coronavirus*.

As things were turning out, it didn't matter anyway. The stock market was a long-term investment. He'd never had the patience. And now he didn't have the time.

He needed to make a killing. Needed to gamble.

The whisper was that the Vancouver Wolves would sign a new sponsor in the off-season. It was a company he'd never heard of.

Intriguing.

He found their details on the Toronto Stock Exchange site. A small cap entity specialising in organic health supplements, insignificant as far as pharmaceutical companies went. It had floated two years earlier with a modest price bump but now it was flatlining and the price-earnings ratio had dipped into negative territory. Which meant the company was spending more money than it was making. Not good for a growth investor.

Or even a gambler.

The Wolves were desperate, that was a given. They'd clutch at any lifeline. But why would a tiny, fledgling concern take a chance on them? What were *they* gambling on?

He pulled up their website. It looked professional enough. He read the blurb – *Mission Statement, About Us* – and then clicked on *Our Key Personnel*. He ran down the list of Executive Officers and Company Directors. Each posed head shot was paired with a brief, flattering profile. He recognised a couple of local names but saw no real heavy hitters.

Selkirk scrolled through the happy snaps, then stopped. He flicked back to a face. He scanned the bio and looked at the photograph for a long time.

Then he said, "You devious prick."

Chapter 18

TOBY FRANKLIN TOLD EVERYONE his name was Tobias, but too many people knew otherwise. It was part of the joke that shrouded his life.

The punchline to that joke was the *Chilliwack Trading Post*. Free to citizens of the town and surrounding area, the *'Post'* was funded by people who sold in the Classifieds, and small local businesses which advertised within its dozen tabloid pages.

Franklin acquired the newspaper through the charity of a now deceased aunt. Her meagre bequest was just enough to let him snap up the failing business, though it didn't enhance his standing in the community. The *Post* was little more than junk mail, and hardly announced its owner as a titan of commerce.

The problem was technology. These days, most people sold their 'knockoffs, castoffs and rip-offs' via the internet. Online transactions and parcel post assured anonymity. It was more convenient and safer, but a dwindling demographic still used the print media.

Small and uncoordinated, Franklin shunned football or other athletic pursuits. Plain featured and awkward, he avoided the nightlife and mainstream social pastimes. Ill-educated and not too bright, he struggled to project charisma.

But balls he had.

Faced with the prospect of losing everything if the paper went under, Franklin worked hard. He engaged an English tutor once a week and took a three-month writing course. He pirated old comics for the paper, and added a puzzle page with weekly prizes that always went to someone nobody knew.

And he learned the power of words. Words in the right place, at the right time, and in the right ears. Words used selectively and without remorse. Why say 'unusual' or 'peculiar' when you could say 'bizarre'?

Control the narrative.

Franklin only printed information from which he could profit. And he considered fabrication a means to that end. Because, for all their sporting prowess and magazine good looks and high-level schooling, most people still wanted to wallow in the muck.

In the misery or squalor or debauchery of others.

So that's what he gave them. Rumour, gossip, hearsay and straight-out invention. The *Trading Post* shouted one outrageous headline every Friday morning, with an equally florid story attached. And demand skyrocketed.

Toby Franklin became a magnate in the currency of lies.

Just after 7:00 a.m. Franklin tipped half a jug of maple syrup over a stack of pancakes at his favourite all-night cafe. He tossed his lank ponytail over a shoulder and forked lumps of the sodden mess into his narrow, pasty face. When he overheard a couple behind him talking about a 'gang of naked men' who 'raped and murdered that poor family' in their car up near Bridal Falls, he almost choked. Here was a readymade headline, no fabrication necessary.

Hold the presses!

The middle-aged pair was from simple mountain stock. They opened up when Franklin flashed his dodgy credentials and hinted at a connection to *60 Minutes*. He learned that an hour before, they had *maybe* glimpsed a naked man in the mountains near a road accident on Highway One. Definitely a white shape, anyway.

Sketchy and unlikely. But it was enough. He grabbed his helmet and backpack and hustled out to the parking lot. He threw a leg over his Moto-Guzzi, growled onto Luckacuck Way, sped onto the Trans-Canada and headed east.

He hammered the bike around T-Can's serpentine bends. What he wanted more than anything as a teenager was a motorcycle, but they cost money and his side of the family had none. Despite his recent fiscal upturn he still wasn't loaded, so the Guzzi was an indulgence.

He'd found it by chance at the back of a leaning hay barn near Surrey. The owner wanted too much, but it was a Le Mans 850 model and he couldn't resist. He scraped together the cash and spent months restoring it with as many upgraded parts as he could find.

Fifteen minutes later, Franklin was trying to decide if he'd repaint the bike its original red or leave it pumpkin orange, when he spotted an Abbotsford cruiser's flashing lights. He swung a U-turn and pulled up inside a row of traffic cones. He took off his helmet and surveyed the scene.

A handful of official vehicles lined the northbound edge of the roadside. Two Mounties waved slowing cars past the accident site. A road crew had cleared what remained of the moose off the highway. The bloody carcass lay heaped on the verge, one crooked leg pointing skyward like a makeshift battlefield cross.

The crew had swept up the chrome and shattered glass and had spread an absorbent mix on the greasy bitumen. A thin sheet of kitty litter now covered a sixty-yard stretch of the Trans-Canada.

Soon after Franklin took over the *Trading Post*, he bought a Canon PowerShot for when he couldn't find generic images on the net. He was never without it.

Now he pulled the camera from his pack. Its main selling point was the 50x zoom lens. More than once he'd taken long shots of couples in an ardent embrace. And if you cropped unnecessary details, and enlarged a photo far enough, it became pixelated and indistinct.

A priceless aid to the power of suggestion.

The morning sun streamed through the treetops but the slope was still in shade. Franklin saw twin furrows leading through the grass to a small silver convertible. He put the camera's viewfinder to his eye and pressed the zoom.

Whoa. Turned out it wasn't a convertible at all.

Moose would do that.

Click.

A blue plastic tarpaulin covered the vehicle's cabin. A gaggle of uniformed officers milled around as a forensic team went over the ruined sedan.

Forensic team?

A raw-boned constable from Abbotsford hiked past Franklin toward the wreck. "Hey, Toby, get a shot of that tree. It'll make a great Sasquatch."

The cop laughed his way up the hillside. The barb wasn't undeserved. Franklin had once passed off a dog's water dish as a UFO.

"It's Tobias – and get fucked."

Franklin crossed the verge but someone grabbed a handful of ponytail and swung him toward the road. He twisted free and almost dropped the camera.

A beefy officer with a porcine face wiped his hand on his uniform trousers. "Watch your mouth, Pulitzer."

"Sergeant Pym. What a surprise."

"Snuck out of your hole for nothing this morning, Toby. What a shame."

The newspaperman stared around at the parked vehicles. "Doesn't look like nothing."

Pym spread his arms and herded Franklin away from the smashed car. "Here's your scoop. Driver hit a moose. Ran into a tree. One fatality. Two if you count Bullwinkle."

Pym's first name was Roland. If you knew him well enough you could get away with calling him Roly, but no one with half a brain called him 'Roly-poly'.

"C'mon Sarge, I need more than that."

"That's the way it happened. Lucky the guy was dead before the wolves got to him. Now, piss off."

Franklin had learned well. He ignored the hypocrisy of his vocation and reverted to the standard line. He got the indignant tone just right. "But people are entitled to the facts."

"Stick to what you do best. Make something up." Pym trudged away and didn't look back.

The local authorities tolerated Franklin because the Police Board said they had to. The Abby PD adopted a 'we' approach, urging co-operation between the force and the community, but it seemed some officers hadn't read the memo. Roland Pym wasn't one to drown you in specifics. Or pleasantries.

Franklin shrugged. "Suit yourself."

He wandered back to his motorcycle, eyeing the silver car in the spruce branches. The sun had topped the ridge and golden streaks flooded down the slope, broken by the elongated shadows of the pines.

Halfway up the hillside, beyond the cluster of activity around the wreck, a jumble of rocks and bleached logs huddled together. A thread of sunlight outlined the small cairn. From afar, through squinted eyes and with a bit of imagination, it could have been a pale, humanoid form.

Franklin snapped a couple of shots. Pym wouldn't like it, but stiff shit. He could quote the couple at the diner. Unless something better came along, that was this week's story.

He packed the camera and straightened the backpack on his shoulders. He pulled his helmet on, fired up the Guzzi and blasted back toward town. As he slithered onto the highway an unmarked car slowed and pulled up inside the cordoned area. He glimpsed silver hair and the shine of bright buttons on a blue uniform. He'd seen the face often enough. The man behind the wheel had aspirations beyond law enforcement.

Franklin roared around a sweeping left-hander, distracted by the new arrival.

The Deputy Chief Constable?

Chapter 19

THE FINISHED ROCK WALL spanned the fence-line and curved up the drive toward the house. Tim hosed out the mixer while Kenny sponged mortar from the last course of basalt blocks. Dene strolled down the driveway.

"Any luck?" said Kenny.

"I left them some cards. We might get more referrals."

"Still no work?" said Tim.

"Only the golf club job. We'll take the week off and start at the club on Monday."

By a stroke of good fortune, the home owner's sister was manager of Abbotsford's Castle Hill Country Club. So impressed had she been by the wall that she contracted Selkirk Stonemasonry to build a new stone feature at the Country club, and low stone walls at the tees on all eighteen holes of their private golf course.

The twins lifted the mixer onto the Ford's tailgate and rolled it against the back of the cab.

Kenny said, "How long before the Wolves sack Bartoli do you think?"

"It's only his third year," said Dene. "And last year hardly counts."

"Geez," said Tim, "it's only the Wolves' third year. They can't be that ruthless. What did they expect?"

"Don't bet on it," said Kenny. "They're four-zip now, and they won't be winning this weekend either."

Tim shook his head. "Harsh call, brah. But hey, there's an upside – if they keep going this well, they have to sign us next season."

Kenny turned to Dene. "Don't know about us, but there's something wrong if you don't get a start."

Dene screwed up his eyes and weaved his head in the 'maybe but don't think so' motion. He'd fallen on his face too many times.

Kenny poked him in the shoulder. "Listen, *haole*. Time for straight talk. We've been playing this game all our lives. You only started four years ago. It's time you made your mark."

"Yeah? I still remember you blokes pissing yourselves when I lined up on the wrong side of the scrimmage."

"Okay, you were average at first. But you've improved out of sight. You run rings around us now."

"Speak for yourself," said Tim. "I'm pushing steel like crazy – I'll look like Arnold soon."

Kenny scowled at his brother. "Won't make you play any better."

"Well, I think I'm a good chance."

"Fat chance you mean."

"No, seriously. They've gotta give us a go. Shucks, I'm so confident, I'm gonna hit that gym right now."

Dene grinned. Tim could be a smart mouth when he wanted to.

Kenny said, "At least the gym at the Wolves didn't cost us anything. I'm pretty sure we won't get our investment back from Andropha."

"Have to admit," said Tim, "it's eating into my entertainment expenses, know what I mean?"

"All I know is I'd rather be making money than spending it."

"The golf club job will pay okay," said Dene. "I'll give us a bonus."

"Hallelujah. That'll go straight to the gym too."

Tim lifted a bucket of wooden stakes and faded fluoro stringlines into the Ford. "Made round to go round, brah." He shoved the bucket up tight against a crate full of hammers and bolsters.

Dene dumped a half-empty bag of cement beside the bucket. "Don't worry. Next year the Wolves will be paying for everything."

Kenny coiled the hose and tossed it onto the tools. "Just so long as someone does."

He threw a whiskery nylon rope over the mixer, and Tim tied it to an after-market cleat with a simple trucker's hitch. The pickup listed hard to port as he yanked down on the rope.

Dene cast an eye over the two line-backers. They were taller and heavier than he was. They moved better. And they knew the game better. If they couldn't make it, how in blue blazes could he?

You'll never be as good as I was.

And in that moment, the idea came skulking back. It was irrational and unethical. So where was he getting these notions?

"Alright Mushy, Wishbone," he said. "Let's head 'em up, move 'em out."

They jammed into the cab, and the Ford clattered away toward Abbotsford.

Chapter 20

PAUL SWIFT CHEWED ON a mouthful of Mars Bar. He worked the confection off his teeth with his tongue and then took a swig of Diet Coke.

David Selkirk arched an eyebrow.

"I know," said Swift. "It's a compromise."

Selkirk admired the office. It was smaller than his own, but more opulent. A pair of cobalt-blue Chesterfields faced off from opposing, latte-coloured walls. The wings of a Cocobolo wood desk kept the couches apart, like a referee between boxers. Framed diplomas hung across the wall behind Swift's head, like a gilded street banner.

The doctor put his snack aside and centred a red-tabbed folder in front of him. He consulted a computer screen, as if verifying details from the hard-copy.

"Dave, this is the situation. Your bone marrow is not producing blood cells. It's a condition called aplastic anaemia." He flipped open the file and ran his forefinger down a page. "Now, it looks like the chemotherapy hasn't had a great effect."

Selkirk hunched into a velvet club chair in front of the desk. "You mean it hasn't worked."

"No. But there are other options. I just need more background from you."

A trace of hope fluttered through Selkirk's eyes. "Would that help treat it?"

"It would mean we don't waste time guessing."

"But there *are* treatments?"

"Yes, there are. Bone marrow transfusions. Stem cell therapy. And there's always new research. Some excellent papers coming out of Vienna."

"Don't make it sound so serious." He gave a weak smile, but it faded with the words.

Swift spread his hands, faintly contrite. "What can I say? You're in serious trouble."

Selkirk pushed himself to his feet. He hitched his trousers and went to the window. He could see the Consulate tower block and a slice of the harbour, shining bright beneath a cornflower sky.

He said, "There was a time when I was a good footballer. I mean really good. But when you're talking World Cup rugby, that's a different level altogether."

Swift worked to finish a stolen bite of Mars Bar.

"Sure," he said. "Same thing happens here. Kids go from superstars in college to rookies in the NFL. Go on."

"The first Rugby Union World Cup was in nineteen eighty-seven. It was a big deal. Everyone was switched on, trying to impress. Half-way through the tournament we ran into a second rower. Whopping great Canuck. He came out of nowhere and played the house down. A few of us asked him his secret. He said a trainer at his club back home helped him out."

"With drugs, I'm assuming."

"He told us this guy had developed a serum. A kind of speed and strength booster. Said it couldn't hurt because it was all natural."

"Yeah," said Swift, "I hear that all the time. So's rattlesnake venom. You got onto this stuff?"

Selkirk nodded at his reflection in the window. "Not many guys knew. We were a secret club."

"How many?"

"By the next World Cup there were fourteen, fifteen? But the Canuck was a no-show. He just fell off the radar. And the serum didn't seem to work for everyone."

"But it did with you."

"Oh, Jesus, I was unstoppable. Thirty-four years old and playing like I was twenty-four."

"And you all took this serum?"

Selkirk wavered. He looked at the doctor.

"Every drop we could get."

Swift unscrewed the cap on his Coke. He took a gulp and wiped his mouth with the back of his hand.

"Well, this is a start." He sat the bottle beside the remnants of his Mars Bar. "We track these guys down. Do some tests. Make some comparisons. Maybe get a clearer prognosis."

"It won't be that simple."

"Meaning?"

"Some of them...had a reaction."

"What kind of reaction?"

"Violent."

"How violent?"

"Very. Uncontrollable."

"I mean violent how?"

"Manslaughter."

"Christ." Swift rattled his fingers over the computer keyboard.

He slowly patted the desktop, then glanced at his patient. "You know I have to ask, Dave. Did it affect you too?"

Selkirk gazed out the window.

He'd left his first wife. His second had left him.

He returned to the chair and sat, his long legs as bent and narrow as a grasshopper's.

"This treatment," he said. "How do we go about it?"

The doctor plucked the lid off a fountain pen and scribbled a note in the folder. "Well, donor blood from a relative has the best chance of success. In the short term."

"And in the long term?"

"A bone marrow transplant could be of benefit. But again, it needs to be a compatible donor. You have family?"

A pause. Barely a heartbeat.

"Not so you'd notice."

Swift held the pen to his lips. "This concoction has probably caused, or contributed to your present condition. Now, it's possible that at some stage your body became dependent."

"Like an addiction?"

"Near enough. If we could synthesise more of the same product, you might delay any further deterioration. For a while."

"This all happened thirty years ago. Serum could have changed. There might not even be a serum anymore."

"Okay," said Swift. "Then the best thing to do is find the guys who used the serum and take it from there."

"Won't be easy."

"You didn't stay in touch?"

Selkirk shook his head.

"Not with any of them?"

Selkirk leaned on the arm of his chair and eyed the doctor for a long moment. "I know where one of them is."

"Well, Dave, you'd better track the rest of them down." Swift recapped his pen and closed the folder. "Better yet, find the joker who made this stuff in the first place. It could be your only hope."

THE EYE STALK

THE EYE STALK

Chapter 21

THE BRILLIANT HEAT OF summer persisted into late July. The Vancouver Wolves slipped to 0-7, but last time out they almost held off an under-manned Toronto.

'No lead is safe.'

Almost.

Industrial fans on creaking pedestals blew musty air over a score of sweating, thickset gym rats. They rambled around the weight room, breathing hard between sets and chugging ergogenic brews.

Pumped up and chirpy.

Lifting heavy.

Gettin' swole.

Tim pushed out squats in a Smith machine. Steady motion. Controlled breathing. Submaximal weight. The bar slid up and down the guide rails with a thin whine. Dene and Kenny stood by and swigged from water bottles.

Dene gazed around the gym. "I thought Switzer might be here."

Kenny swallowed a gulp. "I've seen him a few times. Same as at the Wolves. He just comes and goes."

Dene saw Marcus Quillan enter from the office area. Two men trailed behind him, one tall and youthful, the other shorter and older. Quillan dodged around racks and benches and approached the Smith machine.

"Ass to the grass," he said. "Good squats. You two fellas keeping Dene honest?"

"He's doin' okay," said Kenny.

"Good to hear. Got a couple of guys for you to meet." He tapped the younger man on the back. "This is one of our instructors, Baird Turley. He won't be far away if you need a spotter or help with anything else."

Turley bumped fists with the new members. He stood inches above all three.

A flake in Thor's body.

Quillan laid a heavy hand on the older man's shoulder. "And this is our sports science guru, Garner Hall. He'll be able to answer any questions for you."

Hall was lightly built, with olive skin, thinning black hair and frameless glasses. He wore an Andropha sweatsuit but had the look of an accountant. His hangdog features managed to form a smile as he shook hands with the twins.

"Hey," said Kenny.

"Howzit," said Tim.

Hall gripped Dene's hand and nodded at the water bottles. "What's that you're drinking?" The mellow timbre of his voice belied his size.

"Just a sugar mix," said Dene. "Maltodextrin, fructose."

"What ratio?"

"Two-to-one."

"Hmm...commercial blend. Try five-to-four and see how that feels. Use a pre-workout too?"

"Branched-chain aminos. Beta-alanine. Some citrulline malate."

Quillan said, "Usual stuff," to no one in particular. "Sounds pretty run o' the mill to me."

"Creatine?" said Turley.

"Yep," said Kenny.

Tim shook his head. "Not me. Cramps me up like a mutha."

"It can do," said Hall. "You're brothers, yes?"

"Ah-huh," said the twins.

Quillan slapped Kenny on the shoulder. The bonhomie looked strained and unnatural. "I bet that's good for some competition."

The twins looked at each other.

"I guess," said Kenny. "I squat more."

"But I bench more," said Tim.

"What do you use for protein?" said Hall.

"Soy shakes," said Kenny.

Turley didn't bother to hide a chuckle. He turned to a pair of giants doing preacher curls. "You hear that? The newbies drink soy."

The giants smirked.

Turley said, "Sure you guys don't belong next door with the *lay-dees*?"

Dene took a quick breath. There was a reason the twins hadn't made it in football. They were genial to a fault, and they lacked true, cut-throat drive. But Kenny was a licensed heavyweight with Hawaii's State Boxing Commission, and Tim hid a volatile streak beneath the playful facade. You didn't want to light the fuse. Especially if they were together.

Kenny put his drink bottle on the bench. "If I want advice from a bunch of muscle heads, I'll ask for it."

Quillan forced a grin. "Take it easy, he's only joking."

Dene kept an eye on the twins. "So, what's wrong with soy?"

"There's some recent research suggesting that it increases oestrogen," said Hall.

Turley beamed.

Tim put his fists to his hips and rolled his eyes. "Just dandy. No wonder the Wolves can't win a game."

"Whey protein is a better choice," said Hall, "but it's digested too quickly. It doesn't support the entire anabolic period."

"Which means what?" said Kenny.

Quillan put one foot on the bench and leaned on his knee. "It means you guys will get better results the old-fashioned way."

"And that is?" said Dene.

"You need meat. And plenty of it."

Tim stared around the gym. "That's all you guys eat?"

"Pretty much."

Tim raised his eyebrows at the monsters working on the preacher rest. They nodded.

Quillan straightened and backed away toward the offices. "And I'll give you another tip. If you're serious about squats, get outta the Smith and into a power rack."

"And lift a decent weight while you're at it," said Turley.

"Don't like the Smith machine?" said Dene.

"It's good for drying towels," said Quillan.

Turley looked over his shoulder. "Or panties."

Hall gave a rueful grin and followed the others out of the room.

Dene and Kenny eyed the gym junkies up and down. Tim squinted at his legs, then at the plates on the Smith machine.

"Steak House, here we come."

Chapter 22

KENT INSTITUTION AT AGASSIZ is one of eight Federal prisons serving British Columbia and the Yukon territory. It is the only maximum-security prison west of Edmonton, and has a rated capacity of three hundred and seventy-eight inmates.

But just one remains in twenty-four-hour isolation.

Forty minutes after lockdown, eight guards tramped two-abreast through the high-risk wing. Most topped six feet and all weighed more than two hundred pounds. Black combat uniforms. Mil-spec boots. Visored helmets. Batons and riot shields. Their synchronised footfalls echoed in the walkway. Intimidating as all get-out.

It was meant to be.

Against corrections safety protocol, four of the team carried Tasers. One had a 20ml syringe of Midazolam, a fast-acting benzodiazepine. He hoped they wouldn't need it. If they did, he hoped it would be enough.

The formation stopped in front of a steel door. The senior guard slid open a port.

"Your visitor has arrived," he said. "What sort of mood are you in?"

A soft bass filled the corridor. Almost a hum.

"I am always the same."

"Yeah," said the guard. "Until someone upsets you. You know what'll happen if you lose it again."

"My mood is calm," throbbed the voice.

Nightlights bathed the visitors' area with a grey-green wash. David Selkirk loitered in the shadows, hands in pockets. He heard murmuring and the rattle of chains as the guards manoeuvred their prisoner into the outer room of the secure contact booth. Tension quivered in his belly.

He wasn't sure what to expect.

The biggest man in Kent's tactical response group stood six-five and weighed two hundred and eighty pounds. Tabu Kainoa had him beat by three inches and a full two stone. His body was the mass of a hundred-gallon propane tank, on legs like wharf pylons. Arms as thick as girders hung from delts the size of kettle-bells. He wore 9XL jumpsuits, their crayon-red fabric denoting a special inmate.

But not in a good way.

Selkirk had asked to meet the prisoner face-to-face rather than confer by video, so Tabu wore a full-harness transport restraint. His forearms were crossed at the waist and cuffed to a nickel-plated belly chain. Another chain connected his waist to steel ankle hobbles. The oversize rig was padlocked tight, but after enduring Thorazine and electric Stun Cuffs, Selkirk guessed it would feel like a luxury.

A clutch of tactical officers guided their charge into the booth. He dragged his slippered feet to a metal table in front of a ballistic polycarbonate window. Even in the 'convict shuffle' he was a formidable sight.

Three guards man-handled him into a seat. Two locked his leg irons to anchors embedded in the concrete floor. Another fixed the high-tensile manacles to the table. With the subject secured, the guards trooped out to the adjoining room.

Selkirk moved into view. "Hello Tabu."

The prisoner peered through the window. A broken nose and wide, flat lips separated his sagging cheeks. Thin grey fuzz covered his scalp, and his head reflected the light like a waxing gibbous moon.

He said, "Davey Selkirk."

"It's been a while. How are you?"

"I am not free. It pains me."

Selkirk slid a moulded plastic chair closer to the window and sat. He aimed his words at a two-way speaker in the window frame.

"You're still classed as a Commonwealth subject. I could submit a personal reference to the Correctional Service." He ran his fingers around the inside of his collar. "Except I don't like what I'm seeing."

Tabu looked down. He shook his wrist and the manacles clacked on the tabletop.

"They fear me. This is not necessary."

"Two dead prisoners and four guards in hospital might not agree."

"That was long ago." Tabu raised heavy-lidded eyes. "Why are you here, David?"

Selkirk considered his old adversary. They were two sad, timeworn men, holding on to nothing. "I'm looking for some of the guys from 'ninety-one."

The big Samoan let out a rolling chuckle. "And I was the easiest to find."

"No, you were the closest. Until...."

The sound of distant refrigeration units and the buzz of fluorescent lighting drifted through the air.

"Until?"

Selkirk needed the man's help. His co-operation. But would it take a carrot or a stick? He knew his next words would stir something, but he wasn't sure what.

He stepped off the ledge.

"I've found Mattson Lampard."

Tabu's eyes hardened. His body tensed like a torsion bar under load.

"He's been under my nose the whole time," said Selkirk. "He runs a gym in Abbotsford."

Tabu leaned forward. The rumble became a growl, the portent of an avalanche. "He's forty miles away? Get me out of here, David. Let me find him."

"Listen, my friend. You don't want to do this. If they think they can't trust you, they'll never let you out."

"Trust me?" The islander closed his hands into fists. "They *never* trust me." He wrenched on the shackles with each sentence. "Once I had a *life*. I had a *family*. Now I have *nothing*. Not even *time*."

The table shuddered and a guard looked through the doorway. Selkirk shook his head and mouthed 'sokay'.

Then he said, "You know, there are others who –"

"I don't *care* about the others. I care about my children. And what they think of me." Tabu lowered his head. A colossus struck down.

Selkirk felt for him. He looked for a silver lining. "You had a great career. No one can say you didn't."

"Until that man put a demon inside me."

"You were the best forward in the game long before he showed up. And for a bloody long time after."

"But who remembers? Not my children. They only know this."

"Plenty of people remember. Some of them said you were the best, full stop. Hell, they said you were better than me."

"You think I care about being the best? I'm not like you, David. I was happy chasing a melon on the beach. And even that he took away. He took everything away. Him and his serum."

"Are you sure that was all Lampard's fault?"

Tabu's face turned to stone. He rose from his seat, straining against the chains. Selkirk heard the links slip and peal like distant bells. The table creaked and groaned.

Then the storm passed. Tabu's rage simmered. He sunk onto the chair. "My wife is dead. Token and Totem shun me. What do you want?"

"I'm sick."

"I can see that."

"My doctor thinks it's because of Lampard's serum."

Resignation spread across Tabu's face. "So, it's caught up with you, too."

"What do you mean?"

"You were always too involved in your own glory. Have you kept in touch with anyone?"

"It's hard. I work a lot."

"So, nobody."

"Of course I have. Johan de Villiers is running for parliament. He joined the –"

"No, you haven't. Because if you had you'd know they're all dead."

"They can't be."

"Roy Rimmington went first. Dane Cronje was next. Marston Clarke. Kakalosi Fifita."

"Everyone?"

"Johan de Villiers passed two months ago, David. They're all gone."

"Cecil van Zyl?"

Tabu nodded. "Even 'Superman'. And soon they'll be joined by the great Davey Selkirk. And Tabu Kainoa."

Silence like a vacuum.

"You too?"

"Amyloidosis. Talisman has checked everything."

Selkirk knew of amyloidosis. It was one outcome Paul Swift had feared. Amyloid proteins in the blood. The disease caused progressive failure of the organs. Without treatment the prognosis was five years, tops, but the treatments weren't always successful. And you never knew how long you'd had it to begin with.

All those supplements.

All that meat.

"You're kidding."

"It's eating me alive. I have eighteen months."

Selkirk blinked. He looked into Tabu's eyes and sat back in his chair. "I'll be lucky if I have that."

Chapter 23

MATTSON LAMPARD'S OFFICE ECHOED his concept of virility. It was a temple to manly pursuits of another time.

Romantic.

Idealised.

Passé.

A cowhide chair faced the door from behind a carved teak desk on a Turkish kilim rug. A row of books filled a shelf behind the chair. An ostrich egg cradled in pewter laurel leaves sat on a shelf above the books, beside a studio portrait of Garbo.

A glass-doored cabinet held ornate silver trophies on Bakelite pedestals. Their tarnished bowls shone in the sallow light from a green-shaded banker's lamp on a leather desk mat.

To the right, a bank of photographs covered half the wall. To the left, a drooping tiger skin, head down, mouth agape. One yellowed fang curved like a cutlass from beneath a snarling upper lip. The other was missing.

Lampard studied the line of books. He ran a hooked finger along the shelf, paused, tilted his head to read a spine, then moved on.

Garner Hall knocked on the doorjamb and carried a sheaf of papers into the office.

Lampard hipped the chair aside and continued his search. Finally he said, "I'm waiting."

Hall placed the papers beneath the lamp light. "I've transcribed last month's applications. We have more footballers."

Lampard swivelled and raised his arms in mock delight. "Ah, we do love our footballers." He swept the pages across his desk in a wide arc, like a magician with oversized playing cards. "Young, dumb, and full o' cum."

"Full of testosterone is what matters," said Hall. "They're still the best template for our work."

"And you convinced our new friends to eat more meat?"

"It went to script."

"So, the seed has been planted. Good."

Hall pushed his glasses onto the bridge of his nose and nodded at the desktop. "You might find the first two of special interest."

Lampard leaned over the desk on hairy-knuckled fists. He peered down. His eyes opened wide and then narrowed, focussing.

"Brothers?"

"Twins. The first we've had."

"Identical DNA."

"Precisely. It should speed things up. Use one as a control, the other as a subject. More accurate results, quicker progress." Hall placed a fingertip on the top sheet. "And here's the icing on the cake."

Lampard pulled the chair beneath his legs and rocked into the seat. He leaned forward, then bent closer and scrutinised the page. His lips parted and flattened against teeth tinged green by the glow from the Emeralite lamp.

"This is excellent," he said. "Most excellent. Though...can we afford another absence? So soon?"

Hall shrugged. "They were cut from the Wolves. Not much of a recommendation. Footballers that end up on the scrap heap are little more than transients anyway."

"But these boys aren't citizens."

Hall pointed at the page again. "They've listed each other as next-of-kin. I doubt they'd be missed."

Lampard pressed his palms to the desk and did a little push up. "Garner, this project represents a major investment for me. And a windfall for all of us if it comes to fruition. I'd be pleased if we can hasten the process."

"You *could* start the next phase right away. After that? Well, exactly how committed are you?"

Lampard smacked the desktop. "I'm sixty-eight years old, dammit. I'm one hundred percent committed. *One hundred percent!* The clock is ticking."

Hall stepped back. He removed his glasses and rubbed the lenses against his track top. "Alright. But if you go in that direction I can only take you so far. I don't have the knowledge."

Lampard watched him slip his glasses back over his ears. "You disappoint me, Garner. Are you saying I need to bring in someone with more expertise? Now?"

"But Benny runs the camp. Surely he can oversee everything?"

"Benny is not a scientist. He's a nurse for fuck's sake. You know what they're like – they learn myocardial infarction and think they're Christiaan Barnard."

Hall rocked from foot to foot. "There might be someone else around. I could let you know in a week."

Lampard stood and hammered his fist onto the desk. "Pah! A week." He swiped away the applications. They rustled through the air and flapped to the floor. "Get out. *Get out.* I'll take care of it."

Hall retreated and vanished down the corridor. Lampard prowled the room, hands on hips. He swooped on the strewn papers, gathered a handful and dumped them on the desk.

As he turned back to the bookshelf, a name caught his eye. He snatched an application from the pile. He considered it for a moment, forehead furrowed.

"Garner!"

Hall's face reappeared in the doorway. He stepped into view but didn't enter the room. "Yes?"

"This one," said Lampard. "Selkirk. His name, place of birth. They're correct?"

"I don't normally make mistakes, Mattson. What's wrong?"

"Nothing. Everything's perfect. Go home."

Hall hesitated for a second, then bowed his head and turned away.

Lampard strolled around the office, gloating at the paper in his hand. "Last name, Selkirk," he whispered. "First name, Hazeldene. Born 1991, London, England."

He stopped in front of the wall of photographs. Rugby teams in banded jerseys. Grappling wrestlers. Bodybuilders captured in elaborate poses.

He stepped closer to an image. A rugby team, all thick necks and flattened faces and malformed ears. His mouth spread into a saggy-lipped rictus and he murmured at a figure sitting tall in the front row.

"No, I wasn't good enough to play the likes of you, Davey Selkirk. Yet I made you – I made you great. And what thanks did I get? Not a skerrick. Well, no matter. Because now I have the next best thing."

He swatted the application against the frame until it tilted. He scowled and hissed at the photograph.

"I have your *son*...."

Chapter 24

ZANELLE BREEZED THROUGH THE squad room sporting newly plaited ash-blonde hair. She swapped 'hellos' and parried a slew of compliments from the duty officers. It felt good to be part of a team.

She swept around the glass partition to the reception counter. Tom Calder leaned on his elbows, replacing the batteries in a couple of TacLight torches.

"Good morning, handsome," said Zanelle. "What's happening?"

Calder did a double take. "Good morning, your cheery self. New wig?"

"Funny man. Just trying something different. I might even let it grow now that summer's over."

"The ice queen look suits you. Goes with the kick-ass style."

"Hah. The only ass-kicking I do is telling off wayward drivers at school crossings."

Calder reached under the counter and pulled a report from a pigeonhole. "This might let you spread your wings then." He spun the single sheet along the counter top.

Zanelle pinned it to the laminate with a clear-glossed fingernail.

"What is it?"

"A couple of hikers found eight dead dogs dumped up in the Fraser Valley yesterday."

Zanelle's body soaked up a jolt of adrenaline. Her eyes flickered over the page. "You're kidding me."

"Nope. Your name is on the missing dog reports, so they want you to work it with the Abbotsford police."

"Did they give you a contact?"

"Must be important. The deputy chief himself wants to brief you."

"Truman Roberts? Alright. Would you be a darling and let them know I'm on my way?"

"Will do." Calder glanced at the report. "Hey, Zanelle? What does 'exsanguinated' mean?"

A frisson trickled down her back like a chilled raindrop. She returned to the counter and read over Calder's bent elbow.

She said, "You don't wanna know."

———◦———

A LINE OF OFFICES behind floor-to-ceiling glazing ran down one side of the Abbotsford Police Headquarters squad room.

The murmur of routine activity filled the space. Uniformed personnel wound their way through a maze of low dividers, juggling paperwork and mid-morning coffees while colleagues conferred or hunched over telephones.

Zanelle sat outside an office two-thirds down the row. She tapped her toes on the carpet, nervous and self-conscious. A trainee constable with the RCMP scarcely rated a glance. Pretty, curvaceous blondes attracted more lingering attention.

A bull-necked sergeant planted himself in front of her. His pate shone through thinning ginger hair and his ruddy jowls hung in ripples like melted wax.

He hooked his thumbs in his belt and splayed his feet, hips thrust forward. "Chief Roberts will see you now."

Zanelle rose quickly. She glimpsed the sergeant's name tag. PYM. He stood too close and stared at her a second too long. Acne scars cratered his face. She wondered if they called him 'Pymples'. Or just plain 'Pymp'. Both suited.

Pym knocked on the door frame and twisted the handle. He held the door open but made no effort to stand aside. Zanelle couldn't avoid brushing against his thighs, or walking through the fust of stale deodorant.

The Deputy Chief Constable of the Abbotsford Police Department read from a slim folder.

Truman Roberts enjoyed a measure of celebrity in the district. He aligned himself with prominent society figures, and had made two unsuccessful runs at local government. He was also angling for the Abby PD's Chief Constable position, a post he felt was overdue.

He looked up and beckoned. "Thank you, Sergeant." He watched Pym leave and then focussed on Zanelle for the first time. "Good morning, Officer...Argus, is it? Have a seat."

She lowered herself onto a chrome-framed chair in front of thin, half-open venetians. The man across the desk was more compact than she'd imagined. Mid-fifties, silver hair. Neat and cold.

"Hello, sir. Thank you for seeing me."

Roberts flipped the folder shut. "Always an honour to assist the Mounties. But they've sent you on a wild goose chase this time."

"What do you mean, sir?"

"You're investigating some missing dogs. And, yes, we've found some. But the cases are not connected."

"With respect sir, I think it's a little more complicated than that."

Roberts scraped a fingernail over the folder. He affected a meaningless smile. "How so?"

"Sir, what you've discovered amounts to a mass grave. I have to wonder how many more dogs are missing. And why?"

"How long have you been with the Mounted Police?"

Zanelle had completed twenty-four weeks of cadet training at the academy in Saskatchewan. Now she was twenty weeks into a six-month Field Coaching Program at Chilliwack.

She said, "Nearly twelve months. All up."

"Twelve months." Roberts pressed his elbows against the armrests and shifted in his seat. "Argus, your dedication to a few stray animals is commendable, but the matter isn't worth a district alert."

"I think the owners might disagree, sir."

"They can disagree all they like, but it won't change things. We see this from time to time. Greyhound trainers have a well-deserved reputation but –"

"Wait a minute," said Zanelle. "These were greyhounds?"

Roberts nodded with exaggerated patience, then continued.

"But if a dog can't run – meaning it can't make money – then it's not worth feeding. Not for a professional operation. It's more practical to knock them on the head. And to be frank, it's probably kinder."

"Sir, these animals were completely drained of blood. That doesn't sound –"

"Normal? Believe me, it is."

"I was going to say professional."

"Perhaps not. But it's still a business decision. And trainers know they can recoup some of their losses."

"I don't understand."

"They sell the blood to vet clinics, and the clinics use it in surgery."

Roberts spread the fingers of one hand and offered it, palm up. Take it or leave it.

He said, "In a racing kennel, some dogs are simply worth more than others. It's distasteful, but it's an economic reality."

"But surely that's a crime."

"Nobody loves animals more than me, young lady, but it's a fact of life. Unwanted creatures are better off being put down." The Deputy Chief stood. "My advice to you, is go back to Chilliwack and find a cause more suited to your talents."

Zanelle blinked. "Sir, I...Sir?"

"That should be all for now, Officer Argus. Yes?"

"Yes, sir. I'm sorry I troubled you."

Roberts waved at the door, then sat and reopened the file on his desk. Discussion over.

Pym lurked outside the office. He led Zanelle down a flight of stairs and to the station entrance. He turned at the doorway and watched her cross the atrium. His eyes drifted from her breasts to her hips and back again.

"They should put you on the beat," he said. "You could afford to lose a few pounds."

Zanelle looked straight ahead and passed him by without breaking stride. "That's okay. At least I haven't had smallpox."

She sashayed out onto Justice Way with a smirk on her lips. Pym's eyes gleamed like black marbles as he watched her go.

Truman Roberts stared at his computer screen. The *Chilliwack Trading Post* didn't have an online presence, so he'd scanned the story from a hard-copy edition and saved it to his personal files. He rested his elbows on his desk and read the article he'd pulled up.

It was grammatically sound, with none of the semantic anomalies that betrayed a lazy trawl through *Roget's* in search of ever more 'sensory' words. The writer could also spell, and had more than a vague understanding of his words' meanings. No 'unchartered' waters, no 'honed' in, no 'unphased'.

But it was the content that concerned Roberts most.

The Deputy Chief knew the value of friends in the right places. And he wasn't above exerting pressure to get what he wanted. The low-rent newsman was no friend – he wasn't even an acquaintance – but that was about to change.

Roberts pulled out his cell and entered a number on the keypad. He leaned back in his chair and waited.

"Mr Franklin? This the Abbotsford Police Department. We need to talk."

Chapter 25

ZANELLE PULLED HER RED Subaru off a steep road on the eastern edge of Chilliwack and bumped over a patched concrete driveway. A two-storey home leaned against the incline. Greige clapboard. Shingled roof. White gutters and window frames. Her rented cottage sat above a garage at the low side of the building.

She snuggled in her seat and checked the messages on her phone. Still nothing from Dene. It had been a while. They tended to stay at arm's length, but it was mutual. It suited them. And he'd shown no sign of boredom with their relationship. Maybe she'd pushed too far this time. Maybe she was just tone deaf.

Not woke. Not good.

She recalled the encounter with Roberts and Pym, and for the first time, questioned her vocation.

Someone should've told her that jobs were scarce for an under-achieving sprinter. Instead, everyone fawned on her and said how much potential she had.

Potential. She wouldn't wish it on anyone.

She starred on the track at high school. She rose through the college athletic system and qualified for the national talent identification program. The future seemed rosy. She would make the Olympics,

win a medal, go on to coach. Maybe try sports journalism. Even a
television career.

Big fish, little pond.

Everyone had been carried away. She was a local sensation. At the
provincial level she was competitive. But at national level, with hot-
shots from every other province chasing a handful of places on the
squad, she struggled to stay in touch. She hung around the margins
for a while, but eventually fell behind the pack. And by then she'd
ditched her degree.

Another lesson learned too late.

The first fall of an early autumn littered a cobbled path that divided the front lawn. Red alder and mountain dogwood. Pale russet and
deep plum red.

A tall, round-shouldered woman with permed blue hair chased
the leaves with a tattered straw broom. Her white fingers sprouted
from a thin, lilac cardigan and knotted around the broom handle like
strands of macramé. The curled leaves scurried away, then swooped
back again on the draft.

Zanelle watched for a moment, then stepped out of the car.

"Jesus Christ," said her landlady. "There's more hair on my fanny
than on this bloody broom."

"Let me try, Mrs Crozier."

Gwen Crozier turned, head on the side, as if peering at rain clouds
from under a porch. "Would you, pet? I'm about done in."

Zanelle took the broom and marched along the path, whacking at
the cobbles. Leaves scattered in the air and then settled where they'd
been before.

"This. Thing. Is. Useless."

"Like tits on a bull," agreed Mrs Crozier.

Zanelle lifted the broom and hammered it into the pathway. The handle cracked and split along its length. The head of the broom broke away and fell onto the grass.

Gwen Crozier puffed her cheeks. "Well, that's one problem solved."

Zanelle leaned on the broom handle, her eyes glistening. "Damn, damn, damn, *damn*."

The old lady reached out and rubbed her back. "Something's bothering you, isn't it, dear. I can always tell, you know."

Zanelle laughed through her tears. She looked up at the backdrop of timbered foothills rising behind the home. The green slopes rolled up the Fraser Valley and merged with the Skagit Range. Lush golden meadows swept from the tree line to the Fraser River floodplain at the edge of town.

"It's nothing," she said. "Just something that happened at work."

"So, not man trouble then?"

Zanelle picked up the broom head, then shook coils of platinum hair away from her eyes. Her voice trembled.

"Who knows? It's been a funny month."

"Tell me it's not that footballer with the nice legs."

"No, we're okay. I thought I was helping him with something, but it seems I wasn't."

Mrs Crozier placed an arm around her shoulders. "Take some advice from this old duck. Don't worry about him – you should be worrying about yourself."

"I'm just not sure where it's going, that's all." She handed over pieces of broom. "I'm sorry. I wasn't much help. I'll get a new one."

She sniffled and headed down a walkway between the garage wall and next door's fence-line. She climbed wooden stairs that ran up beside the garage. Short, split logs lay stacked beneath the stairs, ready to fire the heater when winter arrived.

To Zanelle, it seemed winter was already here.

Mrs Crozier's neighbour on the downhill side stepped over a low hedge and waddled across the lawn. A stout woman in her sixties, Vera Bell wore flat-soled shoes and a sky-blue nurse's uniform with a Red Cross badge. She pinned a name tag on as she walked.

"You need a new broom."

The landlady nodded at her tenant disappearing through the cottage door. "I think she's having man trouble."

"Not that footballer with the nice legs?"

"Mmm. She's quite upset."

"I'd be upset too. Plenty of pushing power there."

Gwen Crozier stifled a squeal. "She needs to swallow her pride."

"If nothing else."

The women burst into cackling fits. Mrs Crozier dangled one arm as though it was an elephant's trunk.

"Bet he's got a *schlong* like an ox-tongue," she said.

Vera shrieked and grabbed a fistful of the other woman's cardigan. "Gwendolyn! Stop it."

Their laughter rose, then stuttered and then fell still. Gwen Crozier nodded sagely. Vera Bell sighed.

Chapter 26

A MIX-UP AT THE quarry delayed the country club job by a week. Then the committee approved design changes at two consecutive meetings. Five weeks work turned into eight, and the temperature dropped fifteen degrees. Shorts and singlets were out, work pants and flanno shirts were in.

Dene and the twins were halfway down the back nine. They finished smoko and stowed their lunch pails in the pickup.

Kenny said, "Where to after this?"

"Not sure," said Dene.

"Maybe these dudes will change their minds again – stretch it out a bit longer."

"It's always quieter in winter. Something'll turn up."

"Hope so. This gym's costing me an arm and a leg."

"I'm eating half a damned cow a week," said Tim. "That's what's costing me."

Dene split a bag of cement with a trowel. "If I remember correctly, it was you two that wanted to try it in the first place."

Tim grunted. Kenny said nothing. He cranked up the mixer and a tinny, clunking gurgle rolled down the green sward of the fourteenth fairway.

THREE HUNDRED YARDS AWAY, a group of men looked across the golf course through a plate glass wall in the president's private suite. The eight individuals formed a Venn intersection of primary stakeholders in the Vancouver Wolves, and majority stockholders of a second-tier British Columbia pharmaceutical firm.

They watched the workers wrestle with granite blocks amid the bridged ponds and old-growth fir trees that mingled with groves of Garry oak.

"We need a couple of strapping lads like that," said one. "Think they can play football?"

"If they could play football they wouldn't be luggin' rocks."

The men turned from the window with a grumble of accord. They gathered around a polished mahogany dining table. One raised his glass of Walker Blue Label and shook it at the rest.

"We need a marquee player, that's what we need."

"We could invite Russell Wilson up," said Scott Jarreau, "but I don't like our chances."

Jarreau was the Wolves' general manager. The CFL's new TV deal promised to push the league's salary cap toward six million dollars. Seattle's was close to two hundred million. The Seahawk quarterback wouldn't be coming.

"Antonio Brown might be on the market," said a real estate franchisee. Jarreau coughed discreetly. The others stared in dismay. "I'm just saying, is all."

"It doesn't need to be a big name," said the president. "He only needs to stand out on the gridiron."

"Precisely. Someone the people can root for."

"What people?" The speaker was a dime-store mogul with a chestnut toupée. "They're either staying home, or they've all found safer things to do since that damned virus."

"If I'm brutally honest," said Jarreau, "that's been to our advantage. It saved us a lot of embarrassment last year."

"It also cost us a bundle in lost revenue."

"Same way it affected the other teams. Levels the playing field a bit."

The president again: "I think we all know this season is down the tubes as well. We need to put everything on the line for next year."

"Hah!" said the toupée. "Get a whole new freakin' roster you mean?"

"Don't overreact. How about we start with just one player? A decent one."

"That's what *I* said – a marquee player."

"Right," said the franchisee. "A drawcard. Someone to bring the crowds in."

"Don't forget the TV ratings."

"They'd better start winning then. And soon."

The drug company's Chief Financial Officer and his top researcher had remained silent throughout. They had less to lose, and much more to gain. The CFO spoke up.

"When the team starts winning, the ratings with take care of themselves. And the crowds will come, you can bet on it."

"I've already bet on it." Blue Label spilled onto the carpet. "A million shares worth."

"I have at least that many. You and your cronies are into me for over two million bucks."

No one asked how a real estate salesman with only three offices had truckloads of cash for the stock market.

The toupée glowed orange over a wispy white fringe. "Not to mention all the money we've sunk into the Wolves."

"You'll get that back ten times over if this comes off," said the CFO. "The Wolves will be sitting pretty, and our stock price will go through the roof. Biomorphi-X will be the darling of the trading floor."

The room fell silent as a waitress brought trays of canapés and laid them on the table.

When she left, the president said, "Aren't we getting ahead of ourselves? I understand the formula still isn't ready for production. It's not even at the trial stage."

"That's right," said the franchisee. "Everything hinges on this serum being –"

"For chrissakes, stop calling it a serum," blurted Jarreau.

As GM, Jarreau answered to the owners, but he had as much to lose as anyone. He'd been antsy from the start.

The researcher chipped in. "Technically, it's a blood booster."

"Then technically, it's illegal."

"If you'd prefer," said the CEO, "we'll be using EPE-1 as a working title."

The researcher saw a bunch of bemused faces. He said, "Exogenous performance enhancement."

"Oh, God, give me strength," said Jarreau. "Performance enhancement? Really?"

"Don't worry," said the CFO. "The marketing people are on it. They'll put something together in time for the release."

"Whatever it's called, it needs to be in the hands of the medicos before next year's training camp. And it needs to work!"

The group murmured assent. The president looked to a small, patrician figure at the top of the table. "You've been quiet."

The man moved his crystal tumbler in tiny circles on the tabletop, leaving a glossy ring of wetness.

"I'm assured," he said, "that the product will work more dramatically than you could imagine. Personally, I consider my money an investment, not a wager. By this time next year we'll be the toast of the CFL." Truman Roberts raised his glass. "And fielding offers from Pfizer."

Chapter 27

BAIRD TURLEY WALKED ONTO the mat as Dene finished his third set of power cleans.

"Mattson wants to see you in his office." Turley eyed the barbell with scorn. "If you feel up to it." He pointed down the corridor. "First room on the right."

Dene flicked sweat from his face and tried to slow his breathing. He entered the hallway, knocked on the open door, and waited.

Lampard stared at a row of photos, meaty arms crossed over his chest. His Andropha T-shirt squeezed his midriff like a tied roast. Loose black trackpants hung over bare, blunt feet in cork-soled slides.

"Mr Lampard?"

The big man turned. He had pale, sparse eyebrows, a pushed-in putty nose and flabby, chimp-like ears.

"Come in," he said, "come in."

Dene crossed the room. He looked around and winced at the tiger skin. He reached out to shake hands but Lampard snatched his limp fingers before he could get a grip.

"And call me Mattson."

"Sure, Mattson. You wanted to see me?"

Great first impression.

Lampard waved at a photograph. "What do you think of that?" A younger Lampard held a silver rose bowl above his head. His chest and arms were as dense as tree trunks. "World record at forty years old." He pointed at the next photo. "Another at fifty."

Dene wasn't sure how to respond. "That's pretty cool."

So lame.

Lampard sat on the edge of his desk and pointed at a trio of Mart Stam chairs assembled on the rug. "Sit."

Dene lowered himself onto the middle chair. He ran his eyes along the bookshelf. Some classic novels; Wells, London, Verne. Lots of non-fiction. A few scientific texts. All hardcovers. Heavy reading.

"To answer your question," continued Lampard, "yes, I did. I like to introduce myself to the new members. I'm sorry it's taken this long. How are you finding things?"

The gym owner's shaven head wrinkled when he spoke. Up close, his eyes were a shade of hazel, like crushed honeycomb. Tiny white scars flecked his scalp; coconut sprinkled on a scoop of ice cream.

Dene said, "Okay, so far."

"And your two friends? How are they doing?"

"I think the butcher's bill has been a shock."

A hoarse laugh escaped Lampard's chest. "Everything comes at a cost." He tipped his head in the direction of the weight room. "Imagine how expensive those supplements are. That's a billion-dollar business. Everyone takes them. But how many make it to the top? Supplements are useless without hard work."

"I know a bit about hard work."

"I'm sure you do. The point is, money isn't all we spend in life. What about deprivation? Misery? Despair? What do you know of those things?"

Dene's mind went blank. The dramatic turn threw him.

You don't see *Gym Owner & Philosopher* on the average business card. The man's eloquence was at once disarming and unsettling. Dene opened his mouth but nothing came out.

"It doesn't matter," said Lampard. "Sometimes I get carried away. I only mention it for perspective. So tell me. What do you hope to achieve here?"

"Well, I want to crack it with the Wolves. It's in my application."

"Yes, I saw that. But what will that give you in a broader sense? How will it enhance your life?"

Dene glanced at the desktop. In his mind, he looked down on the scene. He saw himself as a customer buying a car. Lampard was the salesman; first leading, then pushing, but always steering.

"If I can make Vancouver's roster I might be able to get ahead a bit. Buy a few things."

"That's more like it. Practical goals are important. Everyone wants money. What else?"

"And...it could get my father off my back."

"Ah, now you're getting down to it. Emotional needs are a far better driver of success."

"I suppose."

Lampard circled behind the chairs and settled on the other end of the desk. His voice took on sly, velvet tones.

"Do you know what's even more effective? Survival. It's a visceral need. Every living creature has it."

"Yeah, I guess."

"You guess? Have no illusions, boy. The entire population of this planet struggles every day to survive. And do you know what drives that struggle? It's fear."

The words hustled, then crawled, in Shakespearian cadence. Persuasive, forceful, compelling.

Dene pictured the man in a green-peaked visor, counting money or dealing cards.

He said, "That's a lot of scared people."

Lampard bounced up. His delivery quickened.

"Bah! Little people. Frightened people. They're everywhere. People are the world's most worthless commodity – they're all expendable. And that's what you've become to those Vancouver Wolves. Expendable."

"They haven't welcomed me with open arms, no."

Lampard pulled out a drawer. "There are ways of enhancing your value, you know." He removed two small bottles and sat them on the desk. "This is something I've developed. Think of it as a tonic. A pick-me-up."

Suddenly Shakespeare was a sideshow barker. Dene hadn't seen this coming.

He shook his head. "I'm not going down that road. Too many guys have crashed and burned."

"But you do understand injections? Johnson? Armstrong? Jones? McGwire?"

"I've seen every jab there is in football."

"Ah," said Lampard, "but that's what everyone's using." He got into the act. Gesticulating, twisting his face, modulating his tone. "And if everyone's using it, there's no advantage. You use more and more just to keep up. It's pointless. It's like heroin or ice. After the first rush, you need a hit just to feel normal."

Dene crossed his arms. A body language giveaway. "I wouldn't know anything about that."

"Trust me. There's no upside. No advantage."

"But that's why I came here. To build up. To get an advantage."

Lampard swung a dismissive arm at imaginary hordes. "They're all here for that. But none of them is going anywhere. And do you know why? Because they're doing what everyone else is doing. If you want to be different, you must *do* something different."

Persuasive. Forceful. Compelling.

Dene's resistance stalled, his resolve faltered.

He said, "I haven't thought about anything like this."

But he knew it wasn't true.

Lampard lounged on the desk. He took a deep breath, dropped his head, and slowly exhaled. The show was over.

Then he slid the bottles nearer to Dene. An encore.

"This is for my own personal use. It's all natural and it works. And for you, it's free."

"I'm not sure...."

Lampard went to a cabinet and turned a key in the door. He lifted a silver bowl from the middle shelf and placed it on the desk. It was the same trophy he held aloft in the photograph.

"It's tough trying to make it on your own," he said. "Believe me, I know." He pinged a fingernail against the rim of the bowl. "Let someone help you for once. Give it a few weeks. If it's not for you, we'll forget all about it."

Dene stared at the bottles. Then he looked up at the photographs on the wall. Grey monochromes. Faded sepias. Some more recent in bleached colour.

His eyes landed on a line of grotesquely sculpted bodybuilders posing on a stage.

"Thanks, Mr Lampard, but I think I'll just forget about it."

Lampard regarded Dene for long seconds, then brought his hands together in a single, sharp clap.

"Your choice," he said. "But that fear we talked about? It works both ways. It can hold you back as much as drive you on. Maybe more so."

Dene pulled the office door closed and walked into the weight room. He looked self-consciously at the scattered groups of men, but no one noticed him. He picked up the clipboard and found a pen to update his workout record.

His hands were shaking.

Chapter 28

Gwen Crozier emptied a glass of red with a flourish.

"Well, that was a nice surprise," she said. "Now I can say I've had vegetarian lasagne."

"I'm glad you liked it," said Zanelle.

"It was certainly better than I expected." The woman stood. She gathered plates and glasses and clattered them into the sink. "Vera's taking me to the blood bank tomorrow. It won't be green will it?"

Zanelle grinned and piled cutlery on top of the plates. "You'll be fine."

Mrs Crozier turned on the water and reached for a dish-cloth.

"No, you don't," said Zanelle. She shut off the faucet and snatched the cloth away.

"But it isn't any trouble."

"Don't even think about it. You've been far too kind already. And thank you for the newspapers."

Mrs Crozier always saved the *Trading Post* for her tenant. She'd brought a box of back issues to dinner.

"Couldn't have you moping around on your own." She patted Zanelle on the shoulder. "Now, you're sure you don't need me to stay?"

"No, I'm okay. It's been a rough few weeks at work, that's all."

Zanelle linked arms with her landlady and the pair walked to the door. "And I don't mind being by myself."

"That's well and good." Mrs Crozier dropped into a conspiratorial whisper. "But don't forget what they say about old boyfriends and televisions."

"And what might that be?"

The woman gave an impish chortle. "If you feel like some company, you just go over and turn them on."

"Oh, behave!" Zanelle opened the door. "But I'll try to remember that. Good night. And thanks again."

"Good night, dear. Sleep tight."

Mrs Crozier gripped the rail and descended the wooden steps. Zanelle watched her disappear around the corner of the garage, then stepped back inside and eased the door shut.

She flopped onto her couch. She pulled her legs up and jammed her feet against the arm rest, then unfolded an old copy of the *Post*.

You never knew what someone had to sell.

She flicked to the sports section. In this edition the Wolves were 0-9, yet the paper still rated them a chance for the playoffs. She didn't know how many games they'd lost now, but it looked like being another winless season.

She wasn't sure if that was good or bad. It was good if it helped Dene make the roster next year. But it was bad that he hadn't made the cut for such a mediocre outfit already.

She turned to the front page, glanced at the throwaway headline and skipped to the classifieds. As the pages floated by, her eye fell on a single column follow-up to the accident on Highway One. Several officers from RCMP Support attended the scene, but they hadn't said much. Road fatalities wore everyone down sooner or later.

She recalled Toby Franklin's original article. A salesman had killed himself when he crashed into a moose. It happened all too often, but Franklin distinguished this event with a gory account of how the victim had been decapitated.

The real hook, however, was a supposed sighting of naked men in the area. The *Post's* owner had actually worked 'cannibals' into the headline.

Zanelle read the re-shaped story.

"The fuck? What's your game, Mr Franklin?"

Chapter 29

ANDROPHA GYMNASIUM CLOSED AT nine o'clock, but the last patrons straggled out around nine-thirty. Quillan had the late shift. It bummed him off, but sometimes he couldn't avoid it. He unloaded a leg press machine.

Lampard appeared from the corridor and helped slide the plates onto a rusty steel weight tree.

He said, "You may need to take on more responsibility."

"What's happened?"

"Garner has doubts about our operation. Which means I have doubts about his loyalty."

"You know I'm up for anything."

The two men walked the gym floor. They straightened benches and kicked mats into line.

"Also," said Lampard, "some of our new clients have interesting backgrounds."

"Is that a problem?"

"Not yet. But I don't want it to become one."

"It won't be anything we can't take care of."

"Even so, keep an eye on the Brit and his friends." Lampard dropped to his haunches between a pair of hundred-pound dumbbells and hooked his hands around the knurled grips.

He straightened his legs and hoisted them from the mat as if they weighed nothing. They thudded into place on a nearby rack. "And I want to know more about those Hawaiian boys. See if our man in blue can connect them to someone named Tabu Kainoa."

"Why are you so jumpy about these kids?"

"It's not the kids. It's their fathers."

Quillan's laugh banged around the empty room.

"Geez, Louise," he said. "The day we can't handle a couple of geriatrics, I'll eat my hat."

A sneer creased Lampard's mouth and Quillan went cold. He realised he'd overstepped the mark.

Lampard bent and cleaned a loaded barbell from the floor. The bar bounced on his collar bones, the steel plates chiming faintly. His dead eyes locked onto Quillan. "You forget, Marcus – they're the same age I am."

He straightened his arms and eased the barbell forward until it grazed his manager's throat. He held it with an overhand grip, arms parallel to the floor. His upper body was rigid. Immobile.

"Are you calling *me* a geriatric?" he said.

Quillan forced himself to meet Lampard's eyes. He refused to look at the plates on the bar. The strength needed to do that wasn't natural. He swallowed. "Okay. Point taken."

Lampard drew the barbell to his chest. He turned and slammed it into a rack. The angle-iron frame rocked and the clang echoed through the gym.

He said, "Change the passwords on the computers. And secure the filing cabinets. I don't want our secrets leaked all over British Columbia."

"But Garner knows everything already."

The pair slid plates off the racked barbell, releasing tension from the steel.

"I'm going to send him up to the camp to help Benny. That way, at least we can watch him. Those twins and their English friend have just become part of our plans. We can't afford any setbacks if Garner bails."

"What will you do if he does?"

Lampard placed a bucket of gym chalk against the wall.

"That's the trouble with jumping ship," he said. "You never know if you'll land among sharks."

Chapter 30

THE STUDIO OCCUPIED A sixty by thirty-foot space above the change rooms of an indoor swimming pool. A rack of dumbbells sat against one short wall, with snarled skipping ropes and a pyramid of rolled yoga mats nestled beneath.

Piles of rubber-coated weight plates cluttered the floor and a beaten, leather heavy bag, stained cocoa brown by years of sweat splash, creaked on a chain in the corner.

Zanelle sat on a gym mat, face-to-face with Tom Calder, ankles hooked around his. The young Indian was taller, but they weighed about the same. They churned out sit-ups, passing a medicine ball back and forth with each repetition. Calder counted the reps.

She paid the pool owner a peppercorn rent in exchange for leading water exercise classes twice a week, supplementing her income from the Mounted Police with personal training. A group of younger women trying to stay healthy. Some older women trying to stay young. A couple of men rehabilitating from injuries.

A few of the women paid for extra sessions, but for the money she'd spent, the business wasn't thriving.

Tom was lucky to get a discounted rate.

"What do you know about Kermode bears?" said Zanelle. "The white ones."

"We call them 'spirit bears'. They're quite rare."

"Must be. I've never seen one but the *Trading Post* –"

"You read the *Post*?"

"I was looking for some cheap gear. Pay attention. Remember the crash up on Highway One? The salesman?"

"Yes."

"The guys on the scene said that wolves got to his body. But the newspaper claimed a pack of naked men had somehow caused the accident. I know, that's typical. Except a few weeks later they published a story that said it was a false alarm. It was only white bears that someone had spotted."

"Makes more sense than a bunch of naked men."

"Not if white bears are never there. And why not just go with wolves? Would have been way more logical."

"That paper's not known for its logic. And wolves aren't news."

"True. But printing a retraction is not like the *Post* either."

Calder frowned. "Okay, I'll see what I can find out."

"Thanks. I just can't shake the feeling it has something to do with those missing dogs."

"I thought you sorted that with Roberts."

"It didn't feel right, Tom."

"Maybe it's exactly what he said – trainers getting rid of slow greyhounds."

"No, he didn't want me getting involved, that's for sure."

"Did you mention the break-in at the vet clinic?"

"At Chilliwack?"

"Uh, huh."

Zanelle grabbed the ball and stopped dead. "Another one?"

"Yep. Highfield. Out on Yale near Carleton Street. Got a whole bunch of drugs and some other stuff."

"I didn't hear anything about that."

"I understand you're keen, but you know they can't give you every job that comes up."

"It would have made sense though. I mean, there could be a link."

She straightened her arms and shot the ball at Calder's chest.

He caught it and settled back into the rhythm. "We just need to worry about all the ketamine that's gonna turn up on the street."

"Be nice if someone had told me before I got steam-rolled by Roberts, that's all I'm saying."

"Eighty-eight," said Calder.

Chapter 31

DENE BLEW HARD. THE bar rose and fell above his chest. His movements slowed with each repetition. Lactate swamped his muscles. His arms trembled and he huffed short, urgent breaths. He fought to finish the set and strained to push the barbell onto the pegs.

He sat up, swivelled off the bench, planted his feet and breathed deeply. He picked up a clipboard and jotted some numbers. The bench press was his weakest exercise. He hated it.

A crack rang out like a gunshot and rebounded off the walls. Dene ducked his head, then jumped to his feet. The clipboard clattered to the floor.

"Jee-*zuzz!*"

Lampard had crept up and smacked a book onto a counter-top. He stood with a mocking grin tacked to his face.

"I thought you could do with some encouragement."

Dene spluttered a laugh. "Could tell I was struggling, huh?" He swung his arms to keep the pectorals loose. "The old muscle memory needs some work."

"Heaven help me," said Lampard. He twirled and did a little dance, flapping his arms up and down, a cartoon vulture in flight. "Muscle memory, muscle memory. More bullshit from the cross-fit nutters."

He jabbed a finger at his temple. "It's all neurological. Muscles are slaves to the nerves. Never forget it!"

Dene sensed a few of the regulars grinning in his direction. They must have seen it before. The guy sure kept you on the hop.

"Sorry," he said. "I didn't realise."

Lampard wrapped thick fingers around Dene's shoulder. "Don't worry about it." He pointed at the book. "Ever read Toffler?"

"In high school."

"You understand his definitions of power then."

"Sure. But I didn't think he was referring to exercise."

"He wasn't. But we can use some form of power everywhere, including the weight room."

Dene scrunched his eyes, casting his mind back. "Toffler's three tiers of power were violence, wealth, and knowledge. I don't see the connection."

"It's not obvious to everyone. Take wealth. Money can be stolen. Then its power is transferred. And it can be counterfeited. So then it becomes artificial power."

"I guess."

Lampard waved his hand around the room. "What about knowledge? Information can be stolen too. But the more people who have it, the more its power is diluted. And knowledge can be counterfeited as well. Think about lies. That's counterfeit information. And that can be a powerful weapon – until it turns on you."

He made a fist and bumped it on the cover of the book. "No, I prefer Toffler's first level of power. Violence. Because violence brings our old friend, fear. And fear is incorruptible. You can't counterfeit true fear. And you can't hide it."

"It's a pretty basic emotion. I mean, even animals smell fear."

Lampard turned it on. The spieling, carney showman in full cry.

"No boy," he said, "animals don't smell fear. They smell adrenaline. Epinephrine. The most potent hormone in the body. The fuel of 'fight or flight'. They sense a first strike. That's why they attack – it's pre-emptive. And that can mean the difference between life and death."

Dene struggled to keep up. Where was this going? If it was a test, he didn't want to fall short.

He said, "What about when they run?"

"That's my point. Fear is good, whichever way it shows itself. It keeps you *alive*."

The broad hand crashed onto the counter again. Dene jumped again. The joke was wearing thin.

"But," said Lampard, holding an index finger in front of his nose, "you must learn to control it. Then you have power over yourself. And you take it *back* from others." He straightened. The enthusiasm drained away and contempt swept over his face. "And if you're going to bench more than pussy weights in my gym, get yourself a spotter."

He turned on his heel and stalked out of the room.

End of the lesson.

Dene was numb. He felt he should have been angry. Annoyed. At least pissed off. Instead, he watched Lampard disappear, then looked at the book on the counter. Alvin Toffler's *Power Shift*. He lifted the cover and let a few pages fall beneath his fingertips.

His hands were trembling again.

Chapter 32

DENE PULLED THE GARAGE door down, but didn't bother to lock it. He plodded to the front door of his unit and slumped inside.

The small living area wallowed in mismatched furniture. All pre-owned, it was durable and well-made, from good quality materials. Dense fabrics, heavy timber, thick leather, fat cushions, deep floor rugs.

Second-hand he could tolerate, as long as he was comfortable.

He shut off his cell and plugged in the charger. Then he unzipped his gym bag and tossed a towel and a wet singlet into the bathroom. He dropped the bag onto the couch.

Chink.

He picked it up and shook it.

Chink-chink.

He combed his fingers around inside the bag. His hand closed on two cold, hard cylinders. He felt glass grate on glass and knew instantly what they were.

Lampard must have slipped them into the bag.

He withdrew the small brown bottles and rolled them in his palm. Twenty millilitres each, they had rubber stoppers with an aluminium seal. Made for inserting needles.

White adhesive labels carried typed instructions. He turned a label to the light.

HCS 2ml IM once every 48 hours until finished.

He strolled a lap of the apartment, rattling the vials in his hand. This time he knew he should have been angry, but still he wasn't. He leaned on the bench in his kitchenette and closed his eyes.

People just couldn't stop telling him what to do.

A knock on the living room window scattered his thoughts. He opened the refrigerator and hid the bottles in the butter compartment, then went and opened the door.

Zanelle leaned an arm against the frame. "Hello gorgeous. Whatcha doin'?"

"Hi. Come in."

She stamped her boots on the mat and entered the apartment.

"Haven't seen you for a while," said Dene. "Love the new look. How's everything at the station?"

Zanelle stepped forward and kissed him, moulding her soft mouth to his. She heeled the door shut. "I need someone to fuck me." She kissed him harder, flicking a hot, wet tongue over the inside of his lips.

"I haven't had a shower."

She pushed him in the chest. "That's fine – I want to get dirty."

She shoved him again. He staggered backward, toward the bedroom.

"Okay," he said.

Chapter 33

LAMPARD ROAMED HIS OFFICE with deliberate steps, head down, fists on hips. Roland Pym lounged on the wall beside the tiger skin. His police uniform strained under his arms and across his chest. He waggled a small notebook with stubby fingers.

"He's Samoan," said Pym. "His name is actually *Kaino* – Kainoa is the Hawaiian version. He married a Hawaiian girl but couldn't get U.S. residency because he has history, so they used his Commonwealth connection and moved to Canada."

"History?"

"Little Tabu was a naughty boy back in downtown Apia. Got in a lotta fights. Broke some windows. Smoked some ganja. Stole a car when he was thirteen. Basic juvey stuff."

"Doesn't sound like Al Capone."

"Hah – then he started growing. Assaulted a couple of corrections officers. Did a proper job on them."

"That's more like it."

"But not something the justice system views lightly. Got himself a record with a big fat asterisk. The kid was seventeen before they let him out."

"That must be when he started to get serious about football. Oh, Lordy, did he shake the rugby world up."

"It could be. Looks like he settled down for a while there. No more in his jacket until the thing with the unfortunate Mrs K."

"What about those twins?"

"Nothing that I could find. Kainoa has been up at Agassiz ever since he killed his wife. If he did have children, they could have gone back to family in Hawaii. Even Samoa. Maybe they were adopted."

Lampard mused at a photograph on the wall. "They'll be his. When does he get out?"

Pym flipped the notebook open and thumbed a couple of pages. "It was supposed to be twelve years but he's had time added. Smashed some guy in the head and broke his skull in four places. By the time the medics arrived his brain was running out his nose. One of the big bad bikies thought he'd step in and help. Dumb move. Kainoa laid him out and jumped on his knees. Didn't matter that he wouldn't walk again. He never woke up from the coma."

Lampard's bald head moved up and down. "That's Tabu alright."

"Get this," said Pym. "He once punched a goat to death in the prison ag plot."

Lampard did a 'talk to the hand'. "Enough. We'll worry about it later. I need to handle Garner first."

Pym stood away from the wall and shoved the notebook into his hip pocket. His pants were tighter than his shirt. "Roberts said you have to be careful with this, Mattson. We can't keep a lid on things forever."

"Benny will take Garner's place here, and Garner will stay at the camp with the subjects until I can deal with him."

"Then what? The subjects can't go unsupervised. It's only a matter of time before they stumble on someone."

"Then it'll be bad luck for someone."

"Bad for us if it's the wrong person. We were lucky nobody got a good look after that car crash."

"When it's time, I'll send Benny back up to keep an eye on everything. Then Garner can...take his retirement."

"And?"

"And I'll find someone to replace him. You're all dispensable you know. Don't think you're not."

Given what he knew about Lampard's activities, Pym thought he probably wasn't, but he didn't put it to the test. He aimed for helpful. "Maybe you could find someone at the university. Someone who wants to broaden their research."

Lampard exploded. "Bah! Fucking academics!" He stormed around the room like a bear. "They tell everyone why something can't be done, and when somebody finally does it, they tell everyone *how* it was done. And then take credit for the discovery. All they do is ride on the coat-tails of true innovators – innovators like me!"

Pym stepped to one side. He looked down, as though noticing the pattern on the rug for the first time.

DAVID SELKIRK FINISHED ON the treadmill and towelled down his arms. He'd strolled through a full episode of *Blue Bloods*, but couldn't remember a thing about it. He had more pressing matters on his mind. In fact, he'd been distracted ever since he left Tabu.

He pulled on a track-top, then took an elevator down to the street. His apartment was close to the Consulate building, and the Zeal & Vigor gymnasium was midway between. When the weather was fine, he did a lot of walking. It gave him time to think.

Which wasn't always a good thing.

His hopes of getting any help from the old team had evaporated with Tabu's news. And Tabu was in as bad a shape as he was. He now knew they'd been guinea pigs all along. His alternatives were shrinking fast. He fished his cell out of his pocket and found the number he wanted.

He waited a few seconds, then said, "What can you tell me about this new sponsor? Biomorphi-X."

The city slowed and settled into its late evening drone. Selkirk took a detour around the Vancouver Lookout while he listened. He ended the call three blocks from his apartment building, barely any wiser.

The grapevine wasn't what it used to be.

A deep blue SUV pulled to the kerb beside him. The window slid down and the driver leaned over.

"Hey, old timer. Need a lift?"

"No, I'll be right, Paul. This is good for the soul. Thanks anyway."

"Sounds like something I need. Okay. Enjoy."

The window eased back up. Selkirk watched his doctor's Lexus cruise away down West Cordova, big and shiny under the lights. It was a 2020 model. The GX460 in Executive spec, acquired courtesy of a research grant to run independent tests on *coronavirus* vaccines.

It's an ill wind....

He walked on, matching the latest information with what he already knew. His mind ticked over, moving pieces here and there across the board. A plan took shape. If he could swing it, it gave him a chance. But it hinged on everyone doing exactly what he hoped they would.

Things they'd done before.

He was sure he could get one of them to play ball. The guy was so full of himself he couldn't resist a challenge. He might be edgy for a while, but he'd come around.

The other party would be tougher to manipulate. He was already on a sticky wicket there. It would take some top-shelf reverse psychology.

He stood beneath a street lamp and dialled another number. No answer. The phone was off. He waited for the recorded message to finish, then cupped a hand around his mouth so the traffic noise wouldn't distort his words.

He said, "Hello, Dene...."

Chapter 34

THE TWO BODIES COILED beneath a patchwork quilt, glowing with heat and sated lust. Zanelle watched Dene's chest rise and fall.

She said, "So, what made you pick Lampard's gym?"

Dene stretched elaborately. He examined his fingernails at arm's length. "A couple of guys at the Wolves mentioned it."

"A couple of Hawaiian twins, maybe?"

"Some others too."

"Then it had nothing to do with your dad."

Dene rolled onto one elbow. "Listen, I know all about Lampard's reputation. It's no big deal. Dad warned me long ago."

"And still you went?"

"Look, I'm not a little kid. I don't just do things because he says I shouldn't."

Zanelle slid from under the quilt and sprang off the bed. "Really?" She picked up her jeans and hopped on one leg while she worked the other into the denim. "You know why I'm having doubts about us? Because you aren't straight with me." She started on the other leg. "And you sure aren't straight with yourself."

Dene didn't need this. She knew him too well. And she wasn't afraid to call him out. He wiped his hand across his face, kneading his eyebrows, his nose, his cheeks.

"Did you hear me?" said Zanelle. "I'm thirty-two next birthday, alright? I don't have time to be fucked around."

But you have time to be fucked, he thought, and immediately bit his tongue. Whatever his problems, they weren't her fault. He swung his legs off the bed and pulled the quilt over his lap. "Okay, okay. Maybe Dad had something to do with it. But I'd already talked about it with the twins. It was a valid option."

Zanelle rocked her hips from side to side and hitched her jeans up. "Why are you that way with your father?"

"He's got a chip on his shoulder because life didn't work out the way he wanted. Do you believe it? A guy recognised all over the world. In a bloody Hall of Fame." He rested his forehead on his palm. "So now he tries to organise everyone else's life. He's always put himself first. I'm sure that's why Mum walked out."

Zanelle's soft white belly held the jeans open, zipper spread wide. Her breasts flattened against her ribs under their own weight.

"Dene, we liaise with the Abbotsford police. A lot. There are whispers about Lampard's set-up."

"So, he's a fruitcake. I see that."

"With extra walnuts."

"Well, all I know is I've never been more motivated. Somehow the bloke gets results."

There. He was being straight.

"But he also burns people out," said Zanelle. "Guys have gone there and never played football again. Has he offered you any kind of supplements?"

"Yeah, he has. Protein, protein and more protein. I'm eating so much meat I can hardly crap."

She sat on the bed. "You know about fibre, right?"

"It's just an expression. My diet's changed a bit, that's all."

"Well, it sounds like an unhealthy environment to me." She slipped her hand beneath the quilt and stroked his thigh. Her tone softened. "I know what this means to you. Just be careful."

"I'm fine. We're only there to bulk up over winter."

And just like that, crooked again. Guilt on guilt.

Zanelle stood. She wriggled her hands inside the waist of her jeans and pushed them down over her hips.

"Thought you were leaving."

"I need more."

"Oh. Okay."

Chapter 35

BENOIT BROUSSARD WAS TALL and wide, but lean as a rower. Wavy flaxen hair fell over his shoulders, framing a thin moustache and a pale, trimmed beard. A red woollen overshirt and a puffer vest topped his hiking boots and cargo pants. He wore black Thinsulate gloves; the camp's medical room occupied the same hut as the chilled storage unit, and was almost as cold.

The huts were quiet, the forest still. His patients – Lampard's subjects – roamed high in the Skagit Range. They'd be back when they found nothing to eat. Starvation drained their will. It was a tether. They knew the camp was home, of sorts.

And there would always be food. Eventually.

Broussard prepared doses of medication; a flagrant euphemism if ever there was one. With his help, the subjects walked an organic wasteland between too little and just enough. Hunger was a potent incentive for all manner of things. The needs of the body always betrayed the wants of the mind.

But so far, it hadn't been enough.

Lampard bought the internment camp from the Canadian Government after an agreement with a glamping start-up fell through.

He then applied to convert it into a 'fitness retreat' linked to his gymnasium. When an inspector came to sign-off on the deal, he was told that Lampard's patrons had expressed their desire for a 'spartan' experience to contrast their otherwise cosseted lives.

The camp sat at the northern end of a flattened ridge that formed a narrow plateau between the peaks. The original access road merged into the network of fire trails that criss-crossed the Northern Cascades. You needed the right transport, but if you knew where to go you could find a grassy clearing bounded by red cedars at the southern end of the plateau.

A secondary track followed the ridge to the camp. It was difficult to find, obscured by low-hanging branches and a dog-leg corner. It bypassed a gravelled turn-in and led to a small parking area behind a machinery shed where vehicles were invisible from the clearing.

The camp resembled a *stalag*.

A sliding, wood-framed gate gave entry to the enclosed compound. Rows of weathered wooden huts in a five-by-four grid sat inside a chain-link fence, surrounded by timber light poles. The windows all had shutters, and those guarding broken or missing panes were nailed down.

The first hut inside the gate was once a processing hub for Japanese inmates. An uncovered porch still overlooked the gateway, but its rooms now housed the retreat's supplies, records and communications gear.

Lampard also installed diesel generators for heating and lighting, and set up a fuel dump for the gas-guzzling four-wheel drives. He turned one hut into the freezer storage and medical facility, and made token repairs the least run-down buildings.

The remaining huts were rotting, dilapidated shacks, but they hadn't been abandoned. Barred windows and brass padlocks on reinforced doors preserved their earlier status as confinement sheds.

One cabin, originally a recreation hall, Lampard stripped bare, floorboards and all. He dug a circular pit in the middle, ten yards across and a yard deep, then ringed it with a waist-high post and rail fence. He mulched the stony ground with sand, then soaked it in sump oil and beat it flat.

The hut became a crude arena. It served as a venue for tests of strength. Or feats of endurance. Or, most often, a place to resolve disputes.

Lampard called it a stadium, but thought of it as a colosseum.

Broussard called it *'l'abattoir'*....

DENE WOKE UP ALONE. He missed Zanelle. He missed morning sex.

He tottered to the bathroom and turned on the shower. Five minutes later, he put on coffee and powered up his cell phone.

He dressed in the bedroom. He could smell the sweat on his mussed-up sheets. As he buttoned a shirt, his phone sounded. He pulled on socks and wandered back to the kitchenette. He put bread in the toaster, then looked at the phone.

A voicemail.

The message was brief. No surprise there – it was from his father.

'Hello, Dene. Just wanted to say that I might have been a bit harsh the other day. Anyway. Just do whatever you think's best. You know I'll back you up.'

He was puzzled. The other day? It was months ago.

You'll never be as good as I was.

He knew the conciliatory tone. It only signalled more wheedling. He'd long decided that his father wouldn't run his life. He didn't need his approval to play football instead of rugby. And he'd go to whatever gym he damn well pleased. He deleted the message.

You don't have the mongrel for a start.

The toast popped up.

Dene unscrewed the cap on a jar of peanut butter and looked at the refrigerator door.

He thought, *I'll show you mongrel....*

Chapter 36

THE ORANGE TAHOE EMERGED from the morning mist like a rising sun. It rolled through the gateway and pulled up in front of the porch. Lampard stepped out and stretched. He filled his lungs with clean, cold air. This was his 'Hole-in-the-Wall' – the place he felt more alive than anywhere else.

He leaned down and pulled a box of flunitrazepam from the footwell. Two boxes of ketamine hydroxide followed. He stacked them on the hood.

Broussard bowled down the steps from the main hut. Lampard pointed at the drugs. "That's all I could put my hands on for now. Make it last."

"No problem."

"Yes, Benny, fucking problem. This gear isn't easy to get. And Roberts is braying like the entitled jackass he is."

"Roberts is only worried because he bought into a rubbish football team."

"I still want him off my back. Why is this all taking so long?"

Lampard triggered the Chevy's liftgate and pulled cartons of breakfast cereal and toilet paper from the cargo area. The few legitimate items inside the cardboard outers were a cover, hiding passive-cooling containers filled with bags of frozen blood.

Broussard slapped the top of a box. "We could start here. It's time we were more sophisticated."

"What are you suggesting?"

"No more greyhound pituitaries, no more hares' adrenal cortexes. No more animals full stop. The subjects have had a taste of two-legged prey. So, we should keep them moving in that direction. We need to adopt targeted nutrition."

Lampard stifled his resentment. Contradiction didn't sit well. First Marcus, now Benny. He needed to reassert control.

"Pah! This batch couldn't feed themselves at Costco."

Broussard shrugged. "And yet they've survived this far."

"Not without our help."

"But they aren't all useless."

"Seriously? Tell me, Benny, what would they do with human prey?"

"Perhaps they only need an example to follow. A demonstration."

Lampard cocked his head. His mind drifted over the bright peaks and the shaded forest. He soared above the wilderness; domain of the grizzly, the cougar and the ash-grey wolf.

You could start the next phase right away.

He said, "How many failures this month?"

"Outright? Three."

"When were they last medicated?"

"Yesterday."

Lampard's eyes glistened like frost in sunlight.

Exactly how committed are you?

"Put them in the stadium," he said. "Then round up the rest. If it's a demonstration they need, a demonstration they shall have."

ZANELLE PARKED A WHITE Taurus by the broken kerb of a street in a rundown part of Chilliwack, north of Highway One. The red, yellow and blue sash of the Canadian Mounted Police swept along the flanks of the vehicle like a candy wrapper.

She stepped out and bumped the patrol car's door with her hip. It closed with a healthy thunk. She liked the Taurus. She promised herself that she'd track one down at a government auction and try to pick it up at a reasonable price. Then it would be 'sayonara Subaru'.

She scanned the house from the roadway. A single-storey home, clad in greying brick veneer. Bands of moss edged a path of concrete flagstones. Yellowed envelopes peeped from the mouth of a wooden mailbox like misaligned teeth. Unopened newspapers littered the porch, and junk mail lay strewn amid a drift of fawn lilies in an overrun garden bed.

Zanelle paced along the path and tramped up three wooden steps. She rapped on a warped fly-wire door, then tucked her blouse into the duty belt and straightened her ballistic vest. She waited a few seconds and knocked again.

"Hello. Mr Ellis? Anyone home?"

Silence.

She walked to the end of the porch. The narrow boards creaked beneath her boots. She looked around the side of the house. She cupped her hands and peeked through a window.

"Mr Ellis? We might have some news about Robber."

She stretched an arm out straight, bent a knee and rested on the door frame. No vibration came through the timbers. She bowed her head, concentrating. No sound reached her ears.

If she was honest, she had no proof that Robber was one of the dogs found in the Fraser Valley. Wildlife had shredded the carcasses.

None had collars, so they were pretty much unidentifiable. Joe Ellis told her that Robber was 'brown with black streaks'. Animal registration wasn't mandatory in British Columbia and brindle was a common greyhound colour.

She hung in for a moment. She could stay longer but there was no point. It looked like he was on vacation. And she didn't want to give him false hope. Or break his heart.

She ambled back to the Taurus.

Chapter 37

THE HUT REEKED OF body odour and ammonia. Two dozen haggard, walking corpses leaned over the fence and drooled fetid, green spittle onto the sand. Some wore tattered pants; some wore ragged shirts. Some wore nothing.

Their eyes darted around like jackals on the veldt, but it was only a neural response. A steady infusion of chemicals kept their minds dull. They hardly even felt the cold.

Each was once a prime specimen of the adult male. Now they were famished and wasted and hollow.

Their bones moved beneath thin sheets of decomposing flesh. The Asians were pus-yellow, the whites were the colour of threadworms, the blacks as grey as bread mould. They pissed where they stood and trails of shit smeared their legs.

Debased beyond salvation.

Three hunched forms wandered inside the ring. Two touched six feet, the other was shorter. They carried no fat and only remnants of muscle. Decaying ectomorphs.

The watchers taunted from above. They stammered abuse in vicious, pidgin baby-talk. Broussard marched into their midst. He held a nine-inch cattle prod in one hand and a bullwhip in the other.

The cattle prod parped a warning and the creatures drew back. They knew what came next.

Lampard pushed through double doors at the end of the hut, and the clamour grew. He ignored the mob and strode to the railing fence. Barefooted and half naked, his skin gave off a sickly sheen. A grimy calico *dhoti* wound beneath his paunch and sagged about his loins. Like an Indian wrestler.

Or a gladiator.

He leered at the figures below. They milled on a makeshift stage, players in their own tragedy. In his script, they were the *noxii*, the bottommost class in Roman society, lower than animals, while he took the role of a *venatio* – one of the *bestiarii*.

A hunter.

He gripped the rail and vaulted into the pit. He prowled a circuit inside the fence, raising his arms, urging the spectators on.

Then he turned to the ravaged shapes beside him. "Oh, you big strong footballers, with all your girls and your money and your fans. You were so popular. Well, just look at you now. Snivelling filth."

The three men cowered. Broussard snaked the whip across their heads. He lashed their backs, herding them to the centre of the ring. They scurried away. Their eyes met in a desperate pact. They understood. They grouped, facing the fourth man. Hesitated.

And then charged.

Lampard weighed as much as the three combined. He stepped aside, then shouldered the taller two against each other. They reeled off balance and ploughed into the sand like drunks. He lunged at the smallest man and grabbed his throat. He locked his left hand around the tendons, the wind-pipe, the blood vessels.

The creature clawed at his captor's arm and kicked with frail white legs. He couldn't cry out. His larynx was crushed, the carotid arteries occluded. The oxygen in his veins degraded to carbon dioxide. Lactic acid flooded his bloodstream and the pH plummeted. His ruined brain asphyxiated.

The fallen men scrambled to their feet. One feinted sideways. Lampard took a step and stomped on the man's kneecap. The joint ruptured like a rotten branch. His scream drowned out the rabble.

The other creature dodged away. He reversed against the edge of the pit, but then had nowhere to go. Lampard clubbed him in the face with a hammer fist. The man rebounded off a fence post and tumbled forward. Lampard drove a knee into his forehead. The sudden backward acceleration, then deceleration of his head fractured the base of his skull. Like a car crash.

He fell face down, unconscious. Lampard leapt onto his back. The man's ribs cracked, and the diaphragm sucked sand into his nose and mouth. His airways clogged. He gagged and choked and died.

The man with the shattered knee whimpered on the ground. Lampard clamped his right hand around the back of the man's neck and lifted him onto his good leg. He raised the limp body in his left hand, then spread his arms wide – and crashed the heads together.

Again and again, he battered the heads, wielding them like cudgels. The faces swelled. The skin bruised and bloated. Noses gushed red. Eyebrows split. Tongues bulged through burst lips. The withered limbs flailed and fragmented skulls flopped on broken necks.

Lampard tired. Sweat and blood splatter trickled from his face. He flung the bigger carcass onto the sand, then trailed the small man's body around the ring, fingers still embedded in the purple flesh of his throat. He looked up at uncertain faces, distrustful eyes. At churning, buried anger.

"And *you*," he said. "You strut around like Gods, but you are false idols. You are nothing. Nobodies." He raised his voice above the din. "Warriors all – hah! Look at your comrades. Where is your loyalty? Never leave a man behind, you say? *Balls*, I say!"

Broussard stood amid the throng, transfixed. Lampard waved his fist and thundered on.

"You don't know Nietzsche. You've never read Binding and Hoche. Never heard of Galton. No, your culture is rap music and comic books and reality TV. You worship mediocrity. So you will always be *slaves*."

He cried out and beat his chest.

Goading.

Beseeching.

"What is *wrong* with you? You are not my children. You are nothing to me. I am not your father; I am your tormentor. Rise up. Attack me. Destroy me!"

His eyes brimmed. Mucus streamed from his nose, across his lips, down his chin. He braced his arms and legs, and shrieked at the top of his lungs.

"*Untermenschen!*"

Tears flowed over his cheeks and into his mouth. He raised the shrunken body in his arms. He pulled back his lips and buried his teeth in its chest.

He locked his jaw and racked his head from side to side, peeling wedges of pulpy skin from the ribs. He sheared gristle from the shoulders. He ripped shreds of meat from brittle bones. He gorged and chewed and swallowed.

The creatures stirred. They gathered and pressed against the fence. Lampard looked up. He spat gore and threads of tissue into their rabid, seething faces.

"Life unworthy of...*life*."

Chapter 38

DENE SWALLOWED A BOTTLE of Gatorade in one pull; he'd put in a solid session.

He wandered into the locker room and removed a soaking wet singlet. He stuffed it into his gym bag, kicked off his heavy training shoes, and stepped out of his trackpants. He pulled on running shorts, then pushed his feet into lightweight racing flats. He sat on a slatted wooden bench and tied the laces.

Garner Hall poked his face around the door. "We're closing up."

"Hey, Garner. Just on my way out." Dene slipped a dry T-shirt over his head. "Listen, I wanted to speak with you about something."

Hall strolled past the empty shower cubicles, then peeped under the toilet doors. "I thought you might."

"So, when's a good time?"

"It has to be soon. I'm going up to the fitness retreat. Not sure when I'll be back."

"Are you working tomorrow?"

Hall jammed his foot against the door. "We can't talk here if it's about what I think it is."

Cautious? Or anxious. Dene couldn't tell.

He stood and said, "You have a lunch break?"

"What if I meet you at two o'clock in the City Walk arcade? You can have a soy latte in peace."

"Ha! Look forward to it. And thanks."

"Don't thank me yet. You don't know what I might say."

The little man walked out and eased the door shut behind him.

Dene stretched his quads. Hall wasn't the cheeriest person he'd ever met. He wondered if there was a reason.

Chapter 39

THE STREETS WERE EMPTY – no blinding headlamps – and the cool air was just right. Perfect for a road run.

Dene ran with soft footfalls and easy breaths. Held his form, relaxed his shoulders, opened his elbows and drove the rhythm with his arms.

He picked up the tempo for the last half-mile. Increased his stride and shifted from a mid-sole to a forefoot strike. His feet popped off the bitumen. He stretched out and ran the final two hundred yards at close to top pace, then eased into a jog as he entered the carpark.

He tapped his watch and ended the workout. He slowed to a walk, put his hands on his hips, pulled his shoulders back and filled his lungs. The cool air whistled in through his nose and whooshed out his mouth.

Training for a running-based contact sport is an endless trade-off. The athlete must maintain a level of endurance while preserving upper body mass, and without compromising speed.

Association Football is king in the conditioning stakes. Dene had tried it as a boy, but his father wouldn't have a soccer player in the house. The rugby codes place different demands on the body, emphasising strength and bulk.

American football is different again. It requires immense power, explosive speed and phenomenal athleticism.

But you still need the base. The foundation.

David Selkirk drummed it into his son from a young age. The stronger the foundation, the higher you can build. If you aren't the quickest, you need to run fast for longer. And to do that, play after play, you must be fitter.

Speed rules, but you can negotiate. To a degree.

Dene walked a couple of laps around his pickup, then lounged on the hood while he checked his heart-rate. It had plateaued at eighty-five beats per minute after sixty seconds. That wasn't right. It should still have been one-twenty after ninety seconds. He slid the watch around his wrist. Must be a poor connection with the skin.

He noted the Tahoe in its usual place, backed up to the roller door. He'd run out of the carpark at nine-thirty and had been on the road for forty minutes. Someone always locked the gym up by ten. A tissue of light spread from the entrance. He strolled over and tried the handle. The door creaked open.

A hard-edged thud echoed from the weight room, then another. Dene wandered down the corridor and peered into the gym. No music played and the hanging lamps were in power-saving mode.

He saw Lampard at his regular station in the corner, curled over a loaded barbell, white head gleaming like a polished doorknob in the half-light. His thick torso sprang erect in one abrupt movement. He paused, then slumped down again.

Count of two.

Up.

Count of two.

Down.

The hiss of controlled breathing rolled across the floor. Dene watched the massive weight rise and then crash back onto the rubber mat.

Lampard spotted his reflection in the mirror and released the bar.

"Good," he said. "You've been doing extra."

Dene pushed against a rack and stretched his calves. "I have to keep my running up to scratch."

"You worry too much." Lampard flipped a towel over his neck and wiped sweat from his face. "Muscle carries its own weight. What you need is power. It's basic exercise science."

Dene squinted, unsure. He recited the mantra. "Strength plus speed equals power."

"Good *God*, boy. What have they been teaching you? Power equals force, multiplied by distance, divided by time."

Lampard wiped his shoulders. Crusty white skin cancers peppered his arms. He said, "How much do you dead-lift?"

"One rep max? Four-sixty." Dene saw the frown. "Four-seventy if I'm lucky."

Lampard eyed the barbell at his feet. He bent and pinched the spring collars open and slid them over the stainless-steel shafts. He pushed a plate off each end of the bar.

"Try that."

"You're kidding."

"Try it."

Dene attempted a quick calculation. "How much is on there?"

"Doesn't matter," said Lampard. "Lift it."

"No straps?"

"You won't need them for one rep."

Dene shrugged. He dived his hands into a bucket of chalk. He ground his palms together, then clapped off the excess powder.

He positioned his feet, set himself, and placed an alternate grip on the bar. One palm underhand, the other overhand. He filled his lungs and tensed. And lifted.

The weight barely cleared the mat. Three red lights. A failure.

An embarrassment.

He stood and rolled his shoulders. "I've done a fair bit tonight. I'm worn out."

Lampard poked his tongue through gaps in his teeth. "You only think you are." He lumbered to a pile of heavy-gauge chain sitting by the wall. "There's another factor in the equation. Acceleration."

He dragged a cluster of chains onto the mat and looped a fistful of metal links over each end of the bar.

"Now lift that," he said.

Dene knew how it worked. The initial phase of a lift is the most difficult. The nearer to full extension, the greater force the lifter can exert. With chains, the weight on the bar is manageable at the start of the lift. Then, as more chain comes off the floor, the weight increases.

It let you bump up your one-rep max, and it helped develop explosive power, but it was a 'cheat'. And there was still more metal on the bar than he had ever shifted.

"I couldn't. No way."

"Lift it!"

Dene studied Lampard's face. No coaxing, no cajoling. No persuasive words to sway his judgement.

It was a demand.

He planted his feet and bent over the bar. He swayed from side to side, aligning his knees and hips. He folded his fingers around the steel. He braced himself and strained. He pushed with his legs and dragged the bar from the floor, but the lift stalled at his shins.

Lampard suddenly lunged forward, face contorted, eyeballs bulging, veins knotted. He stamped his foot and roared into Dene's ear.

"Lift it! Lift it! Lift it!"

Dene gritted his teeth. He pulled his shoulders back and heaved. His legs straightened and the bar rose past his knees. He squeezed his buttocks and thighs, driving his hips forward and his torso upward. He straightened to lock-out and stood, rigid, shuddering with exertion.

He let his shoulders slump and released his grip. The chains rattled and the barbell crashed to the floor. He drew sharp, deep breaths.

Lampard stomped around the mat, hunched forward, arms spread, eyes blazing. "Five hundred and twenty pounds!" He thrust a twisted forefinger at Dene. "Speed. Strength. And *fear*."

The man stopped and eased himself upright. He raised his head. A curtain of tranquillity fell across his face. When he spoke, his voice was soft. Resigned. Almost forlorn.

"Never say you can't do something again."

Lampard turned and crossed the room. He disappeared down the corridor to his office and closed the door behind him.

Dene's arms quivered. The tremor purred through his chest. Exhilaration, mingled with fatigue.

He tipped his head back and laughed.

Above him, twin skylights gazed down from the gloom beneath the warehouse roof, like a pair of empty black eyes.

THE CHASE

Chapter 40

ZANELLE TURNED OFF THE main street and drove along a one-way service road. She cruised past Chilliwack's Highfield Vet Centre and eased to a stop in front of the adjacent building, a store that sold hunting equipment.

The two businesses sat side-by-side; identical structures separated by a common parking area. Even the signs above their doorways matched. Same size, same font. Only the message was different. A comic book archer aimed his big red arrow at a small blue puppy thirty yards away.

A study in irony.

She unbuckled her seatbelt and listened to the Subaru's heater fan flutter against the autumn cold. She'd bought the little hatch because it looked stylish and cute. It was only five years old, but had lived a hard life. It used a pint of oil a fortnight and was out of warranty. She was the second owner, but if she'd known the first was a jockey at Hastings Park, she wouldn't have touched it with a barge pole.

She pondered a set of questions scrawled in her duty notebook. She needed answers, but wasn't sure which direction to take. What was more important – the stolen drugs or the stolen blood? And would they lead to the same place?

Activity along the road dwindled. Shop doors closed and the late afternoon traffic thinned. By the time the street lights blinked on, just a single vehicle remained in the vet clinic's carpark.

She grabbed a blue parka from the back seat. She already wore her RCMP trousers and boots, and hoped she looked official. She stepped out of her car and bustled toward the blue puppy.

A glass door opened into the fluorescent glow of the clinic. Ornate certificates dotted the walls between displays of medication, chew toys, collars and leads. The odour of antiseptic and chemical cleaners filled the air; more than a hospital, less than a morgue.

A slim woman in her fifties dragged a twenty-pound bag of dog food from a shelf and dumped it onto a flat-top trolley. Long grey plaits dangled over her shoulders, and beaded yoga bracelets circled her wrists. She wore no makeup, but didn't need to. A lifelong flower child, glowing with brown rice and flax seeds.

The woman turned. "Hey, babe. We're closing soon. How can I help?"

Zanelle approached, all business. She whisked her creds through the woman's eyeline and slid them back into her pocket.

Don't give them time to think.

"I'm with the Mounted Police," she said. "We have more questions to ask about the break-in."

"I take it you haven't found them then."

"Not yet, but we'll catch a break soon. That's why we follow up. People often recall little things afterward."

The woman pushed her beads up each forearm, then spread a dozen metal bowls on the trolley.

"I'm busy," she said, "but if you want to tag along, go for it. I'm Tonia by the way."

"Hi. My name's Zannie."

Would it sound like Annie? And not Officer. Not Constable. No need to get in deeper than she already was.

She said, "Tonia, we want to widen our search a little. What's canine blood used for?"

"Well, patients after surgery of course, but there are various transfusion therapies too. Disease. Poisoning. Infection."

"How much would you use in, say a year?"

Tonia sliced the bag of dog food with a box-cutter. She scooped out cups of kibble and tipped them into the bowls.

"Depends on how many procedures we do. Size of the animals. Eight, nine hundred litres? Maybe more."

"Wow." Zanelle was genuinely surprised. It wasn't the biggest clinic around. "How do you replace it all?"

"Canine blood banks. They're always calling for donations, so we should be fine."

Zanelle made a show of jotting in the notebook while she read the next question from her script. "Why is greyhound blood so popular?"

The woman paused. She flicked a plait over her shoulder. "You've done your research."

She pushed the cart down a hallway, past consulting rooms, to the rear of the building. Zanelle followed her into a kennel-cum-storeroom. Steel mesh cages stacked two-high lined the room, all about the size of a small washing machine.

Dogs yapped and twirled and yowled, and leapt against the wire. Some were convalescing, others were boarding while their owners enjoyed a vacation.

No greyhounds.

Tonia opened cage doors and swapped empty feed bowls for full.

She said, "For one, greyhounds have a high concentration of red blood cells. But the main reason is that they're a kind of universal donor. Eighty-five percent of them, anyway."

"Type O?"

"We don't call it that, but dogs do have different blood types."

Zanelle scribbled. "We had several reports of missing dogs this summer. Could wolves have taken them?"

"It's possible. Wolves sometimes come into the suburbs looking for garbage. If a dog's unlucky enough to run into them, well...."

"So, has the wolf population increased?"

"Probably not. Predator numbers tend to stabilise if there's a reduction in prey. And they wouldn't come into town if there was plenty of food."

"Hunters? I mean, could they affect the prey levels?"

Tonia withdrew a retractable hose and topped up each dog's water dish. "Well, they're supposed to be regulated – permits, quotas – but who knows with those inbred gimps."

"I hear you," said Zanelle. "What else might take their prey?"

"Cougars, perhaps? I don't know. It's complicated. Animals that develop a specialised diet are vulnerable to any reduction in that diet."

"So, theoretically, they could eat themselves out of existence."

"If they didn't adapt to another food source, yes."

Tonia let the hose wind up, then manoeuvred the cart into place beside a garage roller door. She dipped a mop into a wheeled bucket and pushed it back along the hallway.

Zanelle quickly inspected the roller door. She saw no damage. Traces of black fingerprint powder remained on the door guides and a few white blots ringed a light switch.

A strip of black and yellow crime scene tape hung from the wall.

Barrage de police. Ne pas traverser.

Police line. Do not cross.

More irony.

She skipped after the nurse. "Then the alpha male would be the last man standing, right?"

"Ah, the fabled alpha male. That's actually a myth. A mated pair leads most wolf packs, and it's often the female that leads the hunt, marks out territory and so on."

"You should spend some time in a gym. Or a police station. The alpha male is no myth."

"You're confusing alpha males with dickless squibs."

Zanelle couldn't stop a snort of laughter. "I think you might be right."

Tonia steered the bucket into the foyer. She started in a corner, then mopped backwards across the room.

"Anything else?" she said. "I'm nearly done here."

Zanelle turned a page in her notebook. Now she was fishing.

"Dogs are descended from wolves, is that right?"

"It is. Thousands of years ago wolves began scavenging from human camp sites. They're not obligate carnivores like cats. They'll eat almost anything if they're hungry. The tamer ones hung around and evolved into the dogs we have today."

"If wolf numbers aren't increasing, could their population actually be shrinking?"

"Oh, for sure. The way we're going, we'll wipe out every wild animal one day."

"But dogs couldn't become extinct. Could they?"

"No, I doubt that'll happen. They're still bred for specific purposes – which basically means they're farmed, like sheep or cows."

"No shortage of those."

"Not yet anyway. As callous as it sounds, the best way to protect a species from extinction, is to eat it."

Zanelle took a moment to reconcile the idea of eating Javan rhinoceros or Vaquita porpoise.

Then she shuddered.

Or mountain gorilla.

She said, "Okay then," and snapped the note book shut. "Listen, thanks for your time. You've been a big help."

"You're welcome." Tonia opened the door. "Say, are you undercover, or is it just casual day?"

Zanelle lifted her eyebrows as innocently as she could.

"Hmm?"

"No uniform," said the vet nurse.

Busted.

"Oh, I'm finished for the day. Just on my way home."

She gave a too-friendly smile as she slipped out the door, then threw a last wave before she hurried toward her car.

Tonia pushed the clinic door closed and snibbed the latch.

She slid bolts into the frame, top and bottom, then watched the blue-clad figure merge with the twilight.

"Of course you are, sweetie," she said.

Zanelle looked toward the roller door at the end of the parking lot.

She knew conventional fingerprint powder came in several forms. Fluorescent, magnetic and bi-chromatic powders were relatively new, but the black, carbon-based product, seen on a hundred cop shows, was still a staple. They used it on lighter surfaces, like the white-painted roller door and its runners.

A titanium oxide mix was used on darker surfaces, such as the red bricks inside the surgery's storeroom. The grubby smudge marks left by the carbon clearly indicated latent prints, but titanium oxide could sometimes be mistaken for other, similar substances. Like plaster dust. Or talcum powder.

Or magnesium carbonate.

Better known to some...as gym chalk.

She ducked into her car and glanced up at the archer on the shop sign. Even she had to concede, that was a long bow to draw.

Chapter 41

THE WOLVES' SEASON ENTERED freefall.

In August they lost two matches in overtime, but that didn't show in the standings.

Twelve-zip.

The horror stretch continued. In September, after a nightmare road trip and a ten-minute locker room rant, Roger Bartoli had a heart attack.

With only vague assurance that his position was safe, he spent a week in hospital while Pete Hoffman took charge of the team.

The change of coach didn't change their luck.

Fifteen-zip.

In the last week of October they finished the season with a 44-3 drubbing at the hands of Hamilton, the Grey Cup favourites.

Eighteen-zip.

DENE STOOD IN FRONT of the stove. Loose denim jeans hung from his hips and a faded, jade-green tee stretched over his biceps. He picked up two scotch fillets with his fingers and laid the chunks of meat in a pan of sizzling garlic butter.

Gentle tapping rattled the window.

"Just a minute!"

He wiped his hands and went to the door, unhooked the chain and swung it open.

"Hi. Can I come in?"

"Sure."

Zanelle stepped inside.

Dene grinned. It was a knack she'd always had – she knew how to keep him off balance. And he wasn't certain why, but he liked it. He closed the door behind her.

"Your hair's getting longer," he said. "Looks good."

"Thanks, that's really nice to hear." She peeled off her jacket and dropped it onto the couch. "I need to talk to you."

Hmm. Which way would this go?

"Only talk? You don't want me to turn these off?"

She glanced at the steaks. "Don't flatter yourself, kiddo." She unwound a scarf and threw it onto her jacket. "I've been following up on some incidents. And I'm not sure I like what I've found."

"What incidents would these be?"

"Someone broke into a vet clinic in Chilliwack a while back. Usually, they're looking for drugs."

"Usually?"

"One thing taken was the clinic's supply of blood. Canine blood."

"I think I know who did it."

"Really?"

"Vampire poodles."

A jarring straight right hit him dead centre.

"Dick brain," she said. "We've had twenty dogs reported missing in three months. And fourteen were greyhounds."

Dene rubbed his chest. "I thought greyhound racing was illegal."

"Actually, it's not. It's only unlegislated. They can race them, but they can't gamble on them."

"Like that's gonna happen."

"Right," said Zanelle. "You know, they make great pets. You should consider one."

"Maybe one day. If I ever get my own place." He watched her eyes wander over his arms as he slid a bottle of Cabernet Sauvignon from a wooden rack. "Would you like something to eat?"

Zanelle grimaced at the crackling pan. "I'll be fine, thanks."

"Sorry. Best I can do." He grabbed a couple of glasses and blew dust off the rims. "You were saying?"

"Well, I thought wolves might have taken the dogs, but apparently the wolf population is stable, which means they shouldn't be that desperate for food. But you can put it another way. Because they're desperate for food, the wolf population is stable. See my problem?"

Dene filled a glass and passed it over. "So, what's the connection?"

She took a quick sip. "Vet clinics use a lot of blood. They mostly get it from animal blood banks, which collect it from donor animals. But guess what blood they prefer."

"Greyhounds?"

"Bingo."

"But why?"

"Because dogs have different blood types. And I'm told greyhounds are a universal donor."

"If it's so important, maybe someone's selling it. Like black-market blood."

"Closer than you think. Earlier this year some hikers found a bunch of dead dogs in the Fraser Valley. They were all greyhounds. And someone drained every drop of their blood."

Dene frowned. "Now that *is* creepy."

He tasted his red, then slipped into a Transylvanian accent. "Vot elze voz taay-ken?" He almost laughed at her pained look. He took a languid swallow and let his eyes linger on hers.

She arched an eyebrow. "You're being unusually playful."

"Because you're being unusually serious."

"I'm always serious, you know that. And this is a serious matter." She slid a hand up Dene's sleeve and squeezed his shoulder. "Are you getting bigger?"

Dene thought his arms had thickened up. If others had noticed as well, he was probably right. He shrugged it off and said, "Okay, I'll be serious too. What else did they take?"

"What?"

She was distracted. He guessed why. He felt the warmth of her fingers spread down through his belly.

"You said *one* thing taken. What else did they take from the clinic?"

"Well, ketamine of course. And all their clenbuterol. You know where that'll end up."

Dene nodded. Clenbuterol was used to treat respiratory problems in racehorses. It worked by dilating the blood vessels, but not just in the lungs. It increased blood flow throughout the body. And that led to faster muscle development.

Despite being a banned substance, horse trainers soon learned how to abuse it. Then the fitness industry caught on. Its use as a weight training supplement had been rife ever since.

"Hmmm," he said. "Bodybuilders. But who wants an anabolic agent...and dog's blood?"

"That's what I'd like to know."

Dene remembered the steaks. He turned them and gave the pan a shimmy. "Tell you what to do. Go to the university and find Tallie Kainoa. She might be able to help."

"Related to the twins, I assume."

"Older sister. She's doing her Master's in chemical biology. And she'd know as much about PEDs as anyone."

"You footballers and your performance-enhancing drugs. What satisfaction do you get from cheating?"

He dropped his head and massaged his jaw. The rough skin of his fingers grated over black stubble. He knew people handled things differently. She'd been through the system. She should have understood that not everyone could deal with the pressure.

And not everyone had scruples.

"Look," he said, "don't get me wrong. I'm not condoning it, but that's how it is in sport today. Only an outsider would call it cheating."

"Alright, let's call it looking for a short-cut."

"Most of them don't even want a short-cut."

"An edge?"

"They're looking for a way to keep up with everyone else. You can take all the drugs you want, but you still need to do the work."

"So that's how you rationalise it?"

"I don't mean it like that. And besides, not everyone uses. The twins have always been clean. They saw what happened to their dad. Now his health is down the tubes, and Tallie's trying to help."

Only the twins? He waited, but she didn't say it. Better get out of this argument fast. He grabbed a pint container of table salt and shook a blizzard of sodium over the sputtering meat.

"Dene!"

"Hmm?"

Zanelle snatched the salt shaker from his hand.

"Jesus, are you trying to poison yourself?"

She slid the shaker out of reach along the benchtop. He leaned for it but she shoved an elbow across his throat and fended him away. Keepings off. Teenage foreplay.

Cab Sav sloshed onto the floor. She said, "Aww, I was enjoying that."

The wine or the wrestling?

He gave up anyway. Mission accomplished.

Zanelle licked wine from the back of her hand. Mischief twinkled in her eyes. "Are you sure you aren't getting out of your depth at that gym?"

Hmph. Maybe not. He shot her a look that said 'shit stirrer', and tossed back his red.

"How many times do I need to say it? I'm only there until training starts up again." He turned off the stove. "And this is my last chance, so I won't go back if I don't make it."

She shook her head. "Something about that place doesn't wash with me."

Dene took her glass and set it on the bench. He gripped her shoulders and kissed her. She fell into the embrace. He felt her palms run across his pecs.

She kneaded the fabric of his shirt, and thumbed his nipples.

"What *are* they giving you? You're definitely getting bigger."

He took her hand and pressed it against the bulge in his jeans.

"That's what's supposed to happen," he said.

Chapter 42

ZANELLE CROSS-CHECKED VICTIM STATEMENTS in the RCMP reception area. She glanced up when Tom Calder walked in.

He said, "I learned some more about the Kermode bears."

"Good man. Let's hear it."

"Whoever wrote that article didn't do their homework. Genetically, the Kermodes are actually black bears. They're a sub-species. But only around ten percent of Kermode bears are born white. The white colouration is a genetic anomaly. It's a recessive mutation."

"Be patient with me here. That means one parent must be white?"

"No, it's a recessive gene, remember. If a bear carries one gene for black fur, which is dominant, and one for white – which is recessive – the bear will be black. So that means both parents can be black, but...if they both carry a white gene, *and pass it on*, they can produce a white cub. It's tricky but that's why the white Kermodes are so rare. If the offspring only receives one white gene, it will still be black. It must receive two white genes, one from each parent, to be born white."

She nodded slowly. Her knowledge of genetics was basic at best. It would help if the kid got to the point.

"And," she said, "I'm guessing that's less likely."

"Right. The thing is, although we *have* seen black bears up in the Skagit Ranges, sightings are relatively uncommon. Here's the kicker though. The entire recorded population of white bears lives on the coastal islands north of Vancouver. That's two-hundred and fifty miles from here. Yes, white bears exist. But sure as shit not in the Skagit Ranges. Lousy research."

Zanelle folded her arms. "Or a cover-up. I wonder if I should have a word with that journo."

A phone trilled beneath the counter. An internal call. Calder picked up.

"Yes, ma'am." He straightened and patted his hair. "No, ma'am." He swallowed. His fingertips drummed on the laminate as he listened. He said, "Right away, ma'am," then put the phone down. He turned a glum face to his colleague.

She saw the chastened look and waves of anxiety rippled up her spine. She lifted her shoulders and spread her hands. "What?"

"Forget the journo," said Calder. "The Inspector wants to see you in her office. Now."

"She say why?"

"Were you bothering someone at a vet clinic the other day?"

"Bothering? Who said I was bothering anyone?"

"You're aware that everyone knows everyone else in this town, right?"

"I was investigating the break-in. So what?"

"Off-duty? Out of uniform?"

"Jesus, Tom, it's a crime isn't it? And you can bet your First Nation nuts that it's connected to those dogs. And probably that damned gym."

"Well, I just had the Riot Act read to me and I only answered the phone. Sounds like Truman Roberts has enquired about you, too."

"Oh, that'd be right. He can't lift a finger to help, but he can interfere when I'm trying to do my job."

Calder grabbed the pile of victim statements. "I'll finish that. You'd better go. And don't push your luck."

Zanelle tossed her head. She'd had gutful. Don't push your luck? Well, she wouldn't be kissing ass.

The glass partition shuddered as she stomped out of the reception area.

"*Fuck* me dead!"

Chapter 43

"You don't look the soy type. If you don't mind me saying."

The pale young waiter set a latte on the table and gave a coy moue. Dene half expected him to flutter his eyelashes. It wasn't the first time an optimistic suitor had reached out.

Dene flashed his grin. A compliment was a compliment.

He looked around the cafe. A few late diners occupied tables, but no one he knew. He guessed Lampard's cohort didn't 'do lunch'.

Garner Hall stirred a cup of black tea and said, "Have you tried the different sugar ratio?"

"Not yet. Think I'll need to mix my own."

"That's good. Learn to improvise. You can get maltodextrin at a home brew supplier. Health food stores should have fructose."

"Will it make much difference?"

"You may only notice subtle benefits, but subtle can have a big effect over a year. Even months. Mix it five-to-four and drink it pre-workout. You should get a nice, prolonged carbo wave. My feedback is that fifteen minutes after a workout you'll feel like you could go around again."

Dene looked out the window. Hall had just described his last three sessions. "Lampard gave me something. Said it was a sort of tonic."

"HCS?"

"That's what the label says. Look, I'm as game as the next guy, Garner, but I'm not sure I want to be using any old backyard potion."

"It's not that bad. He's worked on it for years, but he isn't getting the ergogenic effect he needs. That's why I'm here. My specialty is high-performance nutrition, but there's a big grey area."

"So, what's in it?"

"Ah, he's a tinkerer when it comes to supplements." Hall tipped more sugar into his cup. "Let's see. Years ago, he discovered the military's EHO programs –"

"Hold on. Too many initials. EHO?"

"Enhanced Human Operations."

"Sounds like something out of Robocop."

"Close to the truth. Think of it as 'training with benefits'. If you thought athletes were off the wall, you should see what the army does. Implanted sensors, anti-sleep drugs, nano-magnetic healing. And they're way down the line with exoskeletons." He sipped his tea. "Anyway, Lampard became fascinated with one of the older technologies. Blood doping. It was his El Dorado. He started using his own blood as a base for various compounds. Not all of them legal. Or safe, I might add."

Dene was lost at ergogenic, but he'd heard of blood doping. They based the protocol on experiments designed to help pilots function at high altitude after World War II.

They withdrew a unit of the subject's own blood and separated the red cells. Those cells were then re-injected. The added red cells increased the blood's capacity to transport oxygen. And that improved performance.

"I'll give you some background," said Hall, dunking a cookie.

"Blood loading became widespread among sports-people in the sixties. Endurance athletes had the most to gain – runners, swimmers, skiers, cyclists. With no foreign substances to detect, it was almost impossible to control. The medical term is 'induced erythrocythaemia'. In the common vernacular, it's called cheating. And for any athletes so inclined, the rewards outweighed the risk of side effects. Pulmonary embolism, heart attack. Even strokes."

Dene cradled his coffee. He had to admit, it was a fascinating topic. And it seemed Garner was only getting started. He didn't interrupt.

"After transfusions, the scientists came up with EPO. Erythropoietin. That's a blood boosting hormone – which the body produces naturally, by the way. They banned it from professional sport in 1990, but didn't start testing until the Sydney Olympics. People jumped up and down after the Lance Armstrong revelations, but then they forgot about it and the sporting world moved on."

"To other ways of gaming the system."

Hall shrugged. "Like I said, a grey area. The biological passports slowed things down a bit, but it hasn't stopped them. So, then they developed synthetic oxygen carriers. They still use SOCs in blood substitutes today. And athletes continue to abuse them."

Dene said, "That's really Lampard's blood in those bottles?"

"No, don't worry. Not entirely. You've seen the weights he lifts? The trophies? That's half him, half extras. He had some success, sure, but he never achieved the results he wanted. Because his body accepted his own blood without needing to adapt. And now he's stopped gaining. That's largely due to his age of course, but he's frustrated, so his focus has shifted to other areas."

"Such as?"

"Oh, I assure you, we're getting to the sophisticated end of town. His latest idea is actually half smart. He's looking for a way to infuse haematopoietic stem cells with biomorphic proteins. But he'll try just about anything."

Dene found himself adrift in the science again. "He should go see the Wolves. I'm pretty sure they'd try anything right now."

"He already has. Mattson is part of the Vancouver Wolves Alpha Pack."

Dene spluttered a mouthful of coffee over the table.

Hall grinned. "Ignore the name – someone let the marketers loose. It's a coterie of backers who provide unofficial support. Mostly goods and services. Low key. All off the books. In return, they're given parcels of shares by the major sponsors. Everyone gets their back scratched. As long as the Wolves start winning. Mattson has guaranteed that his serum will transform enough players to turn the Wolves around, but he needs *one* bona fide success to convince the others they should persevere. And it needs to be soon, or everyone's going to take a big financial hit."

Dene mopped up the spill, thinking. Hall had misread. The name wasn't the problem. Without knowing it, Dene was linked to Lampard the whole time. He didn't believe in fate, but....

He wiped his mouth. "The magic formula is proving to be elusive, that it?"

"The formula is only part of it," said Hall. "The subject must then respond to the serum. And respond in optimal fashion. But if they do, it's off to the races."

"Have you seen anyone respond? Optimally?"

"No, can't say I have, but I've only been here a few years. We've seen a range of outcomes across the performance spectrum though. Improvements in speed, strength, reaction time. But Mattson says he can count on one hand the number of total successes he's had."

"So, what happened to all the failures?"

Hall swirled the dregs around his teacup. "Some subjects went backwards from the start. Some showed early promise, then fell away. Some...." He shrugged again.

Dene said, "So the odds aren't in my – anyone's favour. If they use this stuff, I mean."

The little man leaned forward. He looked over his glasses and lowered his voice.

"Don't misunderstand. It won't produce miracles. You still need the basic athletic components. But if you were one of the lucky ones, it could take you to the top. And let me be clear on this. I mean the big league. The NFL."

Chapter 44

DENE PATROLLED A STRIP of carpet in the middle of the gym, hands on hips, catching his breath. Gas heaters had taken over from the cooling fans, but he wasn't cold.

Kenny and Tim stacked cast iron discs onto a heavy-duty fitness sled. The apparatus sat at one end of a twenty-yard track, loaded with two dozen forty-five-pound plates. The twins added six more.

Tim said, "Man, you are movin' some serious shit. What's your record?"

"Not sure."

"Well, you won't shift this in a hurry," said Kenny. He glanced at a clock on the wall. "Ten seconds."

Dene lined himself up with the sled. He gripped a pair of bars and bumped his shoulders into protective pads. He wondered if Lampard was watching. The place hummed on Saturday mornings and he knew the owner liked to keep his finger on the pulse. He lowered his eyes and leaned against the weight.

"Go," said Kenny.

Dene drove his legs into the carpet and shoved. The sled didn't budge. He groaned and rocked from side to side.

The sled moved half a foot.

"Alright," said Kenny. "Dig it in. Dig it in."

Quillan stopped wiping a bench and stared. A few of the gym rats gathered beside him.

Dene gulped a breath and held it. He heaved the sled forward.

Three feet.

"C'mon dude, move that fucker." said Tim.

Another step, then another. And then one more.

Five yards.

The banter in the gym went down a notch. Quillan strolled toward the action. He stepped onto the sled track and yelled into Dene's ear.

"Pain is only *weakness* leaving your body!"

Ten yards.

Dene dropped his head and growled. The steps came faster.

Tim skipped sideways, waving his arms like a traffic cop. "Here it is, Dene. Get over this line. Get over this mutha-fuckin' line!"

Fifteen yards.

Dene's face glowed crimson. He lifted his feet, planted them, and then pushed, one after the other, extending each leg with a violent thrust until the sled jerked and clanked across the line.

Twenty yards.

Tim clapped his hands. "Alright!"

Dene collapsed to his knees. His back throbbed. The veins in his calves burst through the skin. His thighs quivered and his glutes cramped.

The members murmured among themselves. A couple dipped their heads in approval as they drifted back to their stations.

Lampard stood in the passageway, shaded from the spotlights, his topaz eyes fixed trance-like on the sled. Quillan caught his attention and gave a nod, mouth pulled down in a 'not too bad' look.

The smooth white head nodded back.

The gym manager sidled up to the twins. "Great workout. Really good. Tell me, you boys doing anything tomorrow?"

Dene rolled onto his back. "Not now," he gasped.

Tim said, "Sunday's my day of rest. What did you have in mind?"

"We might be able to help put some meat on the table. Whadda ya say?"

Tim's eyes widened. "Rest I can do without. Steak I can't."

"Sounds good to me," said Kenny.

"Fine. How about we pick you up around ten?"

"We'll be ready," said Tim.

"Okay, see you then. And make sure you wear something warm."

Quillan sauntered back to the gym junkies. Kenny and Tim hoisted Dene to his feet. He tilted an ear. "Did he just say, 'pain is only weakness leaving your body'?"

Tim's face wrinkled into a grin. Kenny shut his eyes and bobbed his head.

"Fucking mirror men."

Chapter 45

Tom Calder walked away from the Mounted Police office. He turned left and meandered north, head bent, ear pressed to his cell phone.

"Is it true?" he said.

Zanelle zig-zagged through mid-morning traffic in the Abbotsford business district. She switched her cell to speaker.

"If you mean, am I suspended, yes, it's true."

"I knew it."

Calder glanced along a line of parked cars. No dark shapes hunched over steering wheels. No tell-tale condensation on the windshields. He stepped off the sidewalk and stooped between a pair of SUVs.

"Listen," he said. "You know that salesman killed on the highway up near Bridal Falls."

"Eckstein?"

"Epstein."

"That's it. His body was eaten by wolves."

"No," said Calder, "it wasn't. His body had been dismembered."

"What?"

"The guy's limbs were missing."

"No fuckin' way. You're shittin' me."

"I shit you not. I found it hidden in a copy of the Abbotsford incident report. The Abby police were the ones who kept talking about wolves."

"You're freaking me out, Tom."

"Well, imagine how everyone would have felt if that got around."

"So, all that rubbish about bears in the paper – maybe they just didn't want to spook anyone."

"Or maybe you were right all along. There could be more to this than meets the eye."

Zanelle cut across a two-lane roundabout and copped the finger. Her mind raced. "But if it wasn't wolves, and it wasn't bears, that leaves...."

"Precisely," said Calder. "Franklin's naked men just jumped to the front of the queue."

"Jesus, no wonder they want to hush it up."

"And that's the real problem. If something's going on, it's connected to someone inside the Abby PD."

Zanelle pondered the new wrinkle. A cover-up in Abbotsford was one thing, but if it reached all the way to the Mounties, that was something else.

"Better keep your head down, boyo," she said. "This might get ugly."

"I think you're the one disobeying orders."

"Hey, I'm suspended. What more can they do?"

"Don't be naïve. They can do whatever they want. So be careful."

"Will do. Thanks, Tom. Gotta go."

She chewed her lip as she turned off toward the university. Why *had* she been suspended?

Was Truman Roberts behind it after all?

LAMPARD CLOSED HIS OFFICE door and stood for a long moment. His skin tingled and his heart drummed. He replayed the spectacle of the loaded sled in his mind. Plenty of men had moved more weight. He'd done it himself. But they were all bigger and heavier than the Englishman.

He picked up his cell, jabbed at the screen and held the phone away from his head while it rang. He knew not to expect small talk.

When the blunt question came, he said, "We'll soon need more blood. And more supplements."

The voice on the line sizzled with irritation. He closed his eyes and rubbed his scalp.

"Because the process is not an exact science. It requires problem solving. And there's a lot of...wastage."

He wandered around his desk, scratching at dry skin on his forearm, only half listening.

"Well, your beloved Vancouver Wolves haven't set the world on fire. Tell me again – how many games have they lost in their celebrated history? Oh, that's right. *Every single one.*"

The reply crackled. Lampard sniggered deep in his throat. He walked along the photos on the wall. "Now, now, don't be nasty. Things might be looking up."

He stopped and scrutinised the thick-necked rugby team. One thing he knew from experience; no young man wants to live in the shadow of his father, whoever he might be.

He said, "I think I've found you a star."

Chapter 46

ZANELLE WANDERED THE HALLS of the science faculty alone. Academics and students were thin on the ground at eleven o'clock Saturday morning.

She found the door at her third try and poked her head into the lab. Clinical worktops jutted from stark, white walls. Silent monitors and shiny apparatus filled neat rows of benches. Finely calibrated instruments slept beneath plastic hoods.

Talisman Kainoa perched on a swivel stool near the centre of the room. She hunched over a workstation and peered into a bi-focal microscope. A white lab coat stretched across her back.

She said, "Be with you in one second." She made some keystrokes on a laptop, then spun to face the door. "Hello there. Come on in. What can I help you with?"

The woman stood. She cut a daunting figure, but her smile was effortless and disarming.

Zanelle guessed she had years of practice putting people at ease. She bobbed forward and extended her hand. Her fingers disappeared into Tallie's gentle grip.

"Hi. My name's Zanelle Argus. I'm a friend of Dene Selkirk."

"From what I hear, you're *the* friend of Dene Selkirk."

Zanelle felt pink blooms spread across her cheeks. "Well, we'll see." Her forehead creased, then recognition dawned. She pointed a finger. "You were at Toronto. Discus."

"Good memory, girl."

Canada hosted the Pan Am Games for the third time in 2015. The event claimed forty-five percent participation by women, but Zanelle missed out.

She said, "I was in our relay squad. They didn't need me, so I watched a few other events. You were colossal."

"Hah. Should have seen me in the shot put rounds. I was a midget next to some of those girls. What are you doing now?"

"I'm with the Mounted Police. Which is why I'm here – I'm trying to make a connection. If you don't mind, I'd like to ask a few questions about your dad. About what happened to him."

Tallie's eyes flattened and a thin eyebrow lifted. "Dene hasn't told you?"

"I don't mean what he did. I was more wondering what caused it."

The big shoulders slumped. "That, I'm not entirely sure about. The process is super-complicated."

"Anything you can tell me will help. I'm struggling to pull this together."

Tallie ambled to the door and pushed it shut with the tip of a middle finger. She grabbed a spare stool and steered it under Zanelle's hips. Zanelle wriggled onto the seat, grateful that it made her a couple of inches taller.

Tallie sat. The stool groaned beneath her weight. She said, "I take it you know of the infamous Mattson Lampard."

"Alarm bells ring every time I hear his name."

"As they should. Okay, where to begin...." She slapped her knees.

"Around thirty years back, Lampard synthesised a blend of anabolic compounds, growth hormones, and blood. But not any old blood. He developed a human-canine blood hybrid. And I don't know how, but he made it compatible with human subjects."

"So, we're not talking a one-off fluke that he couldn't replicate."

"Oh, no. There were definite results, and with multiple subjects. But the science was hit and miss. They were amateurs. They didn't understand what they were doing, or what was happening."

"Trial and error."

"Absolutely. Lampard was heavily involved with the fitness industry – such as it was back then. He only played low-grade rugby, but he positioned himself as a sort of conditioning guru. Eventually he became a top ranked power lifter. And that meant whatever he said was taken as legit. He ran with bodybuilders, wrestlers, even circus performers. And rugby players like my dad. Now, by accident or not, Lampard had some success – at least by his standards – and he advertised it among his contacts. Wasn't long before he had scads of eager subjects to experiment with."

"But it can't be natural. I mean, dogs' blood? How can you be sure it wasn't just the growth hormones kicking in?"

Tallie tapped the counter with buttercup yellow fingernails.

"There's no published science, obviously. There aren't even any records unless Lampard kept track of everything. And the results aren't measurable. But the empirical evidence is there."

"Do you have any idea how it worked?"

"I suspect it occurred by a process of gradual substitution – more and more canine blood replaced the human component. Of the administered serum anyway."

"But why use animal blood at all?"

"I admit, that's a stumbling block. Maybe it was just easier to get."

"It all sounds like science fiction."

"Actually, it isn't such a stretch. We already perform transfusions between dogs and cats. And transfusions between pigs and humans are possible, in theory."

Zanelle leaned forward, elbows on her knees. She said, "We're not dealing with werewolves are we?" and instantly regretted it.

Tallie closed her eyes and shook her head.

"Dogs and humans are both omnivores, albeit at opposite ends of the carnivore spectrum. A minor genetic change could increase the appetite for meat. Or it might be the other way around – a shift in the source, or quantity of protein, may trigger a change at the genetic level."

Zanelle had an olfactory flashback; she smelled the salty warmth of Dene's steaks sizzling in the pan.

"What happens with these human subjects?"

"That's where the problems start. I don't know how many people this junk ruined. Even killed. I've tried to follow as many leads as I could. Dad knew all the guys who played rugby that used the serum, but it's like the dark web. It's a closed book. And now they're all gone."

"Gone where?"

Tallie stared down.

"Oh. Gone."

"Anyway, the effects weren't consistent. And they sure as hell weren't predictable."

"Best guess?"

"As far as I can tell, and I'm only postulating here, there are two distinct adaptations to the HCS."

"HCS?"

"Hyper-Carnivore Serum – that's what the sicko called it. One manifests through the heightened senses of the carnivore. Sight, smell, hearing. Speed, strength. Agility."

"That's how it affected Dene's father."

"Right," said Tallie. "He was a natural sportsman anyway, and he might have been great at anything he tried, but after getting hold of this serum he became a super athlete. Almost a freak."

"So, it depends on what raw material Lampard had to work with in the beginning."

"But that's the same with any athlete. Given the same training and equal conditions, the natural athlete will ultimately produce better performances. The more gifted individual has a greater rate of acquisition."

"*Citius, altius, fortius.*"

"If you like."

"And the second adaptation?"

"Well, that's where we get into Frankenstein territory. That one manifests via the basal instincts of the predator. Territoriality. Hierarchy. Hunt. Kill." Tallie took a breath. "That's what happened to my dad. Dene's father got all the good stuff. Mine got all the bad."

Zanelle gazed at the countertop and fluttered her fingers on her knees. She wanted to cover all the bases, but it was tricky.

"Please don't take this the wrong way," she said, "but is there a chance the serum magnifies pre-existing psychological tendencies? Any negative traits?"

"It might. But it would be impossible to quantify."

Tallie rubbed her temples.

She said, "There could be something I'm missing. Something that amplifies the effect. But nothing stands out."

"How about some kind of vaccine. An antidote. Is that possible?"

"Maybe, but I've had no luck. The first step in finding a cure is to learn the cause. And you'd need buckets of blood. I do this on my own time and out of my own pocket. And I ain't rollin' in money, honey."

"Do you ever get discouraged?"

Tallie stood and leaned her arms on the counter, arching her back and rolling her shoulders. "They won't set my father free unless he can prove he's a different man. If I can change his blood chemistry – and show that it's changed – it would go a long way toward his release."

"And then you could cure him."

"No, I think it's too late for that now." She rested her elbows on the bench. "Your turn. What are you working on?"

"It all started with missing dogs. Now, it's stolen blood. And stolen drugs. Whatever's going on, it's escalating."

"Whatever's going on," said Tallie, "it sounds like you're a good chance of tracing it to Lampard."

"That's what I think. Well, that's the plan anyway."

Then an idea occurred to Zanelle. She frowned and swung her stool in tiny arcs. "If you could reverse it, you could make it work again too, right? Make another serum?"

Tallie straightened. She pressed her lips together. Her nostrils spread as she took a slow breath. Her shoulders drew back and her breasts rose, straining the fabric of her lab coat.

She said, "Girl, don't be makin' jokes like that."

Chapter 47

A LACY MANTLE OF snow draped the western slopes of the Skagit Range. High along the crests, surging updrafts fanned sheets of frost into slender, feathered fingers, reaching up to a bright blue sky. The snowfall had reached the lower altitudes a little early. Canada's winter was baring its claws.

The forest below was still and calm. A white-tailed deer foraged in the undergrowth. It lifted its head, suddenly alert, then bounded into the sun-mottled cedars.

The growl of an ORV thrashing up the fire-trail ballooned off the hills. A blood-red Trail Boss erupted from the trees and careened over a rise.

Dene clutched at the grab-handle above his head and watched Baird Turley tussle with the wheel. Kenny and Tim bounced in the back seat like unlashed barrels in a cargo hold.

"This place was an internment camp for the Nips during the war," said Turley, slinging the truck into a slide. The Chev lurched to a stop in a clearing on a flattened knoll.

"Nips?" said Tim.

"Canardlys."

"Canardlys?" said Tim.

Dene knew Tim understood what Turley meant.

The two Hawaiians had long experience of the Japanese, a refined and courteous people who brought much to the fiftieth state. He wondered how far Turley's intolerance would go.

And how much the twins would abide.

Turley put his forefingers to the corner of his eyes, then pulled outwards. "Canardly *see*. Get it?" He shrugged at the two deadpan faces. "Anyway, it's a great spot to get back to the wild."

"You're quite the wild man yourself, aren't you," said Kenny.

"Oh, yes indeedy I am."

Turley swung out of the cab. He slammed the door and whooped at the sky. Dene hopped off the footplate and gazed up at the mountain tops. The twins tumbled out the rear doors on unsteady legs.

Kenny stretched his back. "So, what are we hunting?"

Tim looked at the empty tray of the Silverado. "And what, pray tell, are we hunting with?"

"No need for guns up here," said Turley.

Dene saw the twins raise their eyebrows. He'd asked himself the same question.

The orange Tahoe appeared over the rise and burbled into the clearing. Lampard, Pym and Quillan stepped down and squinted against the sunlight.

Lampard fixed his eyes on Turley.

"It's not a rally course, Baird." Lampard prodded him in the chest. "And this camp is not your plaything. If you attract attention, you'll be the first one out on your ear."

Turley gave a lame grin. He looked about to speak when a battered white Hi-Lux poked through a stand of pines on the downslope side of the clearing. A hooded gas barbecue and a steel ice-chest sat in the cargo tray, cardboard boxes jammed into the space between them.

For a moment, Dene forgot Turley, and ignored the barbecue and ice-chest. He was more interested in a metal crate that filled the front half of the tray. It had a door at each side and was stacked with logs, but he recognised what it was.

A dog carrier.

Garner Hall and another man disembarked the vehicle.

Lampard said, "Everything under control?"

"No problems this end," said Hall.

"Benny?"

"All good," said Broussard.

Dene gave the new guy a quick once over. Nordic blond with a trimmed beard and moustache. Athletic, well-muscled, above average height. He fit the template.

Lampard had quite a crew.

Hall dropped the Toyota's tailgate. He said, "I'll get started on the fire."

Then Dene heard Tim give a grunt. A non-verbal 'what the fuck'. He and Kenny turned as one. All three frowned.

Lampard and his men had shucked off their boots and socks. Dene and the twins watched them undo buttons and belts, and peel off their heavy shirts and pants. The men stepped out of boxers and briefs – Pym wore no underwear at all – then bundled up their clothes and tossed everything into the vehicles.

The five stood in the clearing, naked as the day they were born. They scratched their balls and rubbed their armpits and fondled their cocks.

Dene looked at his feet and smirked. He wouldn't be making any comparisons, but the twins had them all covered.

He said, "Those the only weapons you brought?"

Lampard missed the joke. "Firearms are for the weak. The fearful. People afraid of the world."

Dene noticed that while the others displayed countless tatts on various body parts, their boss was a 'clean-skin'. It was something he and his father agreed on. He saw no point in creating a perfect physique, and then defacing it. The Greeks would be appalled. It was incongruous. Obscene. Like graffiti on an opera house wall.

Once again, Lampard had surprised him.

The big man swung his arms in circles. Turley and Broussard did a couple of lunges. Pym performed a clumsy *kata*.

Quillan lifted a bucket from the back of the Toyota. He passed it around and the men gouged up handfuls of lard and swiped it over their bodies. A faintly rancid odour wafted on the air.

"So what happens now?" said Dene.

"Now," said Lampard, "we hunt as God intended. Now we *prevail* as God intended."

Quillan dropped the bucket next to the twins. They took a wary step backward.

Tim spread his hands. "Are you serious?"

"It changes the scent," said Quillan. "Confuses 'em."

"Aznuts, brah. It's freezing."

"Man, I'm from fucking Hawaii," said Kenny.

Pym strode to the edge of the woods. "Turley. Quillan. On point."

"Hurry lads," said Lampard. "You'll miss the action."

The naked men bounded up the slope. Pale bare backs and round white buttocks merged with patches of snow.

Tim said, "I gotta see this." He took off up the rise, weaving between the trees and ducking low boughs. Kenny hiked after him.

Dene looked around. Hall was tossing logs in a pile and whistling to himself. He looked back up the hill.

Finally, he shook his head and followed the others into the forest.

Chapter 48

THE VALLEY COMMUNITY BLOOD Bank took up a ground floor annex of the Regional Health Service building on the outskirts of Chilliwack. It operated three and a half days a week, and shared a staff lounge with the Health Service clinic.

Magazines lay strewn across an island of low tables in the centre of the room, surrounded by a collection of Naugahyde recliners in autumn shades. Peanut brittle, faded Jaffa, soft mint green.

Vera Bell held a pair of mugs beneath a gurgling hot-water urn. Zanelle watched the stout figure, her quick movements and deft handling of spoons and condiments. The flippant woman who lived next door became efficient and businesslike once she donned her uniform. Capable and trustworthy.

Zanelle wondered if people judged her own performance by the same standard; if they saw a different person away from the police station.

"I really appreciate this, Vera," she said.

"No trouble, dear. Just tell that Gwen Crozier she can't hide forever. I've already made her next appointment."

Zanelle shunted a couple of wooden-armed recliners toward a table and kneed them together.

She grinned and said, "I'll see she gets the message."

Vera carried two steaming coffees to the table. She passed a mug to Zanelle, then squatted on a green vinyl seat and flopped backwards, like a scuba diver tumbling off a boat. Zanelle settled into the sagging springs of the chair beside her.

"Have you been a nurse for long?"

"Oh, I retired from nursing years ago. Now they call me a Dedicated Blood Specialist – two days a week anyway." She took a swallow and balanced her mug on an armrest. "Okay, how can I help?"

"I need anything you can tell me about blood. Little things. Something people don't know."

Vera pressed her hands against her ribs and ran them down her uniform, straightening the wrinkles across her waist.

"I might not be the best person to speak with," she said. "It's a complex subject. We did basic haematology when I was training, but the advanced stuff is beyond me."

"Let's start with something simple then. What's the most valuable blood? The rarest."

"Hah. It's funny how anyone with a rare blood type thinks their blood is special. In a practical sense, it's the other way around. The most common types are O positive and A positive, so statistically, more of those people will require surgery, have accidents, get sick."

"How common are they?"

"Combined? Roughly seventy percent of the population. We need a lot of Type O and Type A."

"That must be good then – having so much Type O. The universal donor?"

"Well, that's not strictly correct. The true universal donor is O negative, but fewer than one in ten people carry it, so it's best if we have the other types on hand."

"Tell me about the process."

Vera sipped her coffee. "Well, these days we screen donors before accepting their blood. We're really discriminating, but with HIV and everything else, we don't have a choice. That's the first step. And you've seen how we collect it – just a standard procedure. After that it's tested, bagged and stored in special refrigerators."

"It seems pretty straightforward."

"Oh, no dear. Then there are all the blood products. They hardly ever use whole blood in transfusion therapy. They separate the red cells, the platelets. And the plasma – there's a bunch of plasma derivatives. And now they're harvesting stem cells as well. It's all getting a bit weird if you ask me."

"How long do you store it?"

"Around six weeks, but it's often used before then."

"I thought you could freeze it."

"Well, you can keep it frozen for up to a year, but they only do that in special circumstances. And it's very expensive."

"What if cost wasn't a factor – wouldn't it be better to freeze all blood?"

"Not really," said Vera. "Sometimes the blood products spoil. We dispose of bags and bags of it. I think that's the reason so little is frozen. And that's why we need a continuous supply of real blood from donors."

The Health Service pushed community blood drives several times a year, and the Mounties were always at the front of the line. Zanelle had donated twice and she'd picked up snippets here and there.

"How about artificial blood?" she said.

Vera took a quick swallow and shook her head. "Uh, uh. One of my nephews is a doctor." She gave a little shudder. "He thinks the artificial stuff just isn't as good."

"In what way?"

"Oh, they can have all sorts of problems."

Vera glanced at the clinic door. She leaned toward Zanelle and tapped the side of her nose.

"Trust me, dear," she said. "Artificial blood should only be used in emergencies."

Chapter 49

A WHITE-TAILED BUCK AND a pair of does grazed in the shady quiet of a sloping dell, mid-way up the Skagit Range.

Their elegant heads hung from thick, smooth-muscled necks. Tightly bunched shoulders and hindquarters tapered to dainty legs. Sprigs of sunlight fell through the crown of cedars and lodgepoles, streaking their hides like cream in warm cappuccinos.

The buck's antlers still carried remnants of velvet, but the growth cycle was almost complete. Each year they thickened and their beam grew wider. Now he was a fully mature male, ready for the rut and the breeding season.

Dene crested a rise and spotted the deer across a shallow gully. He steadied against a tree trunk and lowered to one knee. Kenny and Tim pulled up behind him, breathing through open mouths. Kenny gripped Dene's shoulder and dropped to his haunches.

"What's the hurry, Usain?"

"Shhh." Dene pointed ahead.

Quillan and Turley crept through the matted brush, a dozen yards beyond the gully. They saw the deer and halted. The men separated, Turley cross-stepping up the slope to the east, Quillan heading downhill, in the direction of Jones Lake.

Lampard, Pym and Broussard emerged from a thicket of deadfall at the bottom of the gully. Lampard spied the grazing animals and crouched. He held his hands low and waved the others to each side. The men spread out and approached the deer in a semi-circle.

The big white-tail's head jerked up. His jaw crunched once on a mouthful of foliage, then he stood still. The does stopped foraging and backed up against the buck. He twisted his head and checked the trees, high side, then low side. He munched again. The does raised their heads, sensing...something.

The men edged closer. Lampard stepped over dead branches, treading only on the damp layer of pine needles and melting snow that covered the forest floor. Pym and Broussard fanned wide, forming a circle. Quillan and Turley met on the far side of the deer and tightened the ring.

Lampard suddenly roared. He exploded from the brush, arms waving and crooked legs pumping. The others yelled and hooted and charged at the deer.

The panicked creatures pranced one way, then another, then bolted for safety. The buck sprang into the scrub. A doe tried to follow. She leapt over Turley but he grabbed a leg and dragged her down. He wrestled to keep the frantic doe pinned, twisting away from her slashing hooves.

Quillan crashed on top of the grappling pair. The doe bawled. He clung to her wither and wrapped his legs around her forequarters. He folded his arms around the animal's head and wrenched backward. He jerked the head sideways until the neck snapped. The deer kicked twice more, then lay twitching in Turley's arms.

The second doe zig-zagged around the tiny clearing. Lampard and Broussard waved and hollered, and the doe spun to face Pym. He scuttled from side to side, arms spread. The other two closed in and corralled the creature, then gang-tackled it from each side.

They linked arms under the deer's girth and threw it onto its back. Lampard and Broussard restrained the doe in a flurry of arms and razor-edged hooves on scything legs.

Pym lunged at the melee and smashed his knees into the animal's chest. Her ribs cracked. She squealed and her eyes rolled white in terror. Pym hammered his fist into the deer's head. Punch after punch, he rained down a frenzied attack until it lay silent, its head a pulped mess of tissue, bone and sodden fur.

The five muddy forms rose to their feet, panting and blood-splattered. They bellowed at the sky in triumph, the collective roar echoing from the hills.

Kenny and Tim stood and craned their necks, wide-eyed and pumped with excitement. They started across the gully.

Toward the slaughter.

Dene hung back. Conflicted. Uneasy. Filled with a discord between the beauty of the forest and the sin he'd just seen.

He gazed around at the woodland setting. Lemon-lime dapples specked the undergrowth like coins in a fountain, while glittering runnels of pink-tinted snowmelt trickled down the slope.

"Jesus," he whispered.

Chapter 50

SHE COULD HAVE SPOKEN with Vera at home instead of at the blood bank, but Zanelle wasn't only after information. She wanted to look behind the scenes. To 'feel the vibe'.

She left the Health Service and idled through the mid-city traffic. She detoured around the downtown core, located the *Trading Post* office and parked a few doors up. It would be closed but Franklin lived upstairs.

Maybe she'd catch him on his way out.

She reached into the back seat and grabbed an old copy of the newspaper. The 'cannibal' issue. She'd found it at the bottom of the box Gwen Crozier brought to dinner. She spread it over the steering wheel and opened the front page. Franklin published his own photo beside the weekly editorial, a three-quarter selfie. She was confident she'd recognise him.

She glanced up just as Franklin passed in front of the Subaru's windshield. He carried coffee and doughnuts in a cardboard tray, his ponytail bobbing behind him. Caught him on the way in.

She scrambled out of the car. "Mr Franklin? Toby?"

Franklin turned quickly. He seemed ready to run.

Zanelle gave him her brightest smile. "Hello, Mr Franklin. Do you have a moment?"

The man eyed her black leather bomber jacket, the snug jeans and toffee-coloured slouch suede boots. "For you, I do."

Zanelle was used to the reaction. She beamed her gratitude and wondered if she should play the Mountie card. It couldn't hurt.

"Mr Franklin – may I call you Toby? I'm with the RCMP. Public relations." She waved the newspaper. "I'm following up this story for our records. I just need some background."

"A Mountie?"

"Uh, auxiliary staff. I saw you walking past and thought you might be free."

Franklin checked out her jeans again. "I have a couple of minutes. How can I help?"

Zanelle held the front page of the paper up to his face. "Did you actually see these hominids?"

The grainy image had been cropped and enlarged. It was inconclusive. It might have been a pale, two-legged creature. Or a cluster of washed-out logs.

"No," said Franklin, "but I interviewed witnesses."

"Oh. So, you didn't take this picture?" She watched him closely and saw his mind racing.

He hesitated, then said, "Of course not. I do most of my work here."

"Then how do you find something like this? I'm sure it's not one of Getty's."

He pulled a phone from his pocket. "Ever seen one of these? The wonders of technology let people send that stuff to me."

"But did you even verify it?"

"Hey, sweetheart, I can't help it if they get carried away."

His tone had turned snarky; the fun was over. Zanelle dropped the smile. "This article may have compromised an investigation. What do you feel about that?"

"What am I supposed to feel?"

"How about guilty? Don't you have a responsibility to look into these stories?"

"I have a responsibility to give people what they want to read. Readers bring advertisers. Advertisers bring money. And I get paid."

"Ah. A man of principle."

"A man who can't live on newsprint alone."

He moved off but Zanelle sidestepped in front of him. "Why did you print the retraction?"

"New evidence. Mistakes happen all the time, but we don't want to mislead anyone. It was just some white bears. Kermode bears."

"That's bullshit," said Zanelle. "So, who put you up to it?"

The million-dollar question. Franklin didn't bite.

"Like I said – I just give people what they want to read."

"Except someone didn't want to read about flesh-eating ghouls roaming the timberline."

He shrugged. "Some readers are more important than others."

"Didn't want to frighten the campers away, that it? The holiday-makers. The tourists."

The newspaperman's eyes opened wide and his eyebrows lifted. A picture of virtue. She'd seen it a hundred times in the interview room.

And they'd all been lying through their teeth.

He said, "Missy, you got it in one. Think what you like, but I don't want to jeopardise the local economy. Why would I? Listen, this coffee's getting cold. Deadlines to meet and all that."

They did the side-to-side dance, then he walked away and left her standing on the street.

She watched him turn down an access lane next to the newspaper office. Nothing about this rang true. Bigfoot and the Yeti had been luring tourists for years.

Some readers are more important than others.

Franklin climbed the stairs to his apartment. He set the coffee on his dinette and grabbed a doughnut. He pushed it into his mouth as he looked down from the second-floor window. The girl slipped into a red hatchback, then she pulled out and joined the flow of traffic.

His animal cunning jangled. He was getting the hang of this business. When people stopped him in the street, he knew he'd touched a nerve. Self-preservation had been a priority more than once. But the girl had surprised him. She was pretty and buxom, and he'd let his guard down. He hadn't even asked for ID.

Was she really with the Mounties? Or was she working for someone else? Perhaps Truman Roberts was checking up on him.

Testing him.

Something was going on, but what? He decided to stay at arm's length.

But he'd keep the story on his radar.

Chapter 51

DENE DRAINED A LONG, steaming piss into a patch of snow, his relief deeper than physical. He rolled his head from shoulder to shoulder and let the tension drop away.

Watching the hunt stirred him more than he realised. Lampard's men had given a view into the prehistoric past, a glimpse at the edge of civilisation. It was primal and perverse.

Primitive.

Barbaric.

Fascinating.

He zipped up and stared into the woods, listening. A distant hum came through the darkness. He lifted his boots over a layer of damp brush and moved toward the sound.

The undergrowth thinned and the earth grew hard underfoot. Dim quadrangular shapes materialised in the gloom. Horizontal lines. Repeated angles. Man-made.

The fitness retreat.

The hum became a thumping drone; he guessed a diesel generator. Rows of long wooden huts appeared. A halo of misty light laid faint shadows across a flat, dirt perimeter.

In his mind he pictured not bonding executives or hard-bitten workout fanatics, but clusters of forsaken prisoners. Guiltless Japanese, shuffling over the frozen ground. Even weeks from the full depth of winter it looked a brutal place. Callous and pitiless.

Man-made.

He continued forward. And marched into a chain-link fence.

"Shit."

A metallic hiss shimmied along the fence-line. He looked up. Taut strands of barbed wire hovered above his head, disappearing into the blackness, strung on heavy cranked poles.

He stood a moment, taking in the atmosphere. The granite-blue sky merged with the mountains, then blended into walls of conifers, lined up like a black palisade. Firelight danced on flecks of snow in the branches. The scent of roasting venison drifted on the air.

He crammed his hands into his old Carhartt and trudged back toward the fire.

Garner Hall had not been idle during the hunt. The four-wheel drives were parked around the fire, like spokes on a wheel. Heavy clay bricks, laid lengthways and stacked two-high, contained the blaze in an oblate ring. A pile of logs sat nearby, and a roasting carcass glistened on a spit above the flames.

Half a dozen bales of straw encircled the steel cooler and the gas barbecue. Rough-hewn hemlock planks laid across trestles formed a pair of crude tables.

One supported wooden steak platters, a salt cellar and a big glass jar of cranberry sauce. The other bore the raw, dismembered remains of the second doe.

Daylight saving in British Columbia had ended that day; the first Sunday in November. Darkness fell an hour earlier by the clock, but Quillan had both deer bled, gralloched and dressed before sunset.

Now he carved slabs of venison on the makeshift bench with a razor-honed hunting knife. Filleted tenderloin, backstraps, and neck meat were parcelled and stacked for the hunters to take home.

Turley tended corn cobs baking in their husks on the barbecue. Between times, he turned the spit and poured an apple cider baste over the steaming flesh. Whole sweet potatoes simmered in a pot, buried among coals at the edge of the flames. The comingled scents wafted on the smoky air. A rustic gourmand's heaven.

Dene stepped over a bale and stamped his feet beside Lampard. He glanced at Kenny and Tim. They laughed and tossed back beers with Pym and Broussard, joining in the merriment with gusto.

Half their stock of cans lay scattered around the clearing, but at least everyone was clothed. Bulky jackets and thick plaid shirts over jeans or heavy cotton work pants kept out the cold.

Lampard opened the cooler lid. He pushed up a sleeve and searched through shrinking ice cubes, parting the slush with sweeps of his hand. He straightened and held out a Molson.

"Thanks," said Dene. "And better keep 'em coming."

Lampard chuckled. "Everyone's a little unnerved the first time."

"Unnerved? That'd be one way of putting it."

"Good. We've shaken you out of your apathy."

Dene took a mouthful and wiped a sleeve over his chin. "Was damn near shaken outta my tree."

Lampard clapped him on the back. A rough 'well done'. A welcome to the band. The big man leaned in close. His cheeks blushed like peaches from the cold and the beer.

He shook a fist beside his jaw. "You must find the essence of your species. Man is *supreme*."

Dene caught Turley's giggle. The kid was past merry and on his way to properly soused. He tossed corn cobs to Pym and Broussard, then swigged from a quarter bottle of Wild Turkey. He called to the sky – "I am supreme!" – and let out a Tarzan yell. The sound rippled up the peaks and floated back again.

The affable mien slid from Lampard's face. His head fell forward on his thick neck and rotated slowly toward the barbecue. He drilled Turley with the cold-eyed stare again.

"But we must evolve," he said, turning back to Dene, "or be left behind."

Dene swapped the beer to his other hand and stuffed damp fingers into a warm, fleecy pocket. "I think I read somewhere that technology has made evolution obsolete."

"No, no, no. Evolution goes on all the time. It's only pushed in another direction. But that might not be the best direction."

Lampard scanned the group beside the fire. Then he spotted Hall returning through the trees.

"Garner," he said. "Come and teach this lad about evolution."

Dene watched the little man approach. He looked even smaller among the lofty cedars. His dejected expression and creased face added years to his age, but he moved with purpose. Hall dipped into the ice and came up with a Sleeman Railside. Mid-strength. A 'session beer'. Wise head.

He popped the top and pulled a swig. Took a breath and held it, then tilted his head, searching his memory. He recited the definition in his sonorous, narrator's voice.

"Evolution begins as a response to environmental stress on a single organism, which is then transferred to the species."

"And," said Lampard, "I think it's fair to say the planet has never been under more stress."

Dene sensed the other two knew where the conversation was headed. He said, "I couldn't disagree with that."

Hall said, "It's less than two million years since homo erectus climbed out of the trees and stood on his hind legs. Eventually Neanderthal man evolved. Then homo sapiens appeared, and just like that – poof – the Neanderthals were gone."

Lampard crowded the pair, enthusiasm in his eyes, a teacher guiding his students to a deduction. "The point is, we need to understand that something *will* take our place."

Dene struggled with a theoretical concept that seemed concrete to everyone else. He knew he was ill-equipped to debate it, but felt himself drawn into the discussion.

The argument.

He said, "But what could overtake a modern civilisation? We have thousands of years head start. Surely Manhattan Man is more advanced than say, the Maasai?"

Hall tipped his can up and poured the dregs into his mouth. Hollow legs. He didn't muck around. Maybe there was more to the session beer.

"You're talking about cultural assimilation," he said. "Like moving from Nebraska to Tokyo. That's not evolution."

"Survival is the truest test of evolution," said Lampard. "The Maasai would survive longer than any of us in his own environment. Strip our technology away and the primitives are more advanced than we are."

"But by that logic, sharks are more advanced than us, too," said Dene.

"And they are. Because they're perfectly adapted. But it took millions of years. We don't have that much time."

"Relatively speaking," said Hall, "man is still in the early stages of his evolution. The question is not 'What will we become?' but 'What will replace us?'"

Lampard continued. "If man was supplanted by some exceptional being – let's call it a hyper-carnivore – then we would no longer be the planet's apex predator. So we have no choice. We *must* evolve, or become subservient. Even extinct."

"The paradox," said Hall, "is that biological evolution is too slow. Science and technology are outstripping our capacity to adapt."

"Ergo," said Lampard, "we use science to accelerate the evolution process."

Dene swallowed the last of his beer. "And what if we can't keep up with science? Or what happens if we run out of food? Don't tell me that's not a possibility. Which way do we evolve then?"

Lampard scoffed. "Run out? God, look around you, man." He smacked his beer onto his palm, emphasising each word. "Eight. Billion. People. All reproducing. *Spawning*. There has never been so much food. And make no mistake, that's what will happen if man is pushed from the top of the heap. He'll be nothing more than a fat, weak, compliant source of food."

He dropped the can, wandered to the edge of the light and relieved himself in the dirt.

Dene stared into the fire. Pensive. Not convinced, but thinking. From Lampard it sounded like the most logical thing in the world. It was only speculation, but like the best science fiction, the conjecture was based on fact. Suspension of disbelief almost took hold, but something jarred in his subconscious. It made sense – yet it didn't.

"Forget about Mattson," said Hall. "Man isn't a predator, not in the ecological sense. He's more of a high-functioning parasite."

Dene nodded. That was true enough. He turned a blank stare to the firelit tableau. Quillan wielded his blade as if he were a fencing master. Pym and Broussard mugged like a redneck Laurel and Hardy.

Kenny and Tim seemed at ease, waving cans of Moosehead and laughing. Baird Turley tossed his bourbon bottle into the flames. A trail of sparks trickled upward and Dene's thoughts dissolved.

Turley suddenly looked up and howled. A response came back from the hills, but it wasn't an echo. And it was unlike any wolf Dene had ever heard. He saw Quillan and Broussard trade a glance.

Lampard ripped his zipper up and whirled. A growl shuddered in his chest. His mouth twisted and his eyes bulged from his head like golf balls. His words erupted like stones hurled onto a tin roof.

"Hell is empty – *and all the devils are here!*"

The Bard riding in on a tempest.

He churned his misshapen legs and kicked through the straw bales and charged toward the barbecue. Turley realised what was coming and put up his fists. He was taller than Lampard, but three stone lighter and three parts hammered.

And that was a problem.

Lampard ducked Turley's awkward swings and lunged for his testicles. He seized his nuts in a fistful of denim and twisted hard. The kid clutched at Lampard's hand but the big man gripped his throat and thrust him backwards onto the barbecue.

Lampard grabbed the handle and slammed the hood shut on Turley's head, then he raised it and slammed it down again. Then again.

And again.

Turley shrieked. His arms threshed. His face smouldered and the stench of burning hair vented across the clearing. Lampard flung the lid back and released his grip.

Turley collapsed to the ground. The nape of his neck bubbled like blow-torched paint and he whimpered through boiled, broken lips.

Lampard stood over the beaten man. "Garner, see to that."

Hall cupped his hands and scooped ice from the cooler. He kneeled down and dribbled cold water over Turley's smoking head.

Lampard backed away. He stood at Dene's shoulder and watched, impassively, as if the pair had just witnessed a minor road accident.

"That's what we have in store if we cannot rule the animals," he said. "We will become animals ourselves."

The eerie howls faded into the night. The men fanned out, to take a leak or find another beer, then drifted back into the firelight.

Subdued chat resumed from beside the spit. They knew Lampard could be hasty. Reckless. Unbalanced. It was nothing. Tomorrow it would be forgotten.

Dene looked around at the hills and up at the silent stars. Abandoned cans of Molson lay about his feet, red maple leaf logos like a trail of bloody pawprints in the snow.

Chapter 52

A SOMBRE EVENING SKY descended over Chilliwack. Moisture hung in the air, diffusing the glow from the streetlamps. Their metal stems stretched along the roadside like electric dandelions, salmon-tinted light trapped in bubbles of falling dew.

Dene jogged along the quiet suburban street beside Zanelle. It was part of a route that she often took, starting and ending at her apartment. They sometimes ran the loop together, to catch up and share some quiet time at day's end.

The pair turned into Airport Road and headed west at a steady pace. The area around the airport was deserted and the businesses were closed, quiet and stark beneath security lights.

Dene said, "What about the suspension?"

They took a dozen steps before she replied.

"Don't wanna talk about it."

It took all Dene's self-control not to snap back. He'd been cotton-mouthed and grumpy all day.

After the hunters picked up their trash and stamped out the fire and loaded all the gear, he'd endured a wild ride back to Abbotsford in the small hours of Monday morning. Quillan subbed in for Turley, and was even more gung-ho behind the wheel.

They arrived home just before sunrise, but the twins crashed at his place and snored until lunchtime. He'd had next to no sleep.

He was pushing his luck, but he pushed anyway. "Zanelle, don't go all Ripley over it."

"I'm not *going* all anything. I didn't deserve to be suspended. Or don't you think so?"

"I think you should let it be and move on."

"Easy for you to say. That break-in stinks to high heaven. And it's not the only one we've had lately."

"I mean it, Zanelle. Don't get in over your head."

"Your beloved gym won't come up smelling like roses either."

A whiff of Turley's scorched hair came back to Dene. "Well, those guys aren't saints. And they won't be all warm and fuzzy about you sticking your nose into their business."

"Having doubts about your new hunting buddies, hmm?"

The playing field tilted. They ran another dozen paces before Dene answered.

"It was a bit...unsettling, that's all."

"You know they're breaking all kinds of laws, don't you? And that's before any ethical considerations."

"It doesn't mean you're right about Lampard. He's got some weird cats working for him and he's got a temper, but he's no Jekyll and Hyde."

"Are you sure? Did you see inside this so-called retreat?"

"I saw the outside. It's just like they said. The place was a disused internment camp from the war."

Zanelle said, "Yeah, right." She pushed ahead. "C'mon – pick it up a bit."

Dene camped on her right shoulder and studied her form. She ran with her hands high against her chest, an economical motion with minimal arm movement. When it came to running, you could do worse than imitate the Kenyans.

He wanted to lighten the conversation, but he couldn't let the camp go. "They've fixed it up so Lampard's members can 'commune with nature'."

"You mean when he's not using it as some nudist ninja hunting lodge."

They passed a timber yard. Then the RCMP Community Office appeared, brightly lit and with a bank of police vehicles in reserved spaces.

"Shit," said Zanelle. "I forgot where we were." She veered across the street, away from the Mountie office, away from the lights. They continued past Chilliwack's passenger complex, then ran past a helicopter charter service and a marine supplies outlet. They recrossed the street, took another turn and reached a winding stretch of road with reflector posts sticking up from tufts of grass beside a tall security fence.

She said, "You know, if I thought anyone would take notice of me, I'd report those guys."

"Don't be so precious. They're just rednecks playing doomsday prepper."

"They're a bunch of Bambi-killing bastards!"

She lifted her knees a fraction and pulled away. The spots from the airport showed up the curves of her thighs and her high, round glutes. Her black Lycra tights gleamed and shimmered.

Dene savoured the view. "Did you know you have the cutest little arse, Miss Bunny?"

"It's an *ass*, toy brain." She upped the tempo and scooted farther ahead. "And I bet you can't catch it."

She stretched into a full stride, her arms now swinging in counter-balance to her pumping legs.

Dene tacked on close behind. Zanelle shifted into overdrive. The asphalt rang with her foot strikes. Dene grinned. Challenge accepted. He eased up beside her and then accelerated. Zanelle put in a surge but couldn't hold on.

Dene suddenly felt better. He decided to blow out the cobwebs. He pinged away, ten, fifteen, twenty yards ahead. He sprinted a hundred yards past the hangars and machinery sheds inside the airport fence, before backing off near the western end of the runways. The airport glittered away to his left. He slowed to a jog and then a walk. He followed the gravel shoulder for a few steps and paused, pondering the security fence.

Zanelle pulled up beside him, her shoes slapping on the damp road. Her breasts rose and dipped in time with her heaving lungs.

"What the fuck?" she said. "I was a national-class sprinter. You've never outrun me like that."

Dene continued staring at the mesh and the fence posts.

"I'm no slouch myself remember."

"But you're not even puffing." She scowled and wiped her fingers over his forehead. "You're barely sweating."

He rested his hands on his hips. She was right. He felt fantastic. No oxygen debt, no lactate. But right now something else held his interest. He looked up at the strands of barbed wire strung along the top of the fence.

He said, "What's that fence for?"

"Huh?"

"What's that fence for?"

Zanelle looked from Dene to the fence, and back to Dene.

"To keep stupid people out, Stupid."

"Right. But an internment camp would have the overhang toward the inside. To keep people in."

"Obviously."

"But why go to the trouble?"

"What are you raving about?"

Dene started back toward the end of the loop, back to the bungalow and his pickup.

"It's been changed," he said.

Zanelle scampered to catch him. "What has?"

"The overhang around Lampard's camp. It's turned the other way. To keep people out."

Chapter 53

GWEN CROZIER WAS A first-rate landlady. She didn't interfere in domestic matters. She didn't hound her tenant for money. She didn't pry into personal affairs. All of which made it easy to accept her friendship.

This vaguely maternal bond also roused Zanelle's protective side. She sometimes cruised past the house while on duty, just to make sure all was well. She worried if something upset the routine. And Mrs Crozier was a stickler for routine. She always left clues to her schedule. It wasn't like her to vanish. Not without dropping a hint about where she was going.

Zanelle skipped onto the porch, pressed the doorbell and waited. She cupped her hands and peeked through the sidelight – the 'break-in window'. She took out her phone and dialled the woman's home number. Again.

A cheery tinkle came loud and clear from the instrument on the kitchen bench inside. Zanelle sighed and waited for the message service.

"Hello, Mrs Crozier. Just wondering when you'll be back. Speak with you soon."

She heard a mailbox lid clang behind her. She pocketed the phone and turned to see Vera Bell jiggling across her front yard.

"I don't think she's home yet, darl," said Vera.

"She wasn't here last night either."

"No, I haven't seen her since Monday."

Zanelle rocked on a loose board. The house was in darkness when she arrived back from her run with Dene on Monday night. It was now Wednesday morning. Too long.

"Where's she gone?"

"I'm not sure, dear."

Zanelle stepped off the porch and marched to the Impreza. She bounced behind the wheel and slammed the door.

"It can't be a gentleman friend," called Vera. She watched the red car spin out the drive, then chuntered back across the lawn. "Gwen would have bragged about that for a week."

DENE RESTED HIS FOREARMS on the kitchen counter. He doodled on a graph pad, estimating how much basalt they'd need for the pillars in a wrought-iron fence around a local park statue. They could start the job next week – if he could find the twins.

Then he thought about another enclosure. The chain-link and barbed wire at Lampard's retreat. Was he making too much of a fence around private property? Did the overhang matter? But why the change if it didn't?

He rolled off the counter top and leaned back against the bench. He wondered about Kenny and Tim. They lived in Chilliwack because the rent was cheaper. Dene wanted his business to be central, so he lived in Abbotsford. If he had work near Chilliwack, he drove over and picked the twins up. If the job was around Abbotsford, they drove to Dene's and left their car at his place.

But where were they? They weren't at the gym. At least Erin had said they weren't. They could be at their unit in Chilliwack but they hadn't answered his calls. He'd need to check, but it was no big deal.

He would stop in on Zanelle while he was there.

He recalled how the two had met. It was after the Mounties knocked back her first application. She was drowning her sorrows at a bar in Abbotsford, and he stepped in to defuse a quarrel with a drunken car salesman. She let the guy have it, and then doubled down on Dene.

After she bought him a drink to apologise, he sat at the bar hours longer than he'd intended. For him, looks and presentation were only the bait. The hook was personality. And she had it in spades.

She was vibrant and gracious and forthright, with a special brand of integrity. When she said something, she meant it. He found it an alluring package, though it didn't make her popular with everyone. But popularity was a double-edged sword. You never knew what people wanted.

An image flashed into his mind. The twins chomping steak and swilling beer with Pym and Quillan. Someone must know where they were. He dialled a number and the answering service cut in. Seemed everyone was busy but him.

"Yeah, Tallie, it's Dene. I guess you're working out. Umm, call me when you get this. Thanks."

He dropped the cell into his jacket. Everything would be fine. Kenny and Tim would be goofing off somewhere.

He opened the refrigerator and grabbed a water, then shuddered with a chill that didn't come from cold air pooling around his feet.

Another image had forced its way into his head.

Pym and Quillan.

And two dead deer.

He saw the butter compartment. He lifted the plastic door and looked at the last bottle of HSC.

And picked up the syringe beside it.

Chapter 54

ZANELLE MADE THE TRIP from Chilliwack to Abbotsford in record time.

The dead dogs. The theft from the vet clinic. Her suspension. The newspaper stories. Her meeting with Tallie. Lampard's reputation. And now Mrs Crozier's absence. It all swirled around in her mind, but she couldn't pull it into focus.

It ate at her insides.

And she'd had enough.

The golfer Bobby Jones once said that people think they're concentrating, when in fact they're only worrying. Whatever Zanelle was doing, she didn't spot Dene's pickup chugging down the Trans-Canada in the opposite direction.

To be fair, he didn't see her either. He had worries of his own.

Fifteen minutes later she pushed through the door of Lampard's gym. Erin high-stepped from the aerobic studio, keeping time with the beat.

"Hi there. I'm Erin. Welcome to Andropha Gymnasium. How can we help you achieve your goals today?"

Zanelle walked straight past without a glance. She looked over the dancers, then returned to the counter.

Erin said, "Our next class isn't till this afternoon but we could –"

"Can it, Tinkerbell. Mattson Lampard."

The perky smile didn't budge. "Oh, he's extremely busy. You'd need an appointment."

Zanelle saw the girl's hand inch beneath the counter. Probably a buzzer. Maybe a flashing light. She had been announced. She skirted a pot plant, and made for the door in the corner.

Erin crab-walked from behind the counter to cut her off and copped a stiff-armed jolt in the chest. The smile morphed into a pout. She rubbed between her breasts with one hand and waved the other as if she held a piece of hot toast.

"Just a minute...my name's Erin."

Zanelle leaned on the door handle and barged up the passage. She stomped into the weight room and glared at some of the biggest men she'd ever seen.

A few of the giants stopped mid-set. A bearded blond raised his eyes from a magazine. He appraised her for a moment, then stood and strutted forward, oozing insolence. Exactly how to get on her bad side.

"I have an appointment to see Mattson Lampard. Where do I go?"

Benoit Broussard rolled his magazine into a tube and made like he was pulling a cock. He tilted his head and scanned her from top to bottom.

"Tasty. He'll be happy to see you. This way."

———◦◦◦———

THE TWINS' UNIT BLOCK was owned by an old Italian immigrant. Reno Calagaz was a retired quarrier with Bob Mitchum looks. He talked old-time boxing with Kenny and sided with Dene whenever

Tim ragged him about rugby. He was in his garden when Dene stepped out of the pickup.

"Ciao, Reno."

"Hey, ciao, Dino."

"Are those lazy employees of mine around?"

"Hah. They're good boys. Don't think they're home today though."

Dene looked at the white Toyota in the carport. "You sure?"

"They left with some fellas yesterday afternoon."

"What'd they look like?"

"Big. Front rowers for sure. Three of them."

"They have a car?"

"They had two. Black Jeep and a red pickup. Not like yours. New and shiny."

"You know where they were going?"

"Didn't say. But they had their cold weather gear."

A wave of nausea flowed over Dene as he fired up the ute.

I'm eating half a damn cow a week....

———◇———

THE OLD F-150 REVVED up the slope toward Mrs Crozier's house. No sign of the Subaru, but a neighbour was raking leaves in her front yard. Dene pulled a U-turn and bumped a front wheel over the kerb. He reached across and wound down the passenger window.

Vera strayed onto the nature strip. "Looking for Zanelle?"

"Yeah, is she home?"

"You've missed her. She took off half an hour ago."

Dene lifted the clutch and gunned the Ford back down the hill.

Vera shook her head. "Yep, she was in a hurry too."

⸺◇⸺

DENE DIDN'T WANT TO head to Abbotsford if the twins were up at the camp. He might need to come back. He dialled a number on his phone, steering and changing gear with one hand.

Voicemail.

He said, "Zanelle, I can't find the twins. Call me when you get this. And stay away from Lampard. He could be involved somehow, and that...can't be good."

He drove past Zanelle's studio in case she was busy with clients, then took a punt and went past the RCMP detachment near the airport.

No luck.

He tried the twins again. No answer at either number. The cell coverage was patchy past Jones Lake. Maybe their phones were off. Maybe the batteries had died. Maybe they were already back and had simply forgotten to turn them on again. It had him stumped.

He stopped at a gas station and filled the tank, then bought a hotdog and a Coke and paid the cashier for the fuel. He pulled into a parking space beside the gas station. He ate and drank, then put his head back and closed his eyes.

As he drifted off, something stuck in his mind. Something about the neighbour next door.

Chapter 55

BROUSSARD LED ZANELLE DOWN the corridor to Lampard's office. She saw him clench his ass cheeks with each step and felt like kicking him in the knee. Her phone buzzed but she paid no heed. There were other fish to fry.

Broussard knocked and opened the door. Zanelle shouldered past him and stepped into the centre of the room. She wanted to make a statement. A huge bald man sat at a desk, documents fanned in front of him. Had to be Lampard. A creepy-looking muscle freak stood at his shoulder. The two looked up and eyeballed her. She had their attention.

"Benny," said Lampard, "I hope this is important."

"It's important to me," said Zanelle.

Lampard leaned back and folded his arms over his chest.

He said, "Well, I'm sure that's all that matters."

"You got that right, bucko. What if I mentioned greyhounds to you? Or stolen blood? What about ketamine? Clenbuterol? I'll guarantee you know all about that."

The one called Benny shrugged. "Said she had an appointment. She's got a dinky studio up at the 'Wack'. She's competition."

So they knew her. Chalk one up for networking.

"Competition?" said Lampard. "I think not. Opposition at best."

Zanelle couldn't argue that. But she had contacts too. "A so-called fitness camp ring any bells?"

The muscle freak whispered into Lampard's ear. She thought she heard, 'gotta shut this down'.

"Good idea, Marcus," he replied.

So the creep was Quillan. Second banana. Alright, she had them pegged. Time to throw out the trump card.

She said, "Or how about...HCS?"

Lampard stiffened. Quillan moved from his side and said, "What exactly is your point?"

She ignored him and took a pace toward Lampard. "If you think this grubby drug-peddling operation has a future, you're in for a shock." She sighted down her forefinger. "And if you've hurt a single one of my friends –"

Lampard slapped his hands against the desktop. "How dare you come in here making accusations! I've hurt no one, yet not only do you insult me, you also threaten me. Very well." He shoved himself to his feet. "If you want to get personal."

A smile crossed her face. She had him on the run. "Feeling the pressure, huh? Well, I haven't even started." She raised her chin at the weight room. "What else are you hiding in this pig pen? What is it you think you're playing at?"

Lampard's teeth gleamed and his skin turned khaki in the lamp-light.

"This isn't a playground," he said, "this is real life. And your little girlie hobby? With your balls and your hoops and your little rubber bands? It demeans the legitimate fitness industry. And it harms a business I've toiled long and hard to build. I do *not* appreciate that."

"Come off it, you jerk. I don't even work in the same town. And I'm only one *little girlie*. Do I really scare you that much?"

Lampard pushed out his chest. "Actually, you don't scare me at all. But more pertinent to this discussion, none of that is your concern."

Quillan stepped to Zanelle's right. Broussard mirrored the movement on her left. Her eyes flickered between the pair. They were calm. Unhurried.

Not a trace of intimidation.

These guys are no saints.

The tables turned in an instant.

"You know I'm a Mountie, right?"

Lampard's face froze, draped with disdain. He breathed a single sentence, each word soaked in hatred.

"I don't give a *fuck* what you are."

Zanelle baulked. Her anger dried up and her assurance faltered. She rallied one more bluff. "Are you sure you want to take on the police?"

"Are you?" came a voice.

She spun. Roland Pym strode into the office and pushed the door shut behind him. The last piece of the puzzle dropped into place. Everything led to Lampard, all connected like strands of a web. But now she was trapped in the middle.

Don't get in over your head.

Lampard eased from behind the desk, a grotesque, bone-headed bear. His eyes glittered like black and gold diamonds. Like a spider's eyes.

Zanelle felt shards of ice skewer her guts.

And knew she was in trouble.

Broussard leapt behind her before she could move. He pinned her arms and hugged her tight to his chest. A hand clamped over her mouth, mashing her nose and crushing her lips against her teeth.

Panic welled and bile flooded her throat. She wrenched and writhed and hacked at the air. She let fly with a boot and caught Pym's shoulder. It felt like she'd kicked a tree.

Broussard hoisted her off the floor and swung her from side to side. Pym grabbed her ankles and rolled her face down.

From the weeping corner of her half-closed eye she saw Quillan tug on the drawstring of his track pants.

He said, "Oink, oink."

Chapter 56

THE SUBARU MADE IT back to Chilliwack on autopilot. Zanelle remembered nothing of the trip. She didn't know that a fleet of four-wheel drives pulled out of Andropha's parking lot five minutes after her, and followed her east. Nor did she notice the convoy roll through town and continue up Highway One, into the mountains.

She didn't go to the cottage. She refused to taint her home – or Mrs Crozier's. It would be a failure. A submission. A surrender.

And that wasn't going to happen.

She walked out of the showers at the indoor pool in a daze, barefoot and bedraggled, wet hair clinging to cheeks still red from the steaming water. People passed by and nodded or called a greeting. She barely acknowledged them.

She'd scrounged fleece pants and a thick hoodie from the lost property bin. Her old outfit was bundled with her boots and jacket. She ditched the sullied clothing in a dumpster beside the pool complex. The jacket and boots would go later, when she finished with them.

She tramped up the stairs to her studio. Her legs throbbed where they'd been clutched and kneed. Her hips ached from being forced apart. Her bruised vagina burned from repeated violations – and from Pym's makeshift douche of water and bleach, introduced with the rancid dregs of a plastic ketchup bottle.

Fucking reptiles!

Lampard had laughed at her warnings. He said she came to them, making threats. Said a high-ranking officer told her to stay away from a case, to drop the investigation. He said she'd disobeyed instructions and gone to the scene of a crime, off-duty and unauthorised.

And then she'd been suspended.

The bastard said she assaulted a staff member and forced access to a restricted area. That she had to be escorted from the premises. That it was the word of a prominent businessman and a decorated senior police officer, among others, against her – a troublemaker. Biased, vindictive and irrational.

An unreliable witness.

She turned the key and nudged the studio door open. She padded over the carpet and tossed her boots and jacket in a heap. She swung her arms and rotated her shoulders, shook out her legs, then rummaged through a tub of hand wraps and training gear. She slipped her feet into foot protectors and pulled on a pair of bag gloves.

Anger seeped into her bones and pushed the shock from her mind. Fuck Lampard and his pack of curs. They thought they were above the law, and the law wouldn't stop them.

Jesus, the fucking law was with them!

She walked to the corner and set up in front of her old heavy bag. Crinkled bands of duct tape held its seams together and the base bulged where the rag packing had sunk. She held her fists beside her temples. Hands up, chin down. She threw a lazy round kick with her right leg, then another with her left. She followed with a string of short, rapid punches. The bag shook and its chains rattled.

Those animals want to operate outside the law? Fine. They'll be dealt with outside the law.

And then the law can deal with the consequences.

She dropped her hands and trotted on the spot, drawing deep breaths. People said vengeance was a dish best enjoyed cold. Well, fuck that shit.

Vengeance is best enjoyed now.

She set herself again and attacked the bag with thumping double kicks.

Right, right. Left, left. Right, right.

She hammered at the target with tightly bunched knuckles.

Left, right, left, right, left, right, left, right.

She wheeled around and circled the room. She forced her puffy lips closed and took long, controlled breaths through her nose.

She saw herself in the mirrored wall. Faint red blotches marked her face. The eyes beneath her shaggy platinum hair shone with rage. She turned and squared up again.

Left kick, right kick, left kick, right kick.

She bombarded the bag with vicious blows. The old Ringside danced and swayed in erratic loops. The tape split and the stitching moaned and the swivel squawked. She launched a jaw-snapping elbow strike behind a brutal knee drive. She slammed venomous lefts and rights into the cowhide, but the onslaught waned. Fatigue finally won.

Then the shame and fear swept over her.

She wrapped her arms around the ragged, scarred leather and sobbed, then sank to the floor and held her knees against her shuddering chest.

Chapter 57

A SIREN DISTURBED DENE'S rest. He opened his eyes in time to see a red cross flash past. An ambulance. Then he remembered what had bothered him. A Red Cross badge on a woman's cardigan. Zanelle's neighbour worked at the blood bank.

And a blood bank stored blood.

He knew people had promoted blood as a COVID vaccine and sold it online during the pandemic. But what else had they tried? The internet was awash with harebrained drivel and bogus cures. Lampard was loony, but how far would he go?

Or was already he ahead of the curve?

Dene had taken a chance with the HCS. He didn't believe the serum would work, but that was okay, so long as it did no damage. There were some sleepless nights, so he recorded his workouts at the gym. He tracked his heart-rate when he ran. He monitored his blood pressure, took his temperature and checked his weight daily. He even filled out his own wellness reports.

He expected to feel flat, even ill. But the data told a different story.

He felt fine.

He felt great.

Except for being conflicted again.

Good versus bad. Right versus wrong. Cognitive dissonance. He tried to get it straight in his head, to justify what he'd done.

What he was doing.

Zanelle was better with that stuff. He'd swing past the studio again and see if she was there. He fired up the Ford. Then his phone chirped and interrupted his thoughts. He didn't want to answer, but he had to.

It was Tallie.

Dene spotted the little red hatch and pulled into the pool's parking lot. He took the stairs to the studio two at a time. The lights were off, but the door was ajar. He pushed it open and peered in. Empty. He took a cautious step. Then he saw the crumpled shape on a mat in the corner.

He crossed the room at a jog. He knelt beside Zanelle and stroked her arm. She twitched awake. She drew her knees up and jerked her gloved fists to her head.

"Easy," said Dene, "it's only me. I've been looking for you."

She hooked his arms and pulled herself into his chest.

"Hey," he said, "it's okay. What's wrong?"

She rubbed her eyes. "It's nothing. I just had a really tough workout, that's all. I'm tired."

She sat up and dragged her gloves off. He noticed that she hadn't wrapped her hands. It wasn't like her. Her knuckles would ache for days. He stroked her cheeks. Her skin was clammy and her face was bloated.

He pushed wisps of hair from her forehead and said, "I've been thinking. If you're right about the gym, and about black-market blood, then Lampard's camp would be the perfect place to store it."

"Like a blood bank?"

"Why not? It's remote. It's snowed in for half the year. I heard generators up there. It's probably self-sufficient. Hell, they probably don't even use it as a retreat."

She propped herself up on her hands. "That would fit. And they'd need somewhere to take the dogs. Tallie said Lampard mixed different blood components and then added a witch's brew of drugs to make his serum. It's all about getting the right blend." She slowly straightened her legs. "Hey, I bet he tests it on those poor saps at the gym."

Dene started to speak but changed his mind.

Zanelle sat upright, animated, on the scent.

"But it's hit and miss, so they'd need to try heaps of combinations. And they'd need to keep it all frozen. Vera said –"

She paused, then crawled over the mat to her jacket. She dug out her cell and worked her thumb across the screen.

"Hello, Vera? Any sign of Mrs Crozier yet?"

Seconds ticked by as she listened.

"No, nothing's happened. I just wondered if you'd seen her. Listen, Vera – what's her blood type?"

She unstrapped the foot protectors.

"Okay. No, not important. Thanks for that. Bye."

The phone went back into the jacket. She pulled her socks out of her boots and wriggled them on.

"Dene, do you know the twins' blood type?"

"Sure. It's part of the medical at the Wolves. They're both O negative."

"So's Mrs Crozier...Jesus Christ!"

She stood and jammed her feet into her boots, then snatched up her jacket and sprinted for the door.

Dene jumped to his feet. "Where are you going?"

"Greyhounds!"

"What?"

"They're using them as greyhounds."

"What are you talking about?"

"Universal donors. It's not a blood bank. *It's a blood farm!*"

THE GRAB BITE

THE GRAB BITE

Chapter 58

THE CHECKER PLATE RANG like a kettle-drum as Zanelle cycled down the steps. She yanked on the Impreza's door handle, backed into the driver's seat and kicked the engine over.

Dene called after her. "Zanelle, don't! You can't go up there alone!"

The tyres squealed as she reversed out. She flattened the pedal and the red car lunged forward, across the carpark and onto the road.

Dene leapt down the steps.

"Fuck! Fuck! Fuck!"

He ran to his pickup and dived into the cab.

Zanelle steadied the wheel with her knees and tapped at her phone.

"Tom, it's – no I'm fine, now shut up. What's the quickest way up to Jones Lake? I'm looking for an old internment camp on the eastern side."

She pressed the phone to her ear and revved through the gears with her spare hand.

"Okay, got it."

The Subaru fishtailed across a lane as she tramped on the gas.

"No, I'll call you when I know what's going on. And Tom? It might be a good idea to keep this under your hat. Just in case I'm wrong."

Chapter 59

FROM HIS OFFICE ON the north-west corner of the Consulate building David Selkirk could see across Coal Harbour to Stanley Park. He stood gazing at the cruise ships docking, and massaged the bandage around his elbow. More blood tests. His left arm was one big bruise.

He pondered his plan. Never clear-cut, now it was clouded with uncertainty. It relied on too much going right. And on people who weren't that helpful in the first place.

He should have been honest from the beginning. Should have put his head down and just worked through it, but now time had run out. He needed money for treatment, and his new Biomorphi-X shares didn't look like coming to the party.

His cell purred. He picked it up and tucked it under his jaw while he rolled down his sleeve.

"Hello."

"Dad?"

"I'm glad you called," said Selkirk.

"Dad, I need some help."

"There's something I have to ask you too, Dene."

"It's gotta wait, Dad. I think Kenny and Tim are in trouble. And Zanelle could be too."

Selkirk fastened the button at his wrist. Trouble came in different guises.

"So why can't the Mounties help?"

"Because Zanelle is...suspended."

"Oh. That's an auspicious start to her career."

"Please don't make this any harder, Dad."

Selkirk knew his son held him in scant regard. It was a concession for him to phone. He also knew that he never panicked and he didn't cry wolf.

Something must be wrong.

"Have you called the police?"

"We can't trust the police, Dad. Do not go to the police, whatever you do!"

"Then what *am* I supposed to do?"

"You're a bloody security specialist – can't you get some people together?"

"I make policy, Dene. I co-ordinate security, I don't enforce it."

"Well, that's a fucking change. Mister Leave-It-With-Me is suddenly too righteous to bend the rules. Alright. At least Tallie will step up."

"Hang on a minute. I didn't say I wouldn't try to help. What are we dealing with here?"

"Some blokes from the gym. They've taken Zanelle and the twins hunting, but there's a camp up there. I don't think that's all they have in mind."

"I'm sure Kenny and Tim can look after themselves."

"You don't know these guys. I've seen them in action. This is serious, Dad. We're gonna need some muscle."

"So where are they?"

"Up near Jones Lake."

"Christ, I'll need a four-wheel drive and a fucking Indian guide."

"Tallie knows the way. Call her at the university. Tell her to wait for you."

"So that's three of us? Great."

"We don't have time to round up a posse, Dad."

Selkirk drummed his fingers on the desk. "Maybe I can get one more. Okay, I'm leaving now."

"Just hurry," said Dene.

His father said, "Take care of yourself, son," but he only heard car horns and tyre noise, and then the line went dead.

Dene tossed his cell onto the seat.

He'd played his last card. And it wasn't a lie. If Zanelle beat him up to the camp, she *was* in trouble.

Then why did he feel bad about deceiving his father? He had no choice. He couldn't say Lampard was at the bottom of it all.

Or did his father already know?

He pounded the steering wheel and pushed the pickup as hard as he dared.

Selkirk wiped his hand across his forehead. He'd skated on thin ice before, but this was something else. This was getting out of control. And his plans had all just gone to shit.

Trust Lampard to cock things up.

He slipped the phone into his pocket and reached for the intercom. "Valerie, I need a twelve-hour Release & Transfer Order from the Kent Maximum Security Unit to the Abbotsford University. On medical grounds."

"Right away, sir."

"And make sure it gets to the warden *before* it reaches the Commissioner."

The intercom went silent. Selkirk knew Val Bedford had served four Security Directors before him, and he'd never heard her utter a word about any of them. One did not become a career public servant without a modicum of tact. He prayed she would stay true to her diplomatic code.

"I'll try, sir," came the reply.

He unlocked a drawer beneath his desk and pulled out a handgun in a pancake holster. The Mounties liked their Smith & Wessons and he'd used a Glock in London, but SIG Sauer's P226 was his favourite. He withdrew the weapon and laid it on his desk, then undid his belt and fed the end through the slots in the holster. He always carried at four o'clock on his waistband, sidearm canted forward.

He grabbed a loaded magazine from the drawer. Would the double stack mag be enough? He paused a moment before grabbing a second. He dropped one into his trouser pocket and heeled the other into the butt.

The gun nestled in his hand like a cold, lethal bird.

He reached for the intercom again. "And Val? Make that transfer order life-or-death."

He slid the SIG into its holster, cinched his belt one hole tighter, worked an arm into his coat and headed for the door.

Chapter 60

THE CONSULATE ID ON Selkirk's government Nissan got him out of a speeding ticket at the Highway 13 Interchange on his way to Abbotsford. It also gave him access to most places, and the university was no exception.

He saw Tallie waiting behind the parking lot gatehouse in a white Chevrolet Suburban. The university's crest adorned its front doors and banners reading PATIENT TRANSPORT VEHICLE ran along its tinted rear windows. It guarded a space near a bank of EV chargers. Tallie reversed and Selkirk turned in. He locked the car and slid into the Chev's front seat.

"Thanks for waiting."

Tallie said, "Let me get this straight – one stop for back-up, and then we find my brothers."

Her brothers weren't his priority, but he needed her help.

"We find Dene and we find the rest. Do you have everything you need?"

"Hey, my job's the easy part. You have to get us in and out."

Not only was his plan illegal, Selkirk knew he'd be found out in the end. And he'd put it together on the fly; he wasn't convinced it would even work.

"We'll be okay," he said.

The Chev rolled out of the carpark and swayed into the traffic. Selkirk watched Tallie swinging on the wheel. Her arms threatened to split the sleeves of her university track top. He struggled with his seat belt as vehicles fled the path of the big SUV.

"Do you know exactly where we're going?" she said.

"I thought you knew."

"How the hell would I know?"

"Dene said it's up near Jones Lake."

"Then put it in the Sat Nav."

Selkirk jabbed at the screen on the dash. "It says Jones Lake Main or Jones Lake West."

"They're camping grounds. What's east of the lake?"

"Mount Cheam."

"Try Wahleach Lake."

"Nope, nothing."

"This rig is ten years old. God knows when it was last updated."

"Use your phone."

"Use yours, Mr Fancypants. I'm on prepaid and I'm all out of credit."

Selkirk looked out the window. They probably couldn't track him, but he didn't want to take the chance.

"Umm...I left mine in the car."

"Damn it. Dene only told me it's off a forest service road, somewhere east of the lake." She swerved away from Highway One. "But I think we can do better than that."

A minute later and three blocks south, Tallie slung a hard left and pulled the Suburban onto a concrete apron beside a cinderblock warehouse. She bounced out of the SUV and said, "You stay here. This thing's full of medical gear I can't afford to replace."

She walked into Andropha Gymnasium's reception area. The studio was empty but the music beat on.

Erin slipped a copy of *Curve* magazine beneath a desk planner. "Hi there. Welcome to –"

Tallie held a finger to her lips and loomed over the counter.

"I'd like to speak with Mattson Lampard."

"I'm sorry, Mr Lampard isn't in."

"Then where might I find him?"

Erin slipped a hand beneath the counter. "He's at our fitness retreat. But that's only for premium members."

Tallie leaned closer. The light from the doorway dimmed.

"Just give me directions. I'll arrange membership myself."

The door behind the reception desk opened. Marcus Quillan swaggered out, shoulders back, pumped arms propped on wide, tensed lats. The standard passive-aggressive stance. Used to make one look bigger. More threatening. A dog with its hackles up.

He closed the gap to Tallie. He looked her up and down and his fat mouth curled into a sneer. "English not your first language, *wahine*. No visitors."

A veil of serenity dropped over Tallie's face. She looked at the First Aid kit, then spoke to the flushed receptionist.

"Does that defibrillator work?"

"Why, I'm sure it does," said Erin. "Everything works perfectly here at –"

Tallie pivoted and drove a straight-armed heel strike into Quillan's centre mass. She made contact two inches below the base of the sternum, at the nexus of nerves called the *solar plexus*. The blow terminated eight inches past the initial point of impact.

Andropha's manager was a walking advertisement for the gym's benefits, but his chest-out posture worked against him.

He couldn't relax his torso in time to absorb the hit.

And Tallie had forty pounds on him.

Quillan slammed into the wall, then juddered to the floor, wheezing and sucking air. He convulsed with shock, rucking up the carpet with his heels as he tried to find more oxygen.

Erin gawped, then looked up at Tallie.

She said, "I'll draw you a map."

Chapter 61

THE LABORATORY AT THE fitness retreat contained fundamental equipment – a centrifuge, microscopes, an autoclave – as well as cutting-edge blood analysers. Test tubes stood in racks, and glass slides in Styrofoam boxes sat on shelves around the walls.

Lampard lounged on a vinyl recliner chair. He daydreamed at a knot hole high on the wall, while a tube drained blood from his arm into a collection bag rocking in a blood mixer.

Roland Pym sauntered in. His police uniform had given way to camo pants and a wool-lined denim jacket. "I think I'd better take a few subjects and have a look around."

Lampard turned his head part way toward Pym, but his eyes remained on the wall, trapped in a private reverie.

"What's happened?"

"Erin just radioed from the gym. Quillan thinks your twins might have a sister."

The hazel eyes flickered. "Does he now? That could be interesting. A three-way comparison."

"Not that simple. She put him down and forced Erin to give her directions to the camp. Quillan's going to follow her. When he can breathe properly."

Lampard looked at the Abbotsford cop and wondered which of his workers was the least incompetent.

"Typical of Marcus," he said. "All piss and wind."

"Evidently she's quite a specimen."

Lampard's head nodded in time with the clicking of the blood mixer. "And evidently quite resourceful, too. I can't wait to meet her."

"As long as she doesn't have any more fuckin' relatives," said Pym.

Chapter 62

COOL, MOIST AIR RUSTLED down the valley, and ashen clouds hung heavy with rain, like skeins of mohair dabbed in damson ink.

Tabu Kainoa rocked gently in the rear of the SUV, squashed between a pair of prison guards almost as heavy. His manacled hands rested on his thighs, fingers curled into fists. Through half-closed eyes he saw a street sign glide past and grunted.

Cemetery Road.

Tallie made her way onto the Lougheed highway, then took Highway Nine through Agassiz and onto the Agassiz-Rosedale Bridge across the Fraser River. She travelled another minute until the traffic thinned and then pulled onto the shoulder near a landfill site.

"Sorry to be indelicate," she said. "Busting for a pee."

The guards looked around, questions forming in cautious eyes. Selkirk opened the glove compartment where he'd stashed the SIG Sauer.

In for a penny, in for a pound. He turned and aimed the weapon at one guard's head.

"I appreciate your help, gentlemen, but I'll be okay from here. Out." He waved his gun at Tallie and tried to sound menacing. "You. Do as you're told and you might stay in one piece."

Tallie made a half-hearted effort to play the game. She scowled at the SIG but she was already opening the rear door on the driver's side. Tabu leaned against the guard and pushed him out of the SUV. Tallie grabbed a handful of uniform and marched him behind the van.

Selkirk dragged the second guard onto the side of the road. He held the gun pointed at the ground. He was in enough shit. No amount of explaining would help if he accidentally shot an innocent man.

"Tasers, please," he said.

The guards offered no resistance and didn't speak. Professionals. They tossed their stun-guns at Selkirk's feet.

"And the phones."

He shook the gun at Tallie. She grabbed their cells and patted them down. She found a cylinder key to Tabu's cuffs. Then she found the key to the padlock on his belly chain.

"Start walking," said Selkirk.

The men hesitated, then looked at each other and shrugged. They turned their collars up against a spitting breeze and headed back toward the bridge and Agassiz.

Selkirk picked up the stun guns and dropped them into his coat pockets. He guessed the guards would raise the alarm long before they crossed the river, but he thought they'd assume the fugitives would travel east along the U.S. border, then detour south and sneak into Washington or Idaho. Or that they'd go back to Vancouver and try to disappear. Maybe escape by boat.

The Suburban wasn't exactly invisible. He hoped they could make it into the hills before police patrols started hitting the roads. He seated himself behind the wheel and put the column shift into 'D'.

Tallie slipped into the back and hugged her father. "I'm sorry about the needle, *Makua kāne*. I had to give you a sedative."

"It didn't hurt." Tabu took a sidelong look at his daughter. "Didn't work, either."

"Wasn't meant to. It was saline."

"So...we're not going to the clinic?"

Tallie unlocked the cuffs. "No," she said, removing the anklets and the belly chain. She reached into the cargo space behind them. A cordless, diamond-bladed cranial saw made quick work of Tabu's ankle monitor and she lobbed it into the grass beside the road.

"We're going to be in trouble, aren't we," said Tabu.

"Big trouble," said Selkirk, taking the north-bound access loop onto Highway One.

Tabu nodded. A faint smile settled on his face.

Chapter 63

THIN MIST CLOAKED THE Cascade timberland. Patches of snow blotched the landscape, like missing pieces of a jigsaw puzzle.

The Subaru pitched and bumped over a rutted fire trail. Jones Lake stretched away below and to the left, black and still. Zanelle came to a junction and took the path that wound upward. A minute later she hit a steep incline. She got partway up and then slithered sideways, wheels spinning and going nowhere.

Damn.

Mud and snow tyres are mandatory in BC from October. She'd meant to put them on but clean forgot.

The hatch red-lined. The temperature gauge climbed and blue smoke poured from the exhaust. It was a four-wheel drive but the two-litre engine needed a couple more cylinders and an extra gear. It gave up at the bottom of the slope.

"Fuck."

She wrenched on the handbrake, checked that she had her keys, then checked her cell.

No signal.

"Faaark!"

She leaned across and opened the glove compartment. A canister of pepper-spray went into a pocket inside her jacket.

Moisture trickled down the windshield and darkness hovered above the treetops. She searched for a landmark to keep her on course. She peered through the passenger window and scanned the forest. Then she looked out the driver's side.

And her heart exploded.

A haunted, slavering face pressed against the window, lips spread, teeth bared. She screamed. The creature leaned back and smashed a fist through the glass. She scrambled across the seat but another hollow-eyed brute thumped on the passenger window. The first thing threw open the driver's door and grabbed her ankles.

Roland Pym appeared in the dim light. He pressed his fists against the hood and bounced the car up and down. The creature tugged Zanelle off her knees. She clawed at the wheel and tried to sound the horn, but lost her grip. She lid over the seat and fell face first into the mud. A bony knee pressed into the middle of her back and she heard Pym laugh.

THE F-150 BUCKED ALONG the track. Dene dropped another gear but the pickup stalled on the slippery grade. He rammed it into first and tried again. Just the whine of rubber on slimy rock. He'd known it wouldn't get as far as Lampard's camp, but at least he'd made it past the lake.

But how far could a five-speed hatchback get?

He glanced at his phone. Nothing.

He swung out of the cab and pulled on his Carhartt. The air smelled of burning clutch. He searched through the tools in the tray and grabbed a pointed quarrier's sledge. He looked around, then jogged up the trail, into the mist.

Chapter 64

A ROW OF SIX beds took up one side of the ward. Three were empty. Garner Hall, Billy Switzer, and Gwen Crozier occupied the others. Tubes and intravenous lines connected them to drips and blood collection bags, and their heads lolled on their chests.

Lampard and Benoit Broussard moved along the row. Lampard's eyes skipped over the three inert forms.

"Where's the old man?"

"Ellis died this morning." Broussard shrugged. "Some patients aren't as resilient as others."

The pair stopped at the foot of Switzer's bed. The defensive back's red-rimmed eyes wept over pallid, sunken cheeks. He murmured in delirium.

"He looks almost finished," said Lampard. "How long?"

"Maybe twelve hours."

Broussard moved to the next bed. Mrs Crozier moaned faintly. Drool ran down her chin. "This one'll be next."

"Try to keep her going a bit longer."

"I can't guarantee anything."

"Then at least the subjects won't hunt for a couple of days."

"But we have to replace these donors."

Lampard clasped his hands and rubbed his palms together.

"Benny, my boy, I think replacements are coming."

He marched out of the ward with Broussard close behind.

Garner Hall remained still until he heard them shut the door and stamp down the steps. He opened heavy eyelids and watched for shadows outside the windows. He waited a few more seconds, then rolled onto his side and fumbled with the needle in his arm.

———◆———

THE TRAIL RODE CRESTS and hollows and bent around huddled groups of conifers.

Dene settled into a short-striding tempo, dodging plates of ice, seeking traction on cushions of pine needles. His eyes flicked from the pot-holed track to the trees ahead, and every few paces he checked the valley behind him.

He found Zanelle's car six minutes after he set out on foot. It was half a mile farther along the route and four-hundred feet above where he'd left the Ford.

A gallant effort.

It rested in a pool of slush on a narrow step in the slope, skewed at an angle to the trail. Clumps of mud clung to the tyre walls. The driver's door hung open and fragments of glass speckled the ground.

Not good.

Dene held his breath and listened.

"Zanelle!"

Silence.

Not good at all.

He tightened his grip on the hammer and pushed on into the hills.

Chapter 65

MATTSON LAMPARD AND BAIRD Turley stood on the porch in front of the main hut, Turley with his scorched head wrapped in gauze. The pair watched a knot of shapes approach along the ridge.

Lampard said, "It could be a long night. Go check the generators. And make sure there's enough ketamine to keep everyone sedated. Then turn on the lights."

Turley jumped off the porch and trotted along the line of huts, toward the northern end of the camp. Lampard rocked down the steps and waited beside the gateway.

The two subjects dragged a mud-spattered figure into the compound. Pym gripped a six-foot nylon leash with a choker chain that squeezed Zanelle's neck until it bled.

"So, little girlie," said Lampard. "You just couldn't stay away."

"Told you she liked it," said Pym.

Zanelle shook free of the subjects but Pym yanked on the leash and pulled her to her knees. "Heel, bitch."

He fumbled through her jacket and took the car keys and phone. Then he patted her down and felt the tubular shape in an inside pocket. He pressed the lump against her breast and squeezed.

"Well, whadda we got here?"

"Tampons," said Zanelle. "Take 'em – you might need 'em, *bitch*."

Pym shoved a boot into her shoulder and she sprawled on her side. "Dirty sow," he said.

"Persistent, isn't she," said Lampard. He stooped and examined her face. "Well, as you're so eager to see what we do, why don't I give you a tour?"

He took the leash and hoisted Zanelle to her feet. The chain cinched her throat, cutting off a ragged yelp. She doubled over and gagged.

Lampard turned to Pym. "Check on Baird – see that he knows what he's doing. Then send Benny out with more subjects. If Quillan's girlfriend is coming, we should make her welcome too."

SELKIRK SWITCHED ON HIS headlamps as blue-black night settled over the Cascades. He looked left and saw pinpricks of light in the gloom. The Jones Lake campsites, four miles away at the northern end of the reservoir.

"So far, so good," he said.

Tallie nestled against Tabu on the back seat. She checked Erin's map. "This is the only road. It must be the way."

A sudden blaze of driving lights flashed in the mirror. Selkirk squinted against the glare and saw a black Jeep Renegade bounding up the trail behind them.

He said, "Someone's in a hurry."

The Renegade closed fast. It weaved left and right, then cut left again. The Suburban couldn't match the Jeep's pace and the black shape loomed up beside the Chev, a cattle dog on a steer.

Marcus Quillan glared out the window. He hooked right and buried the corner of his bull-bar in the side of the SUV.

"Whoa," said Tallie. "Angry man to port."

Quillan side-swiped them again.

"Jesus, man! There goes all my funding."

Selkirk fought the wheel. Twenty years of rugby had taught him plenty about the laws of physics. And the Suburban was like a barge to a dinghy.

He swung three tons of metal across Quillan's bow. He burst the four-by-four's right front tyre, peeled the fender clean off and buckled the radiator. The Jeep yawed into a pine trunk, spun one-eighty, then tipped onto its side.

"Sod you, ya *Berk*."

"Temper, Davey," said Tabu.

"Fuck 'im," said Selkirk.

He dropped the SUV into haul mode. Three hundred and twenty horse-power roared as he coaxed the heavy van up the trail.

The headlamps painted a wall of ghostly trees ahead. Here and there, the skeletons of lightning-split cedars marked the way.

Chapter 66

DENE NEARED THE RETREAT. He slogged up the hill, heading for a purple glow in the darkening sky. He stopped. A high-pitched moan diffused through the mist. Machinery. But what kind?

He heard muted crumps from the valley below. Metal on metal. He glanced around and moved sideways across the slope. Toward the light, but off the path of any approaching vehicles.

Snow crunched beneath his boots. He stopped dead, straining to hear the slightest noise. A dry whisper reached his ears as something pressed into a bed of pine needles.

A foot?

No. Feet.

A spark of electricity jumped between his shoulder blades. He sniffed the air and caught a hint of something familiar.

It changes the scent. Confuses 'em.

He raised the sledge and spun to see a clutch of shapes emerge from the shadows. The wave of wasted bodies surged forward, greasy torsos gleaming in the murk.

He swung the hammer and split the first creature's head like a melon. The thing teetered sideways and dropped beside him.

He lifted the hammer into another creature's chin and splintered its jaw. It reeled away, screeching, mouth dribbling blood, tongue almost severed.

The pack charged on. Human animals. Half ape, half jackal. Dene backed up for another swing but stumbled over a tree-root. He dropped the hammer and the creatures gang-tackled him as one.

He launched a whirlwind volley of hooks and uppercuts and short-armed jabs. He grabbed frantically at slippery limbs but the creatures wrestled him to the ground.

One leapt onto his back while another hugged his legs. Another pinned his arms and tied him up in a 'gator roll'.

Sacked.

The horde growled and snarled, and hurled clubbing blows at their victim's body. He drew his knees up and covered his head. The barrage continued until Broussard picked up the sledge and drove the butt into his temple.

A dazzling tiara of stars winked once, and he slipped into the welcoming darkness.

One of the creatures yowled at the sky, then the others joined in. A keening, feral wail floated through the trees.

"A perfect replacement," said Broussard.

———◆———

LAMPARD SHOVED HIS HOSTAGE against the beds in the collection ward. The three patients slumbered on, their breathing irregular and hoarse.

Zanelle spotted her landlady. She hooked her fingers under the choker chain and hissed, "What've you done to her? I will –"

"You'll do nothing," said Lampard. "Just like you did nothing the last time you threatened me."

"Don't bet on it, buster."

Lampard jerked on the leash. Zanelle staggered forward and he smacked the heel of his hand into her forehead.

"Pay attention," he said. "It all starts with the blood. And these are our donors."

Zanelle blinked hard, trying to ease the ache behind her eyes. She needed to think fast. She bent forward and tried to yell. Someone might hear.

"You fucking...*creep!* Do you know how absurd this is?"

The big man snatched a look at Switzer. "I admit I've had failures, but even they can contribute."

"They're not failures! They're victims!"

Lampard's eyes widened. He pulled his shoulders back and inhaled through drawn-back lips. His chest grew and his jowls quivered. Spittle arced from his mouth as he bellowed at the rafters.

"They are a necessary sacrifice – because they failed me! And they do not deserve to live!"

Zanelle recoiled in disgust. She battled a rising dread and tried to collect her thoughts. Clearly yelling wouldn't help.

She said, "Like those mutants you created?"

Puzzlement crossed Lampard's face, as if he'd lost his place in the script. Then he rallied; an actor suddenly remembering his lines.

"Mutants? They're not mutants. They're prototypes. But I agree – the process is flawed. I must go to the next phase."

He pulled her closer and gripped a breast, bouncing the flesh on his fingers, feeling the weight. He rubbed his thumb across the fabric, looking for a nipple. "And for that, we need surrogates."

Zanelle's skin turned to ice. This was as close to madness as she'd ever been. She leaned back on the chain, swaying from side to side, evading his touch. Her voice was as raw as her throat.

"You...are a rolled-gold...lunatic!"

Lampard raised his arms and lowered his chin to his chest.

The saviour on a cross.

"But think of it," he said. "You'll be worshipped. Exalted. You'll be the next 'mitochondrial Eve'."

A rattling laugh came from deep in his throat, wet and sour, like a babbling drain. He lifted his head and spoke to imagined disciples, voice soaring, triumph blazing in demented eyes.

"You'll be the mother of mankind...!"

Chapter 67

AT THE SAME TIME Zanelle straggled out of the ward and followed Lampard to the next line of huts, Broussard led the five remaining subjects along the ridge to the camp. Two of the creatures dragged their dead comrade by the ankles, the corpse trailing after them like a ritual travois. His body would feed the rest for a day.

The thing with the shattered jaw lagged behind. It was aware it couldn't eat, but didn't realise the fate that would follow. The others were already eyeing the film of blood and lard that covered its chest.

The last pair laboured with Dene, fourteen stone and out cold. They hauled him through the gate, his boots leaving twin trails in the gravel.

Pym met Broussard at the edge of the compound. The group stood rinsed in yellow light, like cadavers hanging in a funeral home.

"Where's Mattson?" said Broussard.

"Busy with that trouble-making slut." Pym bent and peered at Dene's bloodied face. "Is this who I think it is?"

"Yep."

"Is he dead?"

"Hope not. He's supposed to be the star of the show."

"Put him in the collection ward until Lampard decides what to do. Full sedation."

Broussard escorted the gaunt figures across the compound, their loads dragging between them.

"And if he doesn't wake up," called Pym, "you'll answer for it."

The subjects laid Dene on the next bed in the row. Broussard inserted a cannula into a vein in his hand and adjusted the drip.

"He won't wake up anytime soon," he said to himself.

He ushered the creatures out of the building. They leered at Switzer's end-stage body as they filed past.

Garner Hall lay quiet until he no longer heard their footfalls, then opened his eyes. He disconnected the tubes from his arm and withdrew his legs from beneath the covers. He sat on the side of the bed, then stood, gripping the iron frame to steady himself.

He crept to Dene's side, stopped the IV pump, and then shook him by the shoulder.

"Dene."

No movement. Hall glanced at the other beds. He considered turning off their drips but Switzer was past help and the old woman might become hysterical. She'd be less trouble asleep.

Dene remained motionless. Time to play paramedic. Hall reached out and rolled his knuckles hard across the sternum.

"Selkirk!"

Dene stirred. He blinked at the ceiling. Disoriented. His eyes did a trip around the hut and landed on Hall. He tried to raise his head. He felt like he'd been shunted by a train.

"Garner? What happened?"

"Easy. You'll be woozy for a while."

Dene patted the hair above his right ear. "How'd I get this lump?"

Hall put his fingertips to the spot. "I'd say you've had a run-in with the hired help. You probably have a concussion."

"Have you seen Zanelle?"

"The girl? She's with Lampard."

Dene worked his elbows up beneath his shoulders and lifted his body. Fuck. He ached all over. "Where are they?"

"Steady down, he won't harm her. And you can't go after them on your own."

"I have friends coming. They must be close."

"Then best we sit tight until they turn up. In case you didn't notice, you're outnumbered here."

"I noticed alright. What *were* those things?"

Hall disconnected the drip and removed the needle from Dene's hand. "They're Lampard's pets. His hyper-carnivores."

"Jesus, what did he do to them?"

The little man stood by the bed, a physician on his rounds.

"It's a long story. He started with soldiers. They were ideal subjects. Eighteen to twenty-five years old, hormones raging, conditioned to take orders. Except they can't go AWOL or there's all kinds of trouble."

He made a finger gun and pointed it at Dene. "Then he discovered footballers. Failed footballers are a dime-a-dozen. You can find them anywhere. They're trained to take orders, too. And Lampard's drugs reinforce that training."

"What sort of drugs? Ketamine?"

"That's one. Flunitrazepam is another."

"What's that when it's at home?"

"Think Rohypnol."

"Roofies?"

"One and the same."

Dene tried to sit up. A rush of dizziness swept through him. He flopped back. "That must be what I'm feeling."

"It *is* what you're feeling, but don't worry. You haven't been on it long enough to suffer any lasting psychosis."

"That what's wrong with those things out there? They're loonies? Nut jobs?"

"In a word, yes. They also lose about forty IQ points – which some of them couldn't spare to begin with. They're virtual imbeciles. Broussard uses force to control them, but he found that they crave meat. You can train them if you reward them with meat."

Dene's brain swirled. "Train them to do what?"

Chapter 68

THE RETREAT'S MAIN HUT contained two large rooms and two smaller ones. A basic kitchen fitted into one small room. Non-perishable supplies filled the other.

One large room was Lampard's private domain. A couch, camp bed, music console. The second opened onto the porch and formed a simple reception and communication centre. Desks, filing cabinets, line-of-sight walkie talkies charging on a shelf.

Pym, Broussard and Turley slouched in chairs arranged around a desk supporting a vintage Hammarlund radio transceiver combo.

The device crackled into life.

'Lampard, come in. Lampard? Is anyone there?'

All three men sat upright. They knew the voice, but he'd never called the camp before. Truman Roberts didn't get his hands dirty.

Pym pulled the mic toward him. "Sergeant Pym here, sir."

'Where's Lampard? You guys have less than thirty minutes to pack up and vamoose!'

Lampard towed Zanelle up the steps of another makeshift ward at the southern end of the camp. The wack job's performance was over, so she used the time to take stock.

She was muddy and her pants were torn. Her neck stung and her nose bled. And she hurt like a bitch.

But she was alive.

"This is our transfusion unit," said Lampard. "And here are our prize exhibits. How are they, doctor?"

A portly man in a rumpled lab coat attended to a patient. He straightened and turned.

"They're perfect," said Paul Swift. "Healthy. Strong. I can't wait to start on them."

Zanelle peeked behind the doctor. Token and Totem lay unconscious on adjacent beds. Padded leather cuffs held their arms and legs in place and IV tubes hung from infusion pumps.

She shook her head and drew back. Away from the two Hawaiians. Away from her captor.

"Oh, boy. Now you're really in trouble."

"So you keep saying," said Lampard.

He coiled the leash around his wrist and Zanelle readied for the pain. Then Baird Turley thumped up the steps and into the ward.

"Big drama," he said. "Truman Roberts just radioed. There's a prisoner loose somewhere in the hills. Half the province is after him."

A feather of hope tickled at Zanelle's core. She saw indecision cross Lampard's face. His frustration simmered, then boiled over. He flung the leash at Turley.

"Bah! Hold her. Come with me, doctor."

Turley caught the leash and Lampard stormed out of the building. Swift toddled after him.

Lampard stood in front of the main hut. Swift eased closer and looked up. He kept his tone low.

"Mattson, you're on the brink of something here. Don't destroy it now."

"I can't take the risk," said Lampard. He watched Pym and Broussard lug jerry cans to the foot of the steps. "Benny, start at the top end. Burn it all."

Broussard hefted a jerry in each hand and headed north.

"What about the donors?" said Pym.

"Burn everything."

"The twins?"

"Everything! Doctor, get the vehicles ready."

"But they might not even be close," said Swift.

"I can't accomplish anything in prison, doctor. And neither can you. The vehicles. *Now.*" He called to Pym. "Roland, I'll let the subjects out – you get the girl. Leave Selkirk's kid to me. He's all we need to start again."

———◦———

THE SUBURBAN SAILED OVER the rise into the clearing on the ridge. The trail ended in a tight turnaround. Selkirk pulled the vehicle into a brake slide and killed the headlamps. Three dark shapes detached themselves from the SUV.

"Where to now?" said Tallie.

Tabu pointed toward a pale radiance on the skyline. The lights of the fitness retreat.

The trio hiked into the trees.

Chapter 69

ZANELLE SIZED TURLEY UP. He glanced at her, then at the twins. He looked back at her and then looked away again. He fidgeted with the leash and licked his lips.

Brickin' it.

She said, "You heard what your boss and his buddies did to me?"

"I heard you got what you deserved."

"Oh, I did. And you know what? I let it happen." She tilted her head back, exposing her throat, eyeing him through lowered lashes. "Because that's how I like it."

She reached into her jacket and rubbed her breast, teasing the nipple erect. His eyes followed her fingers. She needed him to look down, just for a second. She wriggled her other hand inside the trackpants and swayed her hips.

"But they were old men," she said. "Not hard like you. You'd give it to me good, wouldn't you?"

Turley's eyes traced the rise and fall of her knuckles in her pants. He dragged her closer. Too close.

"I'd make sure you didn't –"

A blast of pepper spray erupted in his face. The capsicum mix seared his eyes and scalded his blistered skin. He clutched at his head and doubled over.

"Fucking hell, bitch! Fucking hell!"

Zanelle swivelled and leaned. She hammered a side kick into his temple and sent him staggering against a wall. She lined him up again as he rebounded off the planks.

"And I was kidding before," she said. She slammed a right cross into Turley's chin and dropped him cold. "*That's* how I like it."

She loosened the choker chain and lifted it over her head. Livid tissue stuck to the metal where her skin had peeled. She glanced at Turley, then tried to rouse the twins. She unbuckled their cuffs and loosened the bedding.

Sudden heavy footfalls shook the building. She sneaked away from the beds and pressed against the wall beside the door.

Pym plodded into the ward, listing to counter the weight of the jerry can in his grip. He dug a matchbook from his pocket and flicked it onto an empty bed.

"Baird, you useless fuck, where are you? We're gonna burn the lot."

Turley shook his head. "Huh?"

Pym saw the shape on the floor. One shape.

"Christ! Where is...?"

Zanelle edged along the wall. Pym turned as she scuttled out the door. She hurdled the steps and bolted across the compound, then flew out the gate and jagged left.

Pym dropped the jerry and sprinted after her. His stumpy legs took him on a wide arc, skating on the grit, hot on her tail.

"When I catch you, you fucking whore!"

Zanelle zig-zagged through the trees. Darkness swallowed the light from the camp and she tripped on a broken branch. She scrabbled forward on her hands and knees, losing ground.

She heard Pym closing and turned. Ten yards, five yards, three yards. He took a long stride, planted a boot and catapulted himself up and forward.

Zanelle raised an arm and cocked a fist.

Ready for the impact.

Ready to fight.

But nothing happened.

All she felt was a gust of hot wind. A wraith surged past her shoulder and met Pym in mid-air. Antlers like combat knives speared into his neck and chest and abdomen. The white-tailed buck rammed him into a cedar and shook him as if he were a doll. It charged again and again, driving with densely muscled quarters and powerful neck.

Pym's skull pounded against the trunk with the sound of an axe biting into lumber. Bark crumbled and branches rattled and whistling snorts pealed through the woods.

The buck drew back, dropped its head and sloughed the snivelling lump from a bloodied, ten-point rack. It pawed once, then vaulted into the trees.

Pym sank to the ground. He toppled face forward, haemorrhaging like a downpipe. He twisted his head to one side, his face as pale as the moon on the blood-blackened snow.

"Help me...."

Zanelle stalked back to Pym's humped body. She shoved a pile of leaf litter under his ear with her foot, tilting and raising his head, forcing a weak cough. She lifted her right leg and pushed off the ground with her left, then brought her right heel down with the full momentum of her weight.

And stomped his fat, lizard neck.

She heard the vertebrae crunch beneath her boot like a fistful of chalk. He exhaled a short gurgle and was still.

Zanelle caught her breath and shuddered, the damp air frosting her face and hair. She found her phone and car keys in the dead man's jacket, then crept back to the edge of the trees and studied the compound.

She sensed activity, but saw no movement. Before she could decide what to do, a hand clapped hard over her mouth and pulled her off her feet. A huge arm pressed on her chest and held her down. She pedalled her legs and pushed with her elbows, fighting to get out from under...Tallie.

When David Selkirk kneeled beside her, she almost sobbed with relief. She stopped struggling and Tallie eased her grip.

"Let me up."

Tallie said, "The girl means business."

"I have to get Mrs Crozier. And your brothers."

Tabu leaned forward. "Where are my sons?"

A shack at the far end of the compound exploded into flames. Sparks and embers rode a rippling heat wave into the blackness.

"In there," said Zanelle.

Chapter 70

Tabu rose like a Kraken from the sea. He waded toward the camp, Tallie in his wake.

Selkirk quizzed Zanelle. "What's happened to Dene?"

"I don't know." She jumped to her feet. "C'mon."

They chased after the long shadows of Tallie and Tabu. Suddenly the shadows multiplied. Two, four, eight. A score of Lampard's subjects teemed from the forest and rushed at Tabu, whooping and baying.

He didn't miss a step or waver an inch. He swung raging, wrecking ball fists, lifting the creatures off their feet and smashing them into the snow.

Tallie and Zanelle flew into the fray, lashing out with knuckles and boots and knees. Shrill curses and muffled grunts echoed off the branches. The stricken subjects fell back, and then regrouped. They charged again, hairless wild-eyed gibbons, swarming through the trees.

Tabu met them head on. He beat them senseless with crushing blows. Tallie hurled them to the ground, cracking heads and bursting lungs. Galvanized by the reinforcements, Zanelle let all her anger go. She pumped her fists with bitter fury, taking retribution from every cruel strike.

A shriek rang out above the scuffling. Zanelle turned and saw Selkirk walking through the melee, shocking creatures left and right with a Taser set on 'drive stun'.

Two turned on him like feral cats. He poleaxed one with a straight left. The other tried to sidestep, but he cleaned it up with an old-fashioned coat hanger.

Huh, she thought. *The old guy goes alright.*

The skirmish lasted thirty seconds. Half the wretched mob scurried for the shelter of the trees. The rest limped or crawled through the deadfall after them. A few would never move again.

Tabu ran his tongue over a split lip, while Tallie rubbed a swollen cheekbone. Selkirk shook out his hands and rolled his shoulders.

Zanelle wiped blood from her nose. She led the others along the track and onto the driveway in front of the camp gate. They hunkered down beside a post and she pointed across the compound.

"The twins are in the last cabin."

Tallie and Tabu followed her directions. They kept to the inside perimeter of the fence, merging with the shadows beneath the lights.

"Mrs Crozier's in the next row," said Zanelle. "I have to get her out."

Selkirk grabbed her arm. "What about Dene? We passed his truck. He must be here somewhere."

Zanelle pulled free. She'd had enough man-handling. "You don't give him much credit, do you? Now come with me, or look for Dene, or create a diversion, but don't get in the fucking way."

She sneaked across the compound as the northern sky turned another shade lighter. Bright orange flames roared from hut to hut, jumping the laneways and leaping into the heavens.

—◇—

TURLEY BLINKED AND WIPED his watering eyes. His entire head stung. The bitch had suckered him. Lampard would fucking *freak*.

He looked around and spotted the jerry can. He rolled onto his hands and knees, then stood on dodgy legs.

Better not screw this up.

He lifted the cap and poured petrol around the sides of the transfusion ward. He ditched the jerry and saw the matches. He struck one and lit the rest, then tossed the whole book at the far end of the room. The fuel whooshed and licked up the walls. Turley made for the door.

Kenny groaned.

Turley stopped. He took a step and stopped again. "Oh, shit."

He ran back to the twins. Kenny groaned again.

"Fuck this," said Turley. He heard the timber crackling and felt the floorboards buckle. Flames flickered into the rafters. He grabbed the jerry can and emptied the dregs over the bedclothes. "Only coconut niggers anyway."

A solemn voice grated behind him.

"Should be you respect the black man."

Turley spun around. He looked up at a gigantic human form. An ogre. A monster. Then another shape stepped into the ward. Two monsters. His brain stopped working.

He closed his eyes.

"Not again," he said.

Tabu splintered his skull with a murderous left hook. He died in mid-flight. The body smashed against a smouldering wall, then tumbled down between the beds. Turley's clothes flared, and his skin curdled and blistered one last time.

Tallie extracted the needles from her brothers' arms, and untangled the tubes from the leather straps. She threw the blankets against the wall and they vanished in the fire.

Tabu grabbed a bedframe in each hand and dragged them away from the flaming walls. He hoisted Kenny off his bed and manoeuvred him through the doorway.

Tallie skipped down the steps. She hooked her brother under the armpits and unloaded him from Tabu, then carted him into the shadows near the fence-line.

Tabu ran back and wrestled Tim over his shoulder. He staggered out of the blazing hut, clumped toward Tallie and lowered Tim to the ground beside his brother. He kneeled between the twins, cradling their heads in two enormous hands. He hunched over, sheltering his sons from the ash and embers that fell from the sky.

Tallie felt for a pulse in Kenny's neck. Tabu's words rumbled over the crackle of burning timber.

"Are they alright?"

"I don't know. They're cold. Stay here. I'm going to get the SUV."

Chapter 71

DENE EASED AN EXTRA pillow beneath Mrs Crozier's head. Hall removed the drips and tubes from her arms.

"I think she'll be okay," he said. "Lampard's protocols aren't as crude as they were."

"Why does he want an old woman when he has a shitload of footballers to suck dry?"

"It's her blood. Your Hawaiian friends, too. They're type O negative. Their blood can go to anyone and cause no side-effects."

"I thought Lampard made that stuff from his own blood."

"In the early days he did. But there were discrepancies with results. More of them bad than good. Then he couldn't keep up supply anyway, so he started experimenting with greyhound blood. That's when the problems started. He still keeps a store of his own blood, but like I said, he's getting more sophisticated. Now he uses O neg as a medium, and the serum seems to have stabilised. He's not using as many booster injections on the subjects. And it's a better carrier for his chemical cocktails."

"Cocktails?"

"He's tried everything – bull semen, Chinese fungus, arsenic, quail eggs. Great at brainstorming, not so much at science. Now he's talking about cross-species DNA binding."

"What species?"

"Apes," said Hall. "Gorilla maybe. If he could get hold of a wolverine, I'm sure he'd try that too."

"He can't do that. Can he?"

"I doubt it. Otherwise the Russians would be working on it. Then again, the Chinese could be doing it already – who knows?"

Dene shook his head. How close had he come to this nightmare?

"Bugger me. I knew footballers were desperate but...."

"You should accept that Mattson doesn't think like everyone else. He's from Kenai on the Alaskan coast. It's not just another world. It's another time. He had a tough childhood."

"Everyone's had a tough childhood."

"I mean really tough. His father worked on the road from Anchorage in the fifties. Between jobs he linked up with a carnival. A proper roughneck. Kept his son in a freak show for three years. In a kennel with wild dogs."

"If that's true, then Lampard knows what slavery is. So he's got no excuse."

"I'm not making excuses. The guy's deranged. But they treated him like shit. Beaten. Starved. He travelled around in a cage for God's sake. And the whole time he was told, 'toughen up, toughen up'."

Dene remembered his father yelling endless abuse from the sidelines. He crossed to a window and peered into the darkness. "Sound's familiar to me."

"Think so? When he was seven years old he killed a dog with his bare hands. And ate it. From then on they billed him as 'Wolf Boy'."

"I can't believe you admire him so much."

"You misunderstand – I need you to appreciate how much shit we're in here. It's us or him. He's come too far now. Someone will need to kill him. Believe me, that's our only way out of this."

Hall turned to Switzer's bed. The body was cold. He disconnected the tubes. "Poor kid."

Dene held onto the window frame and looked through the dust-smeared glass. The sky was getting lighter. Had he been out all night? He tried to concentrate on what Hall was saying. Perhaps he *was* concussed.

He said, "You mean Lampard? Or Switzer?"

No reply. He heard a soggy crunch and looked over his shoulder.

Lampard stood by the bed with his arms locked around Hall's neck. The little man's face was as purple as a plum. His dead eyes popped and one foot tapped a spasmodic beat. Lampard released his grip and the body crumpled like a puppet.

He said, "Now we'll never know, will we."

Dene fought a tide of rage. He twisted on unsteady legs. "Here he is – the man afraid of fear." He pointed at Hall. "Real fuckin' hero, you are."

"The reward for disloyalty."

"You fucking psycho! Where's Zanelle? Where are the twins?"

"Come lad, you know the rules." Lampard beckoned with both hands. "To the victor belong the spoils!"

"That how you want to play it? Okay *hognose*, you pathetic gutless poser."

Dene shaped up and circled to the centre of the room. A middle-weight against a heavy-weight. He'd sparred with Kenny, so he knew what to do. He needed to stay out of range. It couldn't be a wrestle.

He swung a wild right but Lampard swatted the blow aside. Too angry. He changed tack and went low. A left rip missed and threw his footwork off. He recovered and poked a couple of jabs at Lampard's chin. They didn't even reach the mark.

He suddenly realised his predicament. His coordination was gone, his depth perception shot to bits.

Survival is the truest test of evolution.

And 'the better part of valour is discretion'. Time to get the heck out of here.

He dodged sideways and tripped on Hall's ankle. He reeled toward the door but Lampard dragged him back by the collar and into a choke-hold.

"Not so fast, boy. You're going to be my *Adam*...."

Zanelle rolled out from beneath the hut.

Trying to stay in the shadows, she'd approached Mrs Crozier's ward from the far side and almost walked straight into Lampard as he came from the shacks at the back of the compound. She just fitted between the stumps and under the bearers in time.

Voices drifted down the alley. She moved toward the sound, then shrugged back against the wall as words turned to grunts and thumping.

She poked her head around the corner and saw Lampard wrangle Dene through the doorway. She waited until the noise faded away, then sneaked up the steps.

Chapter 72

DAVID SELKIRK CREPT BETWEEN the cabins, toward the growing firestorm. He held the SIG Sauer by his thigh, but kept his finger curled around the trigger. Bollocks to safety protocols.

He reached a crossway and saw movement down the alley to his right. A tall, bearded man, blond as a Viking, splashed fuel onto a diesel generator at the end of a hut. Above the generator a refrigeration compressor sat on a rickety, angle iron bracket bolted to the timber wall.

Selkirk raised the SIG. He framed the foresight with the man's upper body and walked toward him.

Broussard froze, then slowly turned his head. "Bit far from the nursing home, aren't you, old fella?"

"Still young enough to teach you some manners."

Broussard smirked. "Well, I'm not armed. How about you put that down and we'll discuss it, man to man."

"Sorry, sport. No time to waste. I'm getting on, remember?"

"So you are. But you won't shoot."

"Won't I?"

"You're not Canadian. You're not even French. You're English. You'd never get away with it."

Selkirk watched the bearded man. He knew he'd try for a diversion. Or perhaps a reaction. "Just keep in mind who saved you lot from the Yanks."

Broussard's head fell back. He affected a weak laugh as he took a half step forward. "Okay, Boomer."

Selkirk showed his teeth. A reaction. He'd heard it all before. Kids who could barely read or write – who couldn't get a pizza order straight – confirmed their common status by throwing insults at people decades their senior.

And a lifetime wiser.

He shifted his aim to the jerry can. Very few people know what it's like to be shot. Everyone knows how it feels to be burned.

"Got a smart mouth for a guy with a bomb in his hand."

Broussard glanced down. He bent his knees and placed the jerry on the ground.

The pistol followed every move. "Good boy. Now, where's Lampard?"

The hut behind Broussard caught fire. Sparking amber flames unfurled up the walls. He cringed at the heat on the nape of his neck.

Selkirk said, "Hot enough for ya? Where. Is. *Lampard*."

Broussard contemplated the SIG. It was as steady as a rock.

"He'll be at the main hut."

"Then lead the way," said Selkirk. "Slowly."

———◦———

LAMPARD STOOD INSIDE THE office doorway. His left arm was folded around Dene's neck. The kid gripped his elbow, but his movements were sluggish and clumsy. Lampard allowed him just enough oxygen to remain on his feet.

He kept an eye on a vast shape towering over two bodies by the fence, thirty yards to his left. Even without the prison jumpsuit he'd have known who it was. And Tabu hadn't busted out on his own, so there would be others. Perhaps more than he could handle.

He weighed up the situation. No Pym. No Turley. Not a hyper-carnivore in sight. And where was Quillan?

Things were getting thorny. And it didn't pay to underestimate Tabu Kainoa. He knew a manhunt must be underway. Armed officers and helicopters, probably dogs, maybe drones. And they wouldn't bring the B team.

The net was closing. But he had the boy.

Selkirk emerged from a lane to Lampard's right, two paces behind Broussard. He planted a shoe on the tall blond's rear and shoved him toward the porch steps.

He spotted Dene hanging in Lampard's shadow. Anger surged, but his training kicked in. First responders learn to stay cool. He moved a step sideways where he could keep everyone covered.

Lampard looked from Selkirk to Broussard. He sneered and nodded. "Where's Pym?"

"No idea," said Broussard.

Selkirk saw movement at the far end of the building. He couldn't miss Tabu. Then Zanelle appeared from the darkness. She carried an old woman, draped in a blanket. Must be Mrs Crozier. She laid the woman down and Tabu spread the blanket over all three shapes on the ground. Then the islander turned and approached the main hut.

Lampard took stock again. Tabu and that interfering slag were to his left. The gate was dead ahead, and wide open. Good. He might need it. Selkirk stood to the right of the steps. And he was armed.

But Lampard still had the key.

"Look who I found, Davey," he said. He lifted Dene by the throat and swung him right and left. "The fruit of your loins. The apple of your eye."

Selkirk raised the gun in both hands. He pointed the muzzle at the sky, away from his son. "And I have this."

"So, it seems we're at a stalemate," said Lampard.

"It isn't a fucking game, Mattson. You're outgunned." The Suburban's headlamps swept across the figures scattered in the compound. The Chev wheeled through the gate and crunched to a stop. "And the odds just got worse."

Lampard's composure slipped. Vigilance turned to agitation. Fuck conflict resolution.

"But I have the golden child," he said. "So put your weapon down, or I'll *snap his fucking neck*."

Selkirk took a pace toward the hut. "God, man, just try to be reasonable for once. It's still all of us against the two of you."

Lampard tightened his elbow under Dene's chin and winched him onto his hip as if he were a baby. He gave Selkirk a grisly smile.

Then the Suburban's front door opened.

And out stepped Quillan.

THE KILL BITE

Chapter 73

GREAT. JUST WHAT SELKIRK needed.

Another 'bovver boy'.

He wondered how many more of the pricks he could handle. Blimey, this one was a sight. A crust of blood masked his face, and his eyes bobbled like a madman's.

And then the guy chucked a spanner in the works.

Quillan braced his legs and dragged Tallie from the SUV. He shoved her arm up behind her back and gouged a hunting knife into her throat.

"Well, well," he said. "Looks like we have all the cards."

He screwed a hank of Tallie's hair in his fingers and marched her to the bottom of the steps, knife poised.

Tabu snarled and trundled forward. Zanelle jumped in front of him. "No, don't!" She leaned against his midriff, feet sliding in the dirt as he pushed her nearer and nearer to his daughter.

Selkirk reassessed. Tabu and Zanelle were now at his side, facing the hut. Broussard and Quillan flanked Lampard.

Three against three.

With Tallie and Dene in the middle.

Quillan's crazed stare settled on Zanelle.

"So," he said, "the little Mountie girl wants more. Did she tell you how we all fucked her?"

Dene writhed in Lampard's grip. He kicked his heels on the porch and his toes scraped against the boards.

Quillan laughed. "Apparently not." His black brows arched. "Hashtag MeToo didn't do you a lot of good, did it, Toots?"

Zanelle threw a look toward the hills. "It's not those things that are sub-human. It's you."

"Keep giving lip, sugar, and next time I'll smash your pubic bone with a brick."

Tallie dug her feet in and half turned, but Quillan pulled her head back. Tabu started forward. Quillan brandished the knife and said, "Take one more step, big guy, and Leilani goes to meet her ancestors."

Lampard raised a hand and shook his head. He took a breath and paused, the great orator looking down on his followers. He set baleful eyes on Selkirk.

"You've destroyed three decades of work, David. Thirty years of my life. What if I just kill the boy now? Would that make us even?"

Selkirk's voice cracked like a glacier. "It won't save you."

"Oh, Davey, I'm proud of you. So ruthless. You were my greatest success. Only Tabu came close. Though you both have...flaws." The carney barker was on a roll. "But I can help you. Dene can help you. Together we could do something truly great."

Selkirk noticed Lampard glance away for an instant. He tensed. No security specialist worth his salt would fall for that. He watched for a signal to Quillan or Broussard, and tightened his grip on the gun.

Lampard continued. "We could be the men who ensured the future of our species. Our evolution. Can you imagine the prestige? Can you imagine the wealth?"

The radio in the office blurted a stream of static, breaking the spell.

'Lampard, come in. Come in anybody.'

Zanelle said, "That's Truman Roberts. He is so fucked."

'Christ!' came the voice. *'The goddam Mounties are on their way. Get out of there, now!'*

The receiver fizzled and went dead. Lampard resumed his sermon with new urgency. He cranked up the fervour and the patter flowed like snake oil.

"But if I should die," he said, "what happens to all that knowledge? All that experience? No, that cannot be! My knowledge must live on. At all costs!"

Selkirk ignored the rant.

He squinted through the doorway of the hut. His eyeline was level with the top of the desk. He saw the empty chairs and the silent radio.

He scowled at the desk.

At what sat on the desk.

A Diet Coke and a Mars Bar.

Chapter 74

SELKIRK WHIRLED AND CAUGHT Swift's arm as the doctor plunged a syringe at his neck. He pulled the shorter man off balance, then swung him against the hut.

Swift squealed and slid down the wall. "Dave, don't – I need this. It's everything I've dreamed of."

Broussard took a step toward Selkirk but Tabu moved to intercept him.

"Stop!" yelled Lampard. He lifted Dene's feet off the porch.

Tabu pulled up between Broussard and Quillan. Both men moved out of reach.

Selkirk trod on Swift's arm. "You fat fuck!"

"Jesus, Dave. This guy's lucked out. He's triggered endogenous gene modification. With chemical cofactors alone."

The pistol prodded Swift's forehead. "Talk sense, you fucking quack."

"It's not a transgene – the subject actually has altered traits. It's the holy grail."

Selkirk waved at the mountain peaks. "You think those things out there are some kind of achievement?"

"But that's why he needs fresh blood," said Swift. "Why he's had so many failures. You can't store the blood or it becomes unstable."

"You lot are as unstable as each other."

"Dave, please. I can't work with anymore fucking mice!"

Selkirk wrested the syringe from Swift's hand. "Well, you sure won't be working with Lampard."

The doctor's head slumped to his chest. "Don't you understand? Lampard used his own blood for the original carnivore serum." He looked up. "Your son's blood won't save you – you need an outcross. Hybrid vigour. You need Lampard's blood."

Selkirk tossed the syringe away. It rolled against the hut wall and for a moment there was silence.

In the same moment, Lampard frowned.

"My blood," he said. "Where's my blood?"

Swift nursed his arm and sobbed. "The refrigeration unit. It was in the refrigeration unit, but...."

The deadlock unravelled into bedlam.

Lampard slung Dene aside. He bounded off the porch and ran for the blazing huts. Tabu stampeded after him. Dene stood on shaky legs, breathing hard.

Selkirk tried to cover everyone at once.

The Viking saw a chance and came at him low. Selkirk turned a hip into the tackle just in time. Dene shook himself awake. He flew down the steps and shoulder-charged Broussard. He missed dead centre and they both went sprawling.

Quillan looked at Broussard, then watched Tabu follow Lampard around the corner of the main hut. For an instant he seemed to forget the woman in his grasp.

Big mistake.

Tallie buckled forward with his fingers still knotted in her hair.

She swivelled and dragged him in a half-circle, then spun back and slammed an elbow into his teeth. He lost his grip and grabbed at his battered mouth.

Tallie seized his arm, rolled the wrist and snapped the radius across her thigh. Quillan howled. The knife slipped from his fingers and he thudded onto his knees.

Tallie grabbed a fistful of hair and yanked his head up. "Not funny when people muss your do, eh?" She looked at Zanelle and said, "Be my guest."

Zanelle stepped forward. She hopped once on her toes, then kicked him in the throat as hard as she could.

The hyoid bone splintered. He spluttered and choked on his ruptured trachea. Tallie did a 'mic drop' and Quillan wallowed to the dirt, his broken arm folding beneath him. A scream gurgled through his larynx, then he rolled onto his back and drowned in his own blood.

Zanelle put her hands on her knees and watched him lose consciousness. "MeToo *that*, fucker."

Tallie looked at the body. "I only meant knock him out, but hey, I'm in." She turned to Broussard, lethal intent branded on her face. "Don't be jivin' the sisters, white boy."

Broussard wobbled to his feet and staggered for the Suburban. Zanelle tried to run interference but he shouldered her aside. She stumbled into the vehicle's open door and slammed it shut. Broussard lost momentum. He veered toward the gate. Selkirk aimed the SIG, but couldn't get a clear shot past Zanelle.

"A pox on that," said Tallie.

She swooped on Quillan's knife. She took a stride and hurled the weapon after Broussard. It turned end over end, flashing like a silver Catherine wheel in the glow from the orange sky.

In the hands of an average man, the fourteen-inch gut hook knife would be a formidable implement. In the hands of Talisman Kainoa, it was a virtual harpoon.

The blade shattered Broussard's skull. It cleaved through the cerebellum and split the brain stem. He pitched face first to the ground and slid half a yard in the hoary dirt. His legs tried to run a few seconds more, until they realised he was dead.

Dene sat up and struggled to concentrate. He was watching a movie in slow motion. He squirmed to face his dad. The man had changed. Sparse grey fronds waved about his head, and his neck emerged from his collar like a pick handle. He hadn't just aged. He was a different person.

The thumping in Dene's ears rose in pitch and he felt the air start to throb. His sight improved and the fog in his head cleared. He saw a bright light outlining his father's long limbs.

And he saw the weapon, still trained on Broussard's body.

The cobwebs dissolved. He scrambled up and knocked the gun hand aside. "Don't Dad! Look."

A police EC120 soared above the trees and circled the camp, brilliant white spotlights beaming into the compound. Fine puffs of dust eddied around the SUV, but the vehicle filled the only safe place to land. The helicopter hovered, then banked away and settled over the clearing to the south.

Then the generators gave out.

And fountains of firelight drenched the sky.

Chapter 75

LAMPARD GALLOPED DOWN A lane between the rows of flaming huts. He leaned into a turn and rushed for the refrigeration unit.

Tabu lost him around the corners but he gained on the straights. He dived and caught Lampard with an ankle tap, and sent him crashing into the steps to the lab. He clambered onto Lampard's back and pinned his shoulders with his knees.

"No, Mattson," he said, "not again. Never again."

Tabu hooked an arm under Lampard's neck. He dragged him up and wrestled him away from the door.

Lampard raged. He snapped his head back, driving his skull into Tabu's chin. Shockwaves stunned the giant's brain. He lost his grip and tumbled backward.

Onto Broussard's discarded jerry can.

The reinforced steel base cracked two ribs. Then Lampard hit him with a gut-busting tackle. Tabu outweighed him, but Lampard had gravity on his side.

He hammered an elbow into Tabu's chest, then swung a haymaker at the side of his head.

They locked arms and brawled like drunken deckhands. The Samoan drove a knee into Lampard's balls. Lampard wrapped iron fingers around Tabu's neck and bit off a chunk of his nose. Tabu raked thumbnails over his opponent's eyes.

The battle see-sawed, but years of confinement had eaten away the bigger man's strength. Tabu bucked and twisted but he couldn't find traction. The jerry had jammed under his hips. The can was more than half full. Fuel leaked from the loosened cap and pooled on the hard ground.

The hut's weakened rafters gave way under the weight of asphalt-coated roof shingles. The timbers crashed in and a torrent of sparks gushed from the doorway. A shank of wood dropped to the ground in a shower of embers. It pivoted on its end, then toppled into the puddle of gasoline....

The jerry can exploded like a mortar round.

The blast scattered shards of metal in a starburst on the frozen dirt. Blue flame enveloped the combatants and they thrashed like frantic wildcats.

The weight of the refrigeration compressor pulled the unsupported wall onto their flailing bodies. The compressor cartwheeled into Tabu's head. Overloaded by concussive trauma, his nervous system shut down. Lampard wrenched his arms free and rolled from beneath the burning planks. He crawled to the middle of the laneway and collapsed in a pile of seething clothes and sizzling skin.

Tabu's tortured body reared. The fire drank oxygen from his lungs. Super-heated air closed his throat. The last threads of awareness glimmered, then mercifully floated away.

He lay amid a bonfire of wood and petroleum and red-hot steel. The red jumpsuit turned orange, then yellow, and then black as it melted into his bubbling flesh.

Columns of smoke rose from the pyre, clouding an inky sky. Sirens wailed in the distance and mingled with unearthly cries that floated from the crags above.

Chapter 76

VEILS OF SMOKY MIST drifted through the tree tops. The snow in the clearing glowed red and blue under the strobing lights of paramedic vans and tactical response vehicles.

Dene folded his arms around Zanelle as they watched a Medevac pilot slide Mrs Crozier into the rear of his helicopter.

He felt her shiver with the chill and residual distress.

"She's a tough old broad," he said. "She'll be alright."

"I should have reported her missing straight away."

He hesitated, then spoke softly. "You have another report to make, don't you?"

Zanelle pulled back. "I'm a big girl. And we got more justice tonight than most people ever do." She pointed a finger. "That's the last I want to hear of it, okay?"

Dene hugged her tight and rested his chin on her head. He was certain they hadn't heard the last of this. He gazed around.

Nearby, Tallie looked on as a waif-like girl and a wiry man tended to Kenny and Tim.

"Was that Dad?" said Kenny. "Is he out?"

"Yes," said Tallie, "he's out now. I'll tell you about it later."

She hipped her way between the paramedics and pulled the girl aside. She pointed to an ambulance. "Is that thing going to live?"

The lass was no pushover. "If you don't mind, that *patient* must be seventy years old, and he has sixty percent burns. He should be dead already."

David Selkirk shrugged into a borrowed police parka. The cold had hit him hard and he looked around the clearing with disquiet.

A female officer filled in some details. Tabu's escape was secondary. The police were now focussed on the kidnappings and a swag of dead bodies. As far as they knew, Selkirk was the father of a victim. They hadn't put everything together, but they would. There was no way out. He'd just have to cop it sweet.

A man with a ponytail approached, heavy riding gear bunched around his slender limbs. He offered a small hand.

"Tobias Franklin. Press. I'm with the Chilliwack Post."

Franklin didn't care that eliminating a word from his paper's masthead was a lie. Tonight he'd hit the motherlode. He'd left his motorcycle a hundred yards along the trail off Highway One. When the police ORVs sped straight past, he cadged a lift up the mountain in a fire truck.

Selkirk ignored the hand. The media dogged him for years when he represented England. "Never heard of it."

Franklin's face dropped, but he recovered. "I think you will after this." He reached toward Selkirk again. Something dangled from his fingers. "You're Dave Selkirk, right? Know that guy in the bracelets?"

Franklin nodded at an Abbotsford patrol vehicle where Paul Swift was being handcuffed. A silver haired officer spoke with the doctor. Their heads were close, as if sharing a secret.

"Yeah, I know him."

"He said to give you this."

Franklin pressed a key fob into Selkirk's hand. It took a moment to register.

Swift's SUV.

"Oh, okay. Thanks. I guess he'll be needing someone to look after it. Did he say where he wants it taken?"

"He just said, 'keep it on ice'. Said you'd know what to do."

Selkirk caught the doctor's eye as they bundled him into the back of a police van. The two exchanged a quick nod. Message understood.

"So, what do you have for me? Care to give us a quote for the citizens of Chilliwack?"

Selkirk looked at Franklin and sighed.

Blackened skin and boiled tissue congealed on the side of Lampard's face. His nerves screamed. The pain cut through a fog of tranquillisers. His eyelids fluttered. He really needed something for that pain.

He lifted his head and blinked. He lay on a folded gurney. His left arm pulsed down to the fingertips, but it wouldn't move. He tugged a respiration mask off his mouth and threw back a silver thermal blanket. A patchwork of gel-coated dressings covered his naked body from knees to scalp.

He looked around the ambulance. He scoured cabinets and drawers with his good hand, turning bottles, frowning at their labels, trying to decipher trade names and generic formulations. He found some Tramadol and some Duragesic skin patches. Then he found something better.

A box of EpiPens.

Epinephrine auto-injectors.

Adrenaline.

He tipped out the box and grabbed an auto-injector. Zero point three milligrams. He ripped off the outer tube and removed the safety cap with his teeth, then thumped his fist against his leg.

The spring-loaded needle plunged into his thigh and he counted to ten. He tossed the pen aside, then repeated the trick twice more. For good measure he emptied another.

Lampard pushed the face mask on and drew a lungful of oxygen. His nostrils opened. He sniffed the air inside the ambulance. Stainless steel. Polyvinyl chloride. Chemicals.

And something else.

He forced his left arm up. He raised it from the shoulder in a round-house motion. The bicep hung like a leg of lamb and his forearm was black and crinkled and swollen. A thin antiseptic salve dripped from the roasted flesh.

Roasted flesh.

Chapter 77

SELKIRK GAVE FRANKLIN THE same version he intended to give the police. He wanted to put a matching record of events in the public domain, even if it incriminated him. It might lend credence to his police report, and he meant to make that as favourable to his cause as possible. He hoped he wouldn't take anyone down who didn't deserve it, but if it couldn't be helped....

"I appreciate your candour, Dave," said Franklin. He stopped recording and stuffed the phone into his jacket. "Not everyone is so cooperative. Listen, good luck with everything. Hope it turns out okay."

This time Selkirk gripped the reporter's hand. He'd just let it go when a muffled yell rolled across the glade.

The adrenaline hit.

Lampard's roar boomed from inside the ambulance. The paramedics screwed toward the sound.

"What the fuck? Why isn't he sedated?"

"He *is* sedated."

The girl dragged on the van's rear door. Her eyes widened and her mouth dropped open. Her stomach heaved but she couldn't turn away in time. She sprayed puke all over the inside of the door.

Lampard squatted beside the gurney, his flayed skin the colour of raw chicken. The charred crust of his forearm hung open like a lab dissection. He worked his jaw and spat a piece of sinew, then bared his teeth and tore another strip of muscle from the bloody, white bones.

He crouched at the back of the vehicle, looking out at stunned faces, grinding his molars and swallowing his own minced flesh. He supped thick yellow plasma from his lips and bayed at the sky.

Now we hunt as God intended.

He leapt down and broke the girl's teeth with a backhand swipe, then dropped a shoulder and dumped her colleague on his ass. He bowled around the clearing, flapping gauze like a wallpapered snowman.

With a dead branch for an arm.

Shouts came from all sides. Zanelle and Dene turned toward the commotion. Lampard swerved at the couple. Dene spotted him first.

Someone will need to kill him.

He pushed Zanelle aside and hurled himself forward.

Selkirk spun away from the reporter. He saw Lampard charge at Dene. And saw his son closing the gap. No chance to think. No chance for precision.

He whipped the handgun from its holster and swung into a hasty Weaver stance. He blazed four rounds in a second and a half – all the time he had.

The SIG was chambered for nine-millimetre and Selkirk used jacketed hollow points. The first round was off. It nicked Lampard's left collarbone. The second chewed through his stomach and lodged in his left lung. The third shredded his liver. The last splintered a rib and missed his heart, but the deformed projectile punched a dime-sized hole in the aorta.

That should have been 'game over'. People don't fall the instant they are shot, but pain and shock soon overwhelm the nervous system. Except that Mattson Lampard was full of epinephrine.

And he was totally insane.

The bodies collided like bighorn rams.

Lampard clutched at Dene's larynx. Dene saw torn, black skin and cords of muscle sliding over the bones of the forearm. He dragged his fingers along the mangled limb.

Lampard roared and slugged him with an overhand right. Dene crunched an elbow across his nose and bashed an uppercut into his chin. He clapped his hands against the drooping ears and burst an eardrum. He stepped into Lampard's pelvis with a jolting knee lift, but the man kept coming.

Dene back-pedalled. Lampard stomped on his foot and shoved him in the chest and sent him spreadeagled to the grass.

Dene threw his feet up to fend off the attack, but Lampard stuttered, then halted. He crumpled to the ground. He shuffled a yard on his knees before flopping backward, legs trapped beneath him. Blood bubbled from his wounds and welled across his chest.

Dene scrambled to his side. The doomed man hung a hand on his shoulder and searched his eyes.

"You," he said. "You could have been anything." He swallowed gulps of blood. "When I watched you move that sled, I saw it – the 'call of the wild'. I saw it in you." He waved his savaged arm. "I saw Buck...mighty Buck. I saw him break that sled out of the ice. I saw him strive and strain...until he dragged it over that line."

Streams of red coursed down Lampard's chin. He coughed once and said, "What a noble thing."

And then he died.

Dene looked up. His father stooped and put the gun on the ground and raised his hands above his head. The police parka saved his life.

"It was better that I finish it," he said.

Chapter 78

In the weeks after the story broke, the *Trading Post's* circulation went through the roof. Toby Franklin worked every angle and chased down every lead. He churned out pages of extra copy and began double print runs. Advertising sales soared.

He'd encountered resistance. Phone calls went unreturned and people slammed doors in his face. He was threatened more than once, but he was used to that.

Now he studied his notes, looking for unused phrases or paragraphs he could recycle. With more digging and judicious follow-ups, he figured he could wring another month out of the story.

Franklin propped his feet on his desk. Regardless, he considered the series of articles on 'The Carnivore Club' the best writing he'd ever done.

And almost every word was true....

THE INVESTIGATION LACKED SUBSTANCE. Evidence pieced together from witness statements was ambiguous and inconsistent.

The authorities suspected it was intentional.

The kidnappings and a string of burglaries were blamed on Lampard and his crew, as were the deaths of Joe Ellis, Garner Hall, Billy Switzer and heaven knew how many others.

The razing of the camp and the demise of Quillan, Turley and Broussard were attributed to the 'hyper-carnivores'. In a psychotic drug-fuelled episode, the subjects had turned on their masters. Their identities remained unconfirmed, and the whereabouts of those not deceased was unknown.

David Selkirk copped the rap for Tallie Kainoa. He confessed to forcing her cooperation. Then the prison guards muffed their testimony, partly out of disgrace at being bested by a woman, even one of Tallie's stature and credentials.

Paul Swift escaped conviction by the skin of his teeth. His claim that Lampard had duped him and welched on a contract for monitoring the health of his staff and gym members didn't hold water, but there was no evidence of wrongdoing on the doctor's part. He recovered the Lexus and spent the next months isolated in his lab.

Tabu Kainoa received posthumous acknowledgment for helping to rout the criminals, single-handedly overcoming Lampard, and saving his sons and daughter. It wasn't redemption, but it helped ease the ache.

Under scrutiny and a cloud of suspicion, Truman Roberts took indefinite leave from the Abby PD to 'focus on his mental health'.

A day later, his younger sister Tonia resigned without notice from the Highfield Vet Centre.

With many questions unanswered, and considerable reluctance, the Coroner listed Roland Pym's passing as 'death by misadventure'.

AFTER THE SNOW MELTED, a spate of calls came in to various agencies. Hikers and campers discovered a graveyard of skeletons scattered over the Skagit Range.

The wildlife had a picnic; not a shred of flesh was left on the bones. But there was nothing else either. No cars, no clothes, no ID.

The remains were finally tabbed as a bunch of back-to-nature survivalists who bit off more than they could chew.

Chapter 79

DENE STEPPED OUT OF his pickup and paced across the stadium parking lot. He dropped the latest edition of the *Trading Post* in a trash can as he went past. There was nothing in it that he didn't already know.

He scanned the press every day for more word on the Lampard incident, but the media had latched onto other things. So far, their story was holding. Only the *Post* refused to let sleeping dogs lie.

Life went on. The Canadian Football League assumed official ownership of the Vancouver Wolves. The move was not unprecedented. The CFL saved Montreal's Alouettes from bankruptcy, but they'd now found an ownership group, freeing the league to take over the Vancouver operation until the franchise could transition to private tenure.

This news brought a fresh sense of optimism to the Wolves' training camp. Dene felt the excitement each time he entered the locker room. He unpacked his training kit and pulled on a crisp, white jersey. The players all wore their newly branded gear with pride. The Biomorphi-X name was prominent and sleeve logos highlighted the forthcoming release of the company's latest flagship product.

CEC...Cellular Energy Catalyst.

Zanelle stacked split wood under the stairs. She stretched her back and rubbed her rounded belly. A brindle greyhound curled about her legs. She bent and kneaded the dog's neck as she eyed the timberline behind the house.

"Easy, little man," she said. "It's okay."

Mrs Crozier poked her head out the cottage door. "You know you shouldn't be overdoing things, young lady."

Zanelle grabbed an axe leaning against the woodpile, swung it over her head with one hand and buried it in a log.

"I'm fine," she said. "All done."

"Come inside then. Dinner's ready."

Zanelle clattered up the steps. She watched the forest all the way.

A slimmer but no less flustered Roger Bartoli oversaw the session. Pete Hoffman and Charlie Tait maintained order in the background. Players assembled on the gridiron and the chatter was keen. Dene joined a group of backs and receivers. It took all of two seconds for Kyle Ovens to pipe up.

"Hey! Sell-cock's here. You jacked, boy. Lookin' sharp."

Dene nodded and let a stony gaze linger on Ovens. Some things didn't change. There's always a loudmouth.

Pete kept an eye on proceedings while Charlie manned the ball-thrower. A young hopeful on the try-out roster took his last catch and trotted back to the line of waiting players.

"Okay," said Charlie. "Who's next? Don't be shy."

Dene stepped forward. He saw Charlie roll his eyes.

"Alright then, let's see what you can do."

Charlie wound the machine back a few miles an hour. He sneaked a grin at Pete. "Don't worry, I won't go too hard on him."

He pushed a football into the thrower. It spiralled toward Dene and landed snugly in his hands.

He sent another.

Catch.

And another.

Catch.

Charlie glanced at Pete and cranked the speed up a notch. He loaded another ball.

"Okay," he said, "getting serious now."

Any time you're ready, thought Dene.

The ball whistled through the air. He snatched it with one hand, then casually tossed it away. The watching players perked up. A few yelled encouragement.

Pete shambled over and turned the thrower up full. Charlie peppered Dene with footballs. They fizzed out of the machine like leather cannon shot. Dene plucked them from mid-air, one after another. Right hand, then left. No gloves.

Clean as a whistle.

Ten in a row.

Woo-hoos and the smack of high fives rang around the bleachers.

"Hey, you guys," called Ovens. "Stop goin' easy on him!"

Dene still held the last football in his hands, but no one saw him spread his fingers over the laces. No one saw him align his hips. They didn't see him step toward the cocky wide receiver.

But they couldn't miss the wind-up.

He hit every link of the chain – the triangle, the L, the zero, the extension. It was a bullet pass.

The ball pinged Ovens dead centre. It caromed off his chest, landed fifteen yards away, and rolled another five. He staggered backward, bent over and retched on his boots.

The line of players stared at Dene in silence. Charlie raised his eyebrows and shrugged. Pete Hoffman pulled up Dene's profile on his tablet.

Chapter 80

TALLIE OPENED A REFRIGERATOR and withdrew a tray of blood-filled vials. She prepared a dozen test tubes and loaded them into a centrifuge, her movements painstaking and deliberate.

There was no longer any hurry.

She watched the glass tubes twirl in a ruby-red blur and reflected on the upshot of recent events. Although the students took endless delight in retelling how she'd lost her vehicle privileges, it wasn't all bad. The university board suspended her during an internal review, but they had no legal basis to expel her. She was behind in her work, though that wasn't a crime. And her brothers now idolised her more than ever.

Despite the loss, she could still count her blessings.

"No rest for the wicked."

She looked up. Dave Selkirk stood in the doorway. She shone a smile. "We science types don't take time off."

They met in the middle of the lab and hugged.

"How long have you been out?" said Tallie.

"A little while. You know how it is. Old man, terminal illness, extenuating circumstances."

She rested a hand on his chest. "I need to thank you again for getting me off the hook. You took a big hit."

"It worked out all right," said Selkirk. "I'd had enough of the consulate anyway." He nodded at the purring test tubes. "What's all this?"

"Just tying up loose ends. For my own peace of mind, I have to put this serum to bed once and for all."

She had petitioned the university to requisition the fitness camp autopsy samples from the Coroner's Office. For educational purposes. Everyone involved was tested, so when the RCMP forensics people finished with their own samples she asked for those as well. They arrived weeks later, with a note warning that the cells' viability may be compromised.

Selkirk loitered at her shoulder. "Have you discovered anything?"

"Not yet. And that means I probably won't."

"You've tested everyone?"

"Almost. There are minor pathological changes in some samples, but no signs of DNA modification."

"But Lampard. He must have shown something."

She placed her hands on the benchtop. "Other than being stark raving mad? Just a couple of markers for poor health."

"So...nothing unusual."

"Not a thing. Some kind of gene expression might have presented in a generation or two, but we can't know for sure. And it won't happen now."

"What about Dene?"

"He's in this last batch, but my brothers were fine, so most likely he'll be okay too."

A gangling male student entered from an adjoining lab.

He said, "Doctor K, I still can't find those new burettes."

Tallie grimaced at Selkirk and shook her head. She wrapped the hapless kid in a playful headlock.

"Come with me, young man," she said, chuckling as she dragged him from the room.

Selkirk studied the tray of blood on the bench. He read the labels and came to SELKIRK, DENE. He picked up the vial and dropped it into his coat. Then he noticed another label. ARGUS, ZANELLE. He pocketed the second vial and slunk out the door.

Tallie waltzed back into the lab. "That boy couldn't find his dick in the dark." She looked around and grunted at the empty space.

"Thank you, Talisman, you've been a great help," she said. "Why, you're very welcome, Mr Selkirk."

———◇———

SELKIRK SLIPPED INTO THE Lexus beside the chubby man with the rosy cheeks. The SUV's rear seats were folded down. The cargo area was empty, but Selkirk knew for sure there was room for a pair of sophisticated blood analysers and some passive-cooling containers.

He burrowed into his pocket and handed over the vials. Swift put them in the cooled centre console.

"Gotta hurry," said the doctor. "I've got a date with the Biomorphi-X boffins, but I need to pick some stuff up first."

Swift steered through the parking lot, back toward the security gatehouse. He activated his phone's Bluetooth connection and made a call.

"Hello Vera," he said. "How's my favourite aunt?"

On the way out of the carpark, Selkirk glimpsed a scrawny guy taking snapshots astride a bike. The kid looked familiar, but then Selkirk realised he'd already seen the bike once today. Should have guessed it was a student.

Who else would paint the fairing of a red motorcycle in pumpkin orange?

Chapter 81

BARTOLI STUDIED HIS TABLET on the sideline. He'd worked out how to brighten the screen, but now he fretted about the battery.

Pete Hoffman walked up beside him. "Have you seen this?"

"Not now, Pete."

"No, you should look at this." Hoffman tapped Bartoli's screen, swiped, and then tapped a couple more times. He pointed. "Good numbers, Bart."

"Yeah, if I had a nickel."

"Might be time to give him a break."

"Are we going through this again, Peter? Because if we are...."

Bartoli sighed. The pre-season testing was almost done. He ran his finger down the screen. Forty-yard dash. Shuttle. Broad jump. Three-cone drills.

A frown puckered his forehead. Bench press?

"Can't be right," he said.

"Charlie said it checks out."

The coach blew a long breath through rubbery lips. "Kid's looking kinda husky, I'll give you that."

"C'mon Roger. It's a massive improvement. Marshawn's not putting up numbers like this on his best day."

"Numbers don't mean squat if he can't play. And I still don't think he's got it."

Hoffman crossed his arms. "One way to find out."

Bartoli fixed a suspicious eye on his assistant, then slowly nodded. He looked around the squad of players.

"Rogalski!"

GWEN CROZIER SERVED EXTRA platters of rib eye and steamed vegetables.

Zanelle reached across the table, stabbed another steak and dropped it onto her plate. She sawed off a piece of meat and stuffed it into her mouth.

"Good girl," said Mrs Crozier. "You need to keep your strength up now you're eating for two." She wiped down the kitchen bench. "I was thinking we should take Robber up to the lake this afternoon. Some exercise might do us all good."

Zanelle didn't speak. Instead, she scoffed down chunks of rib eye as fast as she could slice it.

The old lady looked on, perturbed. "Anyway," she said, "you keep going – he can have my scraps."

She began to clean the stove, then stopped and watched Zanelle take a prime cut of medium-rare beef in her hands.

And rip it apart with her teeth.

THE SQUAD LINED UP to watch Dene and Rogalski face off. They'd heard how Dene drilled Ovens with a rocket.

Now they wanted to see how he'd handle big Eddie.

Ovens tried to salvage some respect. "Looks like we're cuttin' players early this year."

A pair of burly line-backers jostled to his side, their elbows hard against his ribs.

"Not the quickest learner, are you," said Kenny.

Ovens opened his mouth but Tim wagged a finger and shook his head. Ovens pouted and grouched away.

Tim said, "Don't listen to him, brah."

"Focus, man," said Kenny.

Dene centred his thoughts on positive self-talk. He'd trained for months. He was well prepared. A lot of people had helped him get this far, whether they knew it or not. Garner. Tabu. Zanelle. He owed them all.

Time to pay up.

"It's okay," he said. "I've been looking forward to this."

He eyed Rogalski and set his cleats in the turf. Bartoli called the play. Dene took the ball and catapulted straight at the defensive tackle. He went low and hard. At the last second he lifted his shoulder. With a vicious snarl, he drove his helmet into the big man's chin.

Rogalski's head whiplashed in the clash of pads and thermoplastic. He bounced off Dene, floated for an instant, then crashed to the ground. He blinked and gasped and rolled onto his side.

"Fuckin' faggot," he wheezed.

The players gawked. The twins beamed like lighthouses.

Dene removed his helmet and checked it for damage. He walked up to Bartoli. "Anything else, coach?"

Pete Hoffman cracked a grin from ear to ear. He turned away and pulled out his phone. He found his contacts, scrolled down to 'S' and tapped on...*Stockbroker*.

Chapter 82

TILES OF INDIGO SHADE and golden sunlight chequered the low-land forest. The wolf sifted through a tier of conifers, her pack arrayed behind.

Their number had grown by two, a male and female, little more than whelps. Spare, sickly wood sprites, flitting among the hardened campaigners, learning the ways.

The Search...

The pack combed a strip of pasture from the tree line to the river flats. Streaks of tawny grey and tea-leaf brown, blending with the meadow grass.

The Eye Stalk...

The wolf spotted her prey, tethered beside a pile of logs. Slender as a fawn. Sleek as an otter. Alone.

The wolves gathered about the alpha pair. The youngsters ranged alongside. They crept toward the bungalow, eight spectres, low and lean.

Robber weaved around the woodheap, mewling at the end of his lead. Zanelle trotted down the stairs. She wiped steak juice from her chin and let the greyhound lick her fingers.

She scanned the open field behind her home and saw movement in the grass. The dog whimpered. She stroked his back and glared at the wolves. "Wanna play, do they, Robber?" She wrenched her axe from the log, swung it in wide arcs, and tracked toward the timberline.

The wolf hesitated. The counsel of a thousand generations thrummed in her veins. Her prey had company. A female, taller and twice as heavy. In her own territory. And carrying young.

The wolves stopped as one. Their tails dropped. The pack was immature, its leaders battle weary. This was a mistake. They milled on the meadow, then scattered and fled to the trees, melting into the shadows.

The Chase...

Zanelle stepped through the waving grass, pacing up the slope. She glowered at the woodland, breathing hard, nostrils flared, axe ready.

A low growl trembled in her throat.

———◇———

THE WOLF LOPED AFTER her clan. She hurdled a fallen bough, then vaulted onto a flat-topped boulder and turned. The she-creature marched on, weapon swinging in a white-knuckled grip.

The wolf's coat had thinned and lightened in the warmth of summer. Her hackles rose and swayed on the breeze. She looked out from her pedestal, an ancient bronze amid towering jade pagodas. A queen in a robe of tobacco-stained mink.

She raised her head, the better to see and hear and smell. She didn't recognise the signs, but instinct told her all she needed to know.

She was being hunted.

THE END

Acknowledgment

My gratitude goes to Graham Schodda of Bellingham, Washington. His advice on the nuances of life in the Pacific Northwest contributed much to this story. As an early reader, he also suffered the worst of my writing with great tact. Any mistakes are mine alone.

COMING IN 2023

Still water runs deep...

PRESSURE WAVE

LAURENCE HAYE

**Read on for a preview of
PRESSURE WAVE**

PRESSURE WAVE

——◆——

JUNE 2034

THE *LODESTAR* RODE A rising swell, eight miles off the California coast. A weathered, pilothouse vessel, she dragged a small mid-water trawl through the waves. Her gallows croaked and her winches moaned as they hauled the catch toward the stern.

Down on the after deck, Callum Sebring leaned over the port side and watched her bow rise and fall across a bleak dawn horizon. He knew the little trawler's voice. Knew if she was happy, and if she wasn't. When he heard the port cable grinding through the pulley he realised something was wrong. He turned to aft. The tow warp's angle was way too steep.

He called to the winchman. "Luis. The otter board's diving."

Luis Legra worked the winches with Popeye arms and mallet fists. He coaxed the twin throttles, balancing the trawl between port and starboard. Between floating and sinking.

"Don't want her twistin', Cal," he said.

Callum set the otter boards himself. He'd checked them twice. It must be a breakage. At last, some excitement.

He pulled a switch and an emerald flush bloomed from spotlights bedded in the stern below the waterline.

"You won't lose her," he said. "I'll take a look."

Lean and supple, brown and hard as a hazelnut, he slipped out of his deck shoes and peeled off his shirt. He stepped onto the coaming. Timing his dive, he leapt out high over the water and knifed into the swell, trailing a shimmer of silver into the gloom. He followed the tow warp down and spotted the problem, then pulled his shoulders back and kicked to the surface.

His head bobbed on the water. Slicked back hair, glistening skin, three-day growth. A dark-eyed model in a swimsuit shoot. He yelled over the slap of the waves and the burring winches.

"The chain bracket's busted."

He hitched a ride on the cable as Luis nursed the trawl toward the boat. Otter boards act as rudders, forcing the net mouth open. Tuning the boards is a marvel of scientific calculation. One malfunction and you can lose time adjusting the gear, or eat into your profit by burning too much fuel.

At least this was an easy fix.

The trawler's captain scanned the sea with pale blue eyes. Skin like steamrolled gravel crusted his face, and hair as thin as paper ash whipped about his forehead. Erik Weber was sixty, but looked a decade older.

He held the big Cummins at a thousand revs, rolling to the diesel's thumping beat. He tipped a dented hipflask to his lips. As he swallowed, he felt the trawler's lopsided pitch, and heard the uneven hum of her winches. He turned and saw Luis feathering the throttle on the port tow warp, and noticed the pool of light behind the boat.

And saw Callum in the water.

"Jesus in a shit storm!"

Weber cut the engine revs to make two knots, then scuttled down the ladder from the fly bridge. He lurched across the deck on spidery legs. "Get outta the water. What do you think you're doing? Get outta the water!"

Callum gave a thumbs up and hid a baffled grin. It wasn't the best time for a swim, but why all the fuss? Couldn't be a shark. When was the last time anyone saw a shark? He dropped off the tow cable and stroked toward the boat in a lazy, head-up crawl. His legs trailed through a stream of colder water and a thought trickled through his mind.

Absence of evidence is not evidence of absence.

Who had said that? Callum didn't remember, but he gave them the benefit of the doubt.

He picked up the pace.

The skipper took a swig and tucked his flask into a pocket. He stalked between the gallows, watching eddies foam and glitter in the stern wash. The drone of the winches merged with the gurgling diesel and the lapping waves.

Then, above it all, came the sonar alarm.

The trawler ran a CHIRP fish-finder array. Compressed High-Intensity Radiated Pulse. Old but effective. Weber could set the alarms for depth, water temperature, and fish size.

This one was big.

He turned to Luis. "Get that net in. Get it in now!"

The burly winchman bounced between the cable drums, leaning on the winch handles, fighting the one-sided drag. The trawl's head-rope broke the surface, steel floats tossing on the swell. And then the alarm changed frequency.

Weber's frown deepened. It wasn't a single fish. It was a school.

"Cal," he called, "get out of there, for Christ's sake!"

Callum was way ahead of him. He'd heard it too. Adrenaline coursed through his system, but not from excitement. It was fear. Abrupt and smothering. His arms thrashed at the water. He surfed a wave of marbled green ahead of the net and surged toward the boat.

Weber scowled at a strobing glow beneath the wake. Luis saw the light shine cherry red, then white, then red again. He crossed his heart and whispered, *"El diablos rojo...."*

THE WATER CHOPPED AND the eddies tightened into whorls. Bubbling springs welled from the deep until a bloody maelstrom roiled behind the *Lodestar*.

Weber and the winchman jostled to reach over the transom.

"El diablos rojo," said Luis. "Get out, get out!"

Callum didn't need an invitation. He ploughed through the wash on churning arms and a six-beat kick. He thrust a desperate hand toward the boat. Weber clutched his wrist and dragged him onto the deck.

The skipper elbowed Luis aside. "Get the net in. We'll lose the catch."

Luis rushed to the shuddering winch drums. Weber manned the derrick, preparing to hoist the trawl from the sea. Callum scrambled to his feet, ready to untie the cod line.

He needn't have bothered.

The net swung over the landing in a ragged tangle of webbing and twine. Shreds of whiting hung from the ruined mesh and remnants of mackerel guts slopped over the deck.

Weber eyed the mess, hands on hips. He cast a sideways glance at Callum and reached for his pocket. He unscrewed the lid and offered the hipflask. "You okay?"

Callum nodded, ashen faced. He took the flask and gulped without thinking. He swallowed hard and almost gagged. He tried to catch his breath. Old salts and their overproof.

Long live tradition.

"What the heck just happened?" he said.

Luis shook him by the shoulder. "*Chico*, you just won the lottery."

Weber said, "You won the lottery twice." He kicked at pieces of offal sluicing across the deck timbers. "The red devils don't hunt in schools. They hunt in packs." He snatched his flask, then shut off the stern lights and the light bar that lit the afterdeck. He tramped back up the ladder, shaking his head and muttering.

"Millennials. So much knowledge." He glanced back at the sea. "So little damned sense...."

The waves rose and fell in sluggish heaves and a murky slick glazed the surface. Callum stared at streaks of briny yellow, frothing in the wake. He blanched and shivered. He watched the net drip puddles of gore onto the landing, then bent forward and tossed up a gutful of salt water and rum.

About the Author

Laurence Haye lives in Australia, where he has written in various formats since his teens. He has written freelance and also on contract. After working in the fitness industry, sales, and the print media, he has now turned his hand to fiction. Hyper Carnivore is his first long-form story.